ZANE PRESENTS

D1190801

Forgive Me

Dear Reader:

Stacy Campbell's debut project, *Dream Girl Awakened*, was a highly successful novel complete with twists and turns. *Forgive Me* is her sequel and as the title suggests, the author explores the quality of forgiveness. Sometimes one can forgive—but they will never forget.

After broken friendships and mishaps, will Victoria Faulk forgive her former friend, Aruba Dixon? Will Aunjanue forgive her mother, Tawatha Gipson, once she is released from prison after five years?

Facing the challenges of marriage and divorce, grief and female bonding, discover if these characters are able to pardon and move on with their lives—together or apart.

Stacy, who listened to her relatives' stories on her family's front porch, spins a wonderful tale that surely will appeal to all readers. Everyone can make a mistake. Everyone has faced the decision on whether to forgive.

As always, thanks for supporting Strebor Books, where we strive to bring you the most groundbreaking, out-of-the-box literature in today's market. If you would like to contact me directly, feel free to email me at Zane@eroticanoir.com. You can also find me on Facebook @AuthorZane and on Twitter @planetzane.

Blessings,

Zane

Publisher
Strebor Books
www.simonandschuster.com

ALSO BY STACY CAMPBELL
Dream Girl Awakened

ZANE PRESENTS

Forgive Me

Stacy Campbell

SBI
STREBOR BOOKS

NEW YORK LONDON TORONTO SYDNEY

Strebor Books
P.O. Box 6505
Largo, MD 20792
http://www.streborbooks.com

ISBN 978-1-59309-458-4
ISBN 978-1-4516-9670-7 (ebook)
LCCN 2013948767

First Strebor Books trade paperback edition February 2014

Cover design: www.mariondesigns.com
Cover photograph: © Keith Saunders/Marion Designs

10 9 8 7 6 5 4 3 2 1

Manufactured in the United States of America

For information regarding special discounts for bulk purchases, please contact Simon & Schuster Special Sales at 1-866-506-1949 or business@simonandschuster.com

The Simon & Schuster Speakers Bureau can bring authors to your live event. For more information or to book an event, contact the Simon & Schuster Speakers Bureau at 1-866-248-3049 or visit our website at www.simonspeakers.com.

This book is dedicated in loving memory of
Lorraine Byrd Lawrence (5/18/1950-10/15/2013),
Sister-in-law extraordinaire and a true friend,
and to all the people who feel life isn't worth living.
It is.

Acknowledgments

I've wanted to write since I learned to read. Stories transported me from my rural setting in Georgia. Thank you God, Sara, and Zane for making my writing dream possible. Thank you also to Charmaine Parker for keeping me in check and on point.

Special thanks to the early manuscript readers: Darlene Lawrence, Andrea Allen, Kimyatta Walker, Devetrice Conyers-Hinton, and Orsayor Simmons. Your input was invaluable and I truly appreciate you taking the time to give me feedback.

To my family, thanks for putting up with my disappearing acts in the writing cave.

To the industry champions and book ambassadors who continue to coax me out of my shell, thank you for your services and your voices. Keith Saunders, Editor Carla M. Dean, Lasheera Lee, Yolanda L. Gore, Johnathan Royal, Ella Curry, Tiffany Craig, Delonya Conyers, Kim Knight, Teresa Beasley, Readers Paradise, Naptown readers, and all the other book clubs and reviewers who took the time to give me feedback and spread the word about *Dream Girl Awakened*.

Victoria Christopher Murray and Renee Swindle: your advice, character interview sheet, and character examination knowledge are making books three and four come to life. Thank you.

To the fellow authors I've met or connected with the past year, thanks for the laughs, wisdom, and support. Sadeqa Johnson, Trice Hickman, Julia Blues, Adrienne Thompson, Author Saundra, Vanessa Harris, Michael July, Phoenix C. Brown, Donneil Jackson, Cathy Jo G., Alvin L.A. Horn, Karen Quinones-Miller, Shamara Ray, Ben Bennassi, Suzetta Perkins, Audrey Ford, Tracy Cooper, Cherlisa Starks Richardson, Curtis Bunn, Shane Allison, and Shelia Goss. I admire your journey and your words.

Special thanks to the Pike Branch of the Indianapolis Marion County Public Library system for the writing room and quiet space. You make writing enjoyable. A big-shout out to the representative of the National Suicide Hotline who provided me with valuable information, and the Marion County Jail officer who explained standard procedures.

Thank you, Peta Gay Campbell, for being the first reader to reach out to me after publication of my first novel to tell you me you enjoyed it. I will treasure your email forever. I appreciate all the readers who've reached out to me and would like to give special thanks to the Atlanta postal workers; my Sparta, Georgia, home-town heroes who attended my first book signing; Sharon Simmons and the patients at Davita Dialysis in Jonesboro, Georgia; and the avid readers who've reached out to me on my website and through Facebook. You keep me going when the words play hide-and-seek. I'm truly grateful that you're taking this journey with me. Stay blessed and take one small step each day toward making your dreams come true. One move makes the difference.

Chapter 1

*T*oday is a good day to be released from prison, Tawatha thought. She gathered her duffle bag and wondered what was taking Royce so long to pick her up. She glanced backward at the Indiana Women's Prison, her home for the past five years. She would miss the few friends she'd made, the Wednesday evening Bible study sessions, and the exchanges among the others who were also confined because of bad love choices.

She still wasn't convinced about spirituality and all the things she learned behind bars, but she was sure of one thing: her girlfriend, Jamilah, pulled a ram out of a bush and set her free. Not only was she free, but she'd also gained a certain measure of respect from the other prisoners—even after killing three of her four children in a house fire.

"Tawatha," a voice called out behind her.

Tawatha turned to see Faithia Perkins, a trustee and mother of the group. She'd embraced Tawatha from the beginning of her stint and kept the wolves at bay after Tawatha's first beating by the other inmates.

"I almost missed you. CO Morris told me you were leaving. I hopped all the way from the infirmary just to say goodbye."

"I was hoping I'd see you," said Tawatha.

"I just wanted to give you a hug and tell you to keep your head up. I don't want to see you back in this place. You've got a second chance to get it right, and I want you to make good on it."

I will not cry, I will not cry. Tawatha opened her arms and let Faithia's embrace soothe her. She would miss the earthy smell of Faithia's skin, the gentleness of her hands when she braided her hair, and all the long talks they had about Faithia's sentence. "I knew saying goodbye to you would be hard. That's why I snuck out."

"No matter what happens, you have to move on. Don't look back; move forward, Tawatha."

Before Tawatha could shed a tear, Royce's Mercedes appeared. He smiled when he saw her and dimmed his lights at the sight of Faithia. He pulled alongside the curb.

Faithia watched the handsome, salt-and-pepper gentleman step out of the stylish car. Tawatha had mentioned her former boss would pick her up, but from the look in his eyes, Faithia picked up on more than an employer-to-employee vibe.

"Mr. Hinton, I'm so happy you're here," said Tawatha. "This is Ms. Faithia Perkins, a prison trustee, and the only reason I survived in this place."

Royce folded his arms, raised an eyebrow, and gave Tawatha a *tsk-tsk* look.

"*Royce*, this is Ms. Faithia Perkins." Tawatha corrected her formal introduction of Royce's name.

"That's better." He extended his hand to Faithia.

"I trust you'll take good care of Tawatha. She's special to me. She's come to be like a second daughter."

"I plan to take the very best care of her." He took Tawatha's bag, popped the trunk, and placed it among the surprises he'd planned for her. He opened the passenger door as Tawatha eased into the seat, unsure of where they were heading.

She waved to Faithia one last time and looked ahead as Royce drove away from the prison. There was no need to look back—only forward.

"So, where are we going?" asked Tawatha.

"Well, I figured you'd want to take a shower and perhaps go out to dinner. I remember you loved Olive Garden. I want you to unwind tonight."

"Did my mother return your calls?"

"She did." Royce sighed. "She said she's not ready to welcome you into her home right now and asked that you give her some time."

Tawatha's countenance deflated. "So where am I supposed to go? She didn't write me in prison, and the few times she came to see me, she just stared at me like I was a monster."

"Calm down. I anticipated this before I picked you up."

"What about Lasheera?"

"Ditto. Since Lasheera and Lake adopted Aunjanue, they feel your presence will disrupt her life. This is Aunjanue's senior year, and well …" Royce's voice trailed off.

Tawatha sat back in her seat, unable to hide her hurt. She almost wanted him to turn the car around and take her back to prison. She wondered about the kind of life would she have if the people she loved treated her like she didn't exist. Jamilah was the only crew member who still communicated with her and had her back. To everyone else, she was a child-murdering ogress who should have been given the death penalty.

"Is that okay with you?" Royce asked, interrupting her thoughts.

"What did you say?"

"The arrangement to stay at my place for a while. You won't actually be staying with me. There's a carriage house in back of my property. You're welcome to live there until you get back on your feet. That is the address I gave the corrections system."

"What about Millicent?"

"Millie and I have been divorced for about two years now. After our daughter died, things were never the same between us. I filed. I don't think she wanted to admit we were through."

"I wish you'd told me that. Millicent was always nice to me when she came by the office. I envied your relationship. How long were you married?"

"Thirty-four years."

"That's a lifetime."

Royce drove past the main dwelling to the carriage house. His in-laws had passed nearly four years ago, leaving the house lifeless.

"Royce, this place is beautiful. Are you sure it's okay for me to stay?"

"Last time I checked, my name was on the deed to both places. Come inside."

Royce removed her bag and gifts from the trunk. He gave her a set of keys to the house and stepped inside the living room, giving her time and space to take in her surroundings.

"Get some rest and call me if you want to go out later tonight."

"Royce, I'm speechless. If it takes me forever, I promise I'll make this up to you." She hugged him and counted the ways she'd show him just how much she appreciated his kindness.

Chapter 2

"Baby, don't fidget. Let me get this tie straight," said Shandy.

"How many times do I have to tell you that I can knot my own tie, Shan?" James joked and swatted Shandy's hand.

"And have us looking crazy at this banquet? No way."

"Oh, I'm representing *you* now, huh?"

"Don't you forget it, either." Shandy kissed James on the lips, grateful for an evening on the town. She hoped that the kiss would be a precursor to a night of passion that kept eluding them.

"Slow your roll, Ms. Fulton. We've got all night to be together," James said, chiding her.

I won't start with him tonight. I'll let things unfold. "So how long do you think this shindig will last? When Isaak gets worked up, he can't stop talking. Even Katrina can't make him be quiet."

"If my mentor wants to talk all night, let him. Sitting at his feet made me the success I am, so you won't hear any complaints from me."

James raked his fingers through his curly mane as he eyed Shandy. His thoughts worked double-time to concoct another excuse *not* to be intimate with her. Although they had grown closer over the past four years of dating, he felt something was missing in their relationship. He knew any man would gladly trade places with him. Shandy became his business partner first, then his lover. She'd moved in with him over a year ago and went to work making his house her own. She never uttered her motivation, but he knew the renovation was to erase all traces of his ex-wife, Aruba.

Maybe Shan could erase traces of Aruba, but he couldn't. Lately, it seemed Aruba was all he thought about. Their divorce ended bitterly after she pursued her friend's husband and won hands down. Aruba waited for him to get his act together, encouraged him to work, and reassured him she'd always be there for him. She held out for ten years, and then swiped back the promise of forever when she discovered his affair with Tawatha Gipson, a secretary at his former job. Tawatha's obsession graduated to insanity when she burned three of her children in a house fire to be with him. He marveled at Aruba's audacity, self-righteousness, and unwillingness to give their marriage a second chance since she crept with Winston as he crept with Tawatha. Who was he kidding? It would have been impossible after the way he'd treated her. If that were not enough, an out-of-wedlock daughter he produced with Tawatha, Jameshia, was still at the forefront of his mind. He always said if he had a child, he wanted to be a part of the child's life. This wasn't how it was supposed to be, and he didn't know how to make things right. The few times he'd visited Aruba in Los Angeles, their son, Jeremiah, refused to talk to him. Little man had grown into a sharp, witty nine-year-old who needed him.

"So, will I have to stage a mutiny for a vegetarian meal tonight?" Shandy asked, coaxing James from his thoughts of Jeremiah and past indiscretions.

"I got that taken care of already. I know how much you detest meat, Shan."

"Keep eating secretions if you like. I want my man to be healthy."

"I'm pure meat and potatoes. Always have been, and always will be."

"I'll wear you down eventually," said Shandy. *Literally and figuratively.* She wanted to know what he was thinking but was too afraid to ask. When she scooted closer to him at night in bed and rubbed the hair or his stomach, he'd turn to her, eyes still shut, and say, "I miss you, Aruba." The only thing she knew about their divorce was that Aruba cheated on him with her girlfriend's husband. She wondered how he could miss a woman like Aruba and why, after all these years, he seemed filled with regret. The last time she broached the subject, an ugly shouting match ensued, James stormed out the house, and he spent two nights in a hotel. There was no way she would mention the subject again. She loved him and wanted to be the new Mrs. Dixon. This summer would be the mother of all tests because his son, Jeremiah, was coming to stay from late-May to August. Her exposure to children was babysitting her niece, Kathryn, whenever she visited Vegas and gave her twin brother, Simeon, a night on the town with his wife.

"Afterward, we can go dancing if you like," said James.

"What did you say?" asked Shandy.

"I said after the banquet, we can go dancing if you like."

"Or we can come home and make passionate love until the sun comes up," said Shandy.

"Is that all I am to you?" James joked.

"Of course not. That's one of many things I like about you, James Dixon."

Shandy twirled around in her teal and black evening gown. She had her shoulder-length hair pulled back in a bun and her makeup done at Makeup by Sparkle, the same studio she'd frequented since meeting James. Shandy hoped James would find the look appealing enough tonight. She always looked good on his arms, but lately she had found it difficult to captivate him behind closed doors.

Tonight has to be different. I can't take this pain much longer.

Chapter 3

"Lake, are you coming out of the office or do we have to come in and get you?"

"I'm almost done typing this chapter, so give me five more minutes. I promise you won't starve by then," said Lake.

"Keep up the jokes and the three of us will leave you here," said Lasheera.

"When will Dad be done?" Zion asked.

"We'll all watch Lake march across the stage next spring. He defends his dissertation soon."

"Will Dad make us call him *Doctor?*"

"You know Lake isn't hung up on titles. Go get Onnie so we can go to Cheesecake Factory."

Lasheera watched Zion walk down the hall to the family room. Tonight's celebration of Aunjanue's academic achievements would be bittersweet for the family. Aunjanue's day was filled with excitement after receiving acceptance letters from Stanford, Spelman, and Bryn Mawr. Those would be added to the pile from Clark Atlanta, Yale, and UC Berkeley. No sooner than she ripped open the letter from Bryn Mawr, her best friend, Tarsha, called to ask if she was watching the news. Before Lasheera could grab the remote from Aunjanue, word of Tawatha's release from prison flooded the living room. Lasheera didn't intend for her to find out about

Tawatha's release—nor was she prepared to reintroduce Tawatha into their lives.

"Onnie, honey, let me…turn the television," Lasheera said as she took the remote from Aunjanue. She turned off the television and went to Lake's home office. She needed his help with this one.

Aunjanue's face froze. She watched the anchor describe the jury-tampering technicality that set her mother free. Memories of her siblings, Grant, Sims, and S'n'c'r'ty, rushed through her mind as she stared at the urn holding their ashes on the mantle. Aunjanue plopped down on the sofa as Zion joined her. He held her hand.

"Onnie, what's wrong?" he asked.

"Remember when I told you about my brothers and my sister, the ones on the photos I showed you?"

"You told me they died."

As she sought the right words to explain her feelings, Lasheera rescued her. "Zion, go to your room. We need to talk to Onnie alone. Straighten your room before we go to dinner. I'll call you down when it's time to go."

Zion walked away. He hated leaving good adult conversation. *What's so important that I can't listen in? She's my sister, too.*

Lake and Lasheera joined Aunjanue on opposite sides of the sofa. They held her hands for comfort.

"Did you know she was being released?" Aunjanue asked.

"I did," said Lasheera. She paused. "We didn't want to disturb your senior year. You've done so well and we didn't want anything to interrupt your progress."

"You know how unstable your mother is," Lake added. "If nothing more, we didn't want her to harm you in any way."

"I hate her. I'll never forgive her for what she did to us. I don't want to see her, and I don't care about the baby she had either.

She's nothing to me." Aunjanue stared at the urn again as she blinked back tears. She'd given Tawatha too many tears already.

As they held her hands, Lake spoke. "You're safe with us. If she comes near you or us, we'll take out a restraining order. If she tries to contact you, let us know and we'll handle her. We're here to protect you, Onnie. You have to know that."

"I don't want to go out anymore. I'm going to my room." She stood to leave as Lasheera touched her shoulders.

"Onnie, don't let her spoil this night. I want you—"

"Give her space," Lake said. "I'll order us some take-out. She needs to be alone with her thoughts, baby."

"Are you sure you don't want to go out?" Lasheera asked Aunjanue once more.

"Positive. I've lost my appetite."

Lake and Lasheera watched Aunjanue as she headed toward the stairs. Lasheera hadn't spoken to Jamilah, their other bestie, since she took up Tawatha's cause and fought to have her released from jail. Of all the first cases on the planet, she didn't understand why Jamilah wanted to set Tawatha free again. *Justice be damned. I'll kill her if she comes near Aunjanue.*

Chapter 4

D arnella tapped on Aruba's door again. The tray of baked chicken, green beans, seasoned rice, and fresh-squeezed lemonade remained untouched next to the latest *Ebony* she had placed outside Aruba's door.

"Aruba, you haven't eaten since this morning. Please open the door, honey."

Darnella wasn't sure what troubled her more, Aruba's silence or her inability to comfort her only child. Aruba moved to back to Georgia six months ago following the death of her second husband, Dr. Winston Faulk. Darnella knew the marriage was ill-fated because Aruba stole Winston from her friend, Victoria. *Friend.* Darnella cringed at the thought of all the secrets and quiet time the women shared as her daughter set her sights on taking Victoria's place. Sure, Aruba's husband, James, wasn't pulling his weight at the time. His chronic unemployment and lackluster desire to keep a job were enough to work any woman's nerves, especially a mother-in-law who hated seeing her daughter Hebrewing to keep the household going. However, Darnella would never have suggested man-stealing as a remedy for a bad marriage. That's why the Western world had divorces. News of the betrayal devastated Darnella the night her mother, Maxine, called to tell her that Aruba's birthday party had turned sour as Victoria revealed to guests and friends that Aruba had been cheating with her husband. *Where did I go wrong raising her?*

Darnella's mind wandered to Winston's funeral eight months ago. His health deteriorated shortly after they'd moved to Los Angeles five years ago. News of his Lou Gehrig's disease took everyone by surprise; he was a noted cardiologist who'd been wooed to Cedars Sinai and was the perfect picture of health. Darnella believed in reaping and sowing, but to see her daughter reap the consequences of her choices was heartbreaking. First, they downsized from a gorgeous mansion to a small townhouse. Afterward, Winston's confinement to a wheelchair left Aruba with no choice but to be his caretaker around the clock. Several nurses came in to assist with his care, but Darnella watched Aruba massage Winston's limbs, adjust his feeding tubes, brush his teeth, and keep his skin bathed and oiled to prevent chafing and bedsores. Jeremiah took a backseat to Winston's care. Two neighbors and their children made sure Jeremiah had playtime, video games, and a loving environment to vent whenever he questioned Aruba's love for him.

Winston succumbed to the disease two days short of their third wedding anniversary. The funeral was a sea of doctors, lawyers, family members, and curiosity seekers. Darnella's shoulders slumped at the memory of Victoria, Winston's ex-wife, rubbing her daughter Nicolette's hair and whispering in her ear as they wept arm-in-arm on the front pew. They both declined a final viewing of Winston's body. Darnella later overheard someone quoting Victoria as saying, "I only want to remember the good times."

Darnella shooed away those thoughts and refocused her attention on Aruba. Aruba seldom came out of her bedroom, and when she was alert, she picked at her food and stared out the window at the flower gardens in a camisole and panties.

"What a tangled web we weave," muttered Darnella.

Darnella stared at her watch. She'd give Aruba five more minutes before entering the room.

She headed toward the den and called out, "Lance, is Jeremiah still across the street at Mama's with George's grandchildren?"

Lance, her husband of almost forty years, looked up from the latest issue of *Auto World*. "Yes. I walked over there a few minutes ago and those boys were upset that Maxine had them watching CNN. She only allows one hour of video games, then nonstop CNN *HLN*. After that, you know it's on to reading the *New York Times*."

"If you can play games, you can learn." They repeated Maxine's words in unison.

Darnella sat next to Lance on the sectional and laced her hands with his.

"Did Aruba eat?" asked Lance.

"Her food is still sitting outside the door. I'll have to reheat it. I didn't want to just barge in, but I'm getting anxious about her behavior."

"She's been through so much, Nella. I feel bad about how all of this ended."

"I feel responsible for this. If I hadn't …"

Lance covered her lips with the tips of his fingers before she could rehash *her* past indiscretions.

"Thank you for forgiving me, Lance. I'm so sorry I hurt you."

"Nella, that was over twenty years ago. We were both young and foolish. I did my dirt, too. Let's move past that time."

"I can't help wondering if Aruba knew about …"

"Please don't say his name. I'm not defending our daughter, but James wasn't exactly the best husband. She got confused and lost her way."

Darnella pulled Lance closer. She looked at him and marveled how good time had been to him. At fifty-nine, he was better-looking now than when they met in high school. He was still "The Towering Wonder," the nickname he was given as Harlem High School's standout forward. Women were always drawn to his smooth, dark skin, muscular frame, and a smile that made them strike up a conversation just to see his teeth. His eyes had the same mesmerizing effect. The Stanton men were generational legends in the conquest department. She realized why Aruba was so drawn to James. He was like her father in so many ways.

"When is Aruba's next appointment?" Lance asked. He rubbed Darnella's shoulder.

"She has a checkup next Tuesday with her podiatrist in Augusta."

"You know what I mean." He stared at her and raised his eyebrows. "You didn't make the appointment, did you?"

Darnella sighed. "She won't agree to seeing a psychiatrist."

"Nella, this isn't up for debate. She's gone past being in a funk. Something's wrong with our daughter that's beyond our control. She needs to talk to someone. I'm not saying she needs to take medication. I ain't with people taking all these antidepressants anyway, but something has to give. She won't eat or bathe. She barely talks to us, and she acts like Jeremiah isn't even here. I'm tempted to reach out to James for help. At least for Jeremiah's sake."

"We will do no such thing!" Darnella snapped.

"Nella, that's the man's child."

Darnella pursed her lips and snatched her arm from Lance's grip. They'd visited Indianapolis last year for Black Expo and were amazed at how successful James's business had become. Make that businesses. As she lay arm-in-arm with Lance at the downtown Hyatt, she wanted to vomit at all the Dixon's Hair Affair television commercials. He now had four locations. One location doubled as a salon and a barbershop. He had a children's shop that catered to boys and girls; a shop that catered to senior citizens only with press-and-curls, haircuts, and Wednesday Bible studies; and he had opened an all-natural hair salon that very week, which was billed, 'the curly girl's cure for kinks.'" Darnella fidgeted for the remote control to turn up the volume when she saw James being interviewed about his meteoric rise to success. Sitting next to him was that bony Shandy Fulton. Darnella watched them finish each other's sentences and discuss how they operated as a team. She rolled her eyes as they rattled off the addresses of the locations. *Aruba should be sitting there*, Darnella muttered under her breath. *He wouldn't be there if it wasn't for our daughter.* Darnella flipped the channel before Lance could protest. Aruba was wrong for cheating, but his whorish ways played a part in her daughter's actions. Darnella burned over the realization that James was living the high life off the seed her child had planted. Now, Aruba was barely coherent and couldn't enjoy the harvest.

"As far as I'm concerned, James doesn't ever have to see Jerry again," said Darnella. Her anger rose at the memory of the commercials and the interview.

"James has been reaching out to Jerry since the divorce. Look at how he went to California all those times to see about him." Lance believed divorce shouldn't equal child abandonment.

Darnella sighed. "We were having a great time until the thought of James got my blood pressure up. It all seems so unfair that he's moved on and is doing well. I don't want to give Jeremiah any false hope."

Lance nodded in agreement but said, "You should know by now life isn't fair. Besides, who knows what the future holds? I think they could have a great father-son relationship if you stop blocking him."

"I suppose you're right. It's taking me more time than I thought to get over this situation. I'll try to be more sensitive, but it feels so...I don't know Lance."

"Baby, I'm going to check on Aruba. I'll let you sit and stew a spell," said Lance. He rose and kissed Darnella on her cheek.

Darnella sat back and thought about how inquisitive Jeremiah had been lately. His mood turned somber whenever the boys in the neighborhood had outings with their fathers. They were gracious enough to take Jeremiah along, but he often bounded home with questions like, "When is my daddy coming to see me again?" or "If I joined the soccer or football team, do you think my daddy would fly from Indianapolis to see me?" Darnella didn't have the heart to tell Jeremiah, Lance, or Aruba that James called weekly to check on Little Man, the nickname he'd given Jeremiah when he was younger. She also didn't tell them about the generous checks James mailed to their home so Aruba and Jeremiah would be comfortable. They came like clockwork on Saturday mornings, and like clockwork, she removed those checks from the mailbox, deposited them into a Cubby Bear account she'd established for Jeremiah, and pretended James didn't exist. The only snafu she had experienced with her charade was Jeremiah's uncanny resemblance to James. Jeremiah had received an equal mix of his parents' good looks. His medium-brown complexion, light eyes, mop of curly hair, and natural swagger often made adults and children do a double take. Amy Russell, Jeremiah's classmate who lived two houses down, declared Jeremiah was her boyfriend as she snuck a kiss during a patio cookout. Marshall Washington, owner of The Banana Man Fruit Stand, an organic fruit vendor in the neighborhood, often asked, "Ain't that boy Ethiopian or Middle Eastern? I know he ain't black." Darnella always responded nonchalantly, "Does it really matter?"

When she looked at Jeremiah, she prayed a silent prayer that when he grew up, he'd have self-control, wouldn't be easily swayed by women's wiles, and that he'd be a man who worked hard and smart. She picked up the picture of Jeremiah sitting on the coffee table and smiled at her grandson's handsome face. She stroked the photo and caressed Jeremiah's face. She leaned forward to set the photo back.

"Nella, help me!" Lance screamed.

Darnella dropped the photo, shattering glass on the floor. She ran down the hall to Lance. His screams grew louder as she neared Aruba's room.

"Baby, get up. Get up, baby." Lance hovered over Aruba's slumped body on the left side of the bed.

Darnella darted next to Aruba's body, fell to the floor, and checked her pulse. She called 9-1-1 as Lance commanded Aruba to move.

"Nine-one-one. What is your emergency?"

"Please send someone now! I think my daughter is dead."

Chapter 5

Victoria strolled arm-in-arm with Emory into The Capital Grille in Buckhead. They had spent so many nights at his house or hers poring over recipes and cooking new items that he insisted they go out on the town tonight. She agreed to The Capital Grille since this was the spot of their first date.

She stood next to Emory's hulking frame and couldn't believe she had actually given another man, not to mention love, a serious chance. It seemed like yesterday she had attended the funeral of her ex-husband, Dr. Winston Faulk, in Los Angeles. She knew she had taken his love and generosity for granted, but she never imagined a *friend* would swoop down and break up their relationship. That *friend*, Aruba Dixon, plotted and schemed until she had her man, a new ring, and an upgraded lifestyle in L.A. But God didn't like ugly, and He wasn't too fond of cute either. Victoria thought of the irony of Winston's Lou Gehrig's diagnosis and how Aruba spent their short-lived marriage taking care of him. She didn't get to enjoy the new lifestyle because most her days were spent in and out of the hospital with Winston. Although the L.A. digs were reconstructed for accessibility, Winston fell victim to a host of infections and was frequently hospitalized. Victoria almost felt sorry for Aruba. Almost. *Serves her right. Backbiting tramp.*

As Victoria stood next to Emory, she blocked the memory of

the letter Aruba had written her. In it, she apologized for breaking up her marriage and asked if they could at least be cordial for the sake of her daughter, Nicolette, and Aruba's son, Jeremiah. When Victoria didn't respond to the letter, Aruba called several times. Once, Aruba called from an unknown number. The moment Victoria answered the unrecognized number and heard Aruba's voice, she ended the call and wondered when Aruba would get the hint they would never be friends again. *I'll forgive her when Hollywood stops making porn.* She was so stuck in the past she didn't realize they had been seated.

Emory held her hand and asked, "Have I told you how beautiful you are tonight?"

Victoria glanced at her watch and gazed into Emory's eyes. "About ten times on the way here. Do you have something to confess?"

Emory rolled his head back in laughter. He shifted in his chair at the sound of Victoria's sweet voice and gazed lovingly at the woman he had fallen for two years ago. Victoria was the toughest conquest he had pursued, but that was fine with him. He'd grown tired of women throwing themselves at him because of his prominence and wealth. In fact, his status seemed to turn Victoria off. Fascinated by the beautiful young woman who moseyed into Haute Love two years ago with the sexiest legs he'd ever seen, Emory Wilkerson knew he had to have her. She seemed out of place in the nightclub. His heart went out to her when he realized she had no rhythm and struggled to dance to the thumping house music blaring through the club. He walked toward her to ask for the next dance when he recognized her sidekick and his former client, actress Marguerite Mason-Richardson. Marguerite's wedding to megachurch pastor, Foster Richardson, had been big news in the

Atlanta Journal-Constitution and the *New York Times* wedding sections. Foster's position as Associate Pastor at Canaan West Baptist Church evolved into his appointment as the Senior Pastor after the former pastor, Bishop Hosea Johnson, retired and moved back to Boston. When Marguerite dated Foster, she brought a sense of style and compassion with her from L.A. Soon, Canaan's membership swelled to over ten thousand members, and naturally, Canaan made sure their beloved pastor wed in style. Emory knew he'd scored another feather in his culinary cap when Foster reached out to him for his catering services. Emory's excitement over being handpicked by Marguerite to cater the affair was the ticket to launching his second baby: Wilkerson's On-the-Go Eatery Services. Emory, a sous-chef and Food Network producer, created WOTGES to help busy professionals enjoy individually portioned meals that were low in salt, fat, and sugar. The heat-within-fifteen-minute meals caught on with celebrities as well. Within no time, Emory had formed a team to deliver his goods throughout the Atlanta metropolitan area. Throughout the last year, he pondered the thought of Victoria being a part of his ventures.

"Sweetheart, don't you think the restaurant is empty tonight? I've never known it to be this quiet," said Victoria.

"Good point." Emory called the waiter over to their table. "Is there something going on tonight? It's usually not this empty."

"Sir, we're expecting a special party tonight. As a matter of fact, I was about to ask the two of if you wouldn't mind moving."

"But we have reservations," said Emory.

"It's okay, Emory," said Victoria. She rubbed his massive hands and winked at him. Her divorce had taught her to relax. Victoria remembered the time she would have insisted a manager be brought out to fire the waiter. Time had taught her to enjoy small moments and to be grateful. "Where would you like us to move?"

They stood as the waiter led them to what appeared to be a private dining area in back of the restaurant.

"See, we'll have more privacy," said Victoria as she rubbed his back.

Victoria followed Emory closely. She loved the way he complimented her, and lately, he accompanied her to the gym to get rid of the twenty-five extra pounds she had gained over the past year. Try as she might since the divorce, she couldn't stop eating. Gone were the vegetarian meals her former nanny, Alva, prepared for her each day. Victoria fell for the South's beauty along with its cuisine. It was nothing for her to scarf down a rack of ribs, coleslaw, steak fries, and half a German chocolate cake in one sitting. Her daughter, Nicolette, chastised her about the food and gently reminded her of Michelle Obama's Let's Move campaign. Thanks to home training, Victoria avoided licking her plate clean. Emory suggested healthier portions of food. She ate them in his presence; however, when he went home or flew out of town on business trips, her toxic inner foodie took over and she couldn't help herself. She knew change was imminent when Emory surprised her with a membership to LA Fitness for Christmas. Victoria reasoned that real-life adjustment caused her excessive eating. The former stay-at-home mom now utilized her social work degree by working Monday through Friday for a health care agency. Although she'd been employed three years, she never adjusted to waking up early, getting Nicolette fed and off to school, navigating the hellacious Atlanta traffic, reporting to management, and obeying office rules. Nicolette's soccer practice, dance lessons, and general day-to-day movement made Victoria's head swim. Her wisely invested, $3 million-dollar divorce settlement was the only remnant of her past life. Gone were the nanny, multiple credit cards, and endless spending sprees from her past life. Were it not for Canaan, and her associate, Yvette Hankerson, she wouldn't make it each day. Victoria wanted to embrace Yvette, but Aruba Dixon taught her that associates beat friends any day of the week.

"After dinner, perhaps we can visit some friends," said Emory.

"What did you say?" asked Victoria. Engrossed in past thoughts, she didn't hear anything Emory said. She held his hand and fell in stride behind the waiter.

The waiter opened the doors to a private area in the restaurant. When he stepped back, Victoria's eyes widened as a sea of familiar faces smiled and said in union, "Welcome." She looked at Emory, unsure of what was going on. He planted a kiss on her cheek.

"This is a special party for the most beautiful, magnificent lady I know," said Emory. Emory extended his arm as if to encourage Victoria to mingle with their relatives and friends.

Victoria's aunt, Marguerite, stepped toward her with a glass of wine. "Do you know how hard it was keeping this secret? Foster just about put masking tape on my lips to keep me from speaking."

"What is going on?" Victoria whispered to Marguerite.

Marguerite opened her mouth to speak but was interrupted by her sister, Lillith. "It's about time you got here. My knee has been bothering me, and I was wondering when Emory would get this thing going. I have plans tonight with one of my gentleman friends, and I can't hang here too long," she said.

Victoria looked at her mother. In Lillith's mind, she stopped aging at thirty, and her outfit was an indicator of her fantasies. She donned a tight, red mini dress that needed relief from hugging the rolls of fat on her stomach. Five-inch stilettos help boost her short stature, but rings on each finger and too much perfume reminded Victoria why she kept her distance from her mother. She held tightly to the cane she'd been carrying since suffering a mild stroke. "And before you ask, Emory asked me for those photos of you when you were little," said Lillith. She tossed her shoulder-length weave to one side and flashed Victoria a wide, veneered smile.

Victoria hadn't noticed the wide-screen television displaying images of herself and Emory on dates, as children, with friends, and alone. She looked to Emory for an answer, but he worked the room with his usual magnetism as he greeted guests.

"Go on and say hello to everyone," said Lillith as she grabbed a glass of Moscato from one of the servers. Lillith bopped her head to the rhythm of the smooth jazz playing.

Victoria worked the room greeting people from her church, the gym, and her office. Two co-workers, Jasmine and Cassidy, gave her the thumbs-up sign and nodded their heads in Emory's direction. When she approached Yvette and her husband, Carl, she hugged her, enjoying the warmth and sincerity of Yvette's joy.

"You look so lovely tonight, Victoria," said Yvette. "I told Carl if I had to pretend I didn't know what was going on for another week, I'd die."

"I'll let it slide this time, but you know I don't like secrets. The last time I was at a surprise party…" Victoria's voice trailed off.

"What happened?" asked Yvette.

"I don't have enough time or liquor to tell you about it," said Victoria.

Yvette observed Victoria walk away with the sullen face that appeared when the past came up. They'd been acquaintances three years, going back and forth to each other's homes, double-dating, and attending Nicolette's games. Yet, there was something missing from their time of fellowship. Yvette couldn't put her finger on it. The few things Victoria shared, she kept them in confidence. She was quick to listen, slow to speak. She wanted Victoria to know she could trust her, but somehow, she couldn't get the message across.

"Carl, did you see her face? I wish I knew what made her so sad sometimes," said Yvette.

"Give her some time, baby. Didn't you say she was divorced?"

"Yes, but I don't know much about it. Whenever the subject comes up, she becomes evasive or stops midsentence about the topic of divorce. I want her to know she can talk to me about anything—especially after tonight."

Carl and Yvette smiled at each other and reflected on the reason they'd all gathered at the restaurant.

Emory stepped to the makeshift stage built a week ago for the occasion. A server handed him a microphone as guests gathered together in a semi-circle. His business partner, Pearson Loft, escorted Victoria to the stage.

Emory held Victoria's hand. He gazed into her eyes and lifted her chin with his free hand. "Your birthday is two weeks away, but I wanted to do something special for you because you deserve so much. You're beautiful, intelligent, and everything I prayed for in a woman."

Victoria looked around at their enthralled guests, still unsure of Emory's motives. He captured her attention once again. "I can't erase all the things that happened to you in the past, but I wanted tonight to be a new beginning for you, for us."

Emory slowly removed a Tiffany ring box from his pocket and got down on one knee. "Victoria Faulk, will you do me the honor of becoming my wife? To share my world, to share my life, to share my vision?"

Victoria's blank stare caught Emory off-guard as did the fresh tears flowing down her face. He knew the surprise would overwhelm her, so instead of waiting for her yes, he slid the ring on her finger.

She took several deep breaths, snatched her arm away, and yelled in a voice unfamiliar to Emory, "How could you be so insensitive?" She plucked the ring from her finger, tossed it at Emory's feet, and ran from the restaurant into the street.

The stunned guests looked at each other, then Emory. Lillith, satisfied that her chit-chat with Victoria two weeks ago had been effective, sipped her Moscato with a smirk, and checked her text messages to see if Bobby responded.

Chapter 6

Tawatha held her urine six hours before realizing the unlocked guest bathroom was safe. Glued to the sectional with her legs crossed, she feared moving. Royce texted to let her know he'd ordered Jimmy John's for her, but she refused to open the door for the deliveryman when he rang the bell. After five rings, he left the food on the doorstep. She sat on the sofa thirsty, hungry, and angry. Royce remembered her favorite sandwich from her Hinton and Conyers days, yet fear kept her stuck to the sofa. *What if the deliveryman recognizes me from the news?* She had been out of jail for eight hours and hadn't decompressed. She waited for a guard to call out her inmate number. She listened for a catfight between inmates whose families didn't visit, or whose families didn't put money on the books. She waited for the hard bang of a steel door closing, which was accompanied by the clanking of keys. She looked around and found only tranquility. Royce had taken great care to make sure her surroundings were soft, genteel. *If only I could move.*

Tawatha knew the real reason for her paralysis: the duffle bag letters. She received many letters in jail from angry mothers, fathers, and siblings who freely spoke their minds about her incompetence and selfishness. After reading several letters, she stopped opening them. The raw language grated her nerves. She collected the letters and brought them from prison as a reminder of past mistakes. The last letter she received two weeks before her release scared her most. The writer researched her mother's name and addressed the letter with Roberta's address in the sender's corner. Thankful her mother reached out to her, she ripped open the letter and found the cryptic words:

Hello, Tramp,

I bet you thought I was your mother, didn't you? Well, think again. Matter of fact, think of the kids you killed who'll never get a chance to have a mother, a basketball game, a snowball fight, a high school graduation, and a wedding. And for what? Just because you were selfish enough to be caught up with a man. That man didn't want you and probably never did. You were an easy lay to him and he moved on to something new. The news didn't say it was about a man, but any time a woman gets a wild hair up her ass and kills her kids, a man is behind it. You messed up bad! You left your oldest daughter alone in the world, and you weren't even woman enough to think about the consequences of your actions. I thought you'd rot in jail and be gone for good, but I look up and see that biracial slut, Attorney Jamilah Greg, has the nerve to be an advocate for your freedom. I'll tell you what. If you see the light of day on the streets, it won't be for long. I will find you and kill you myself for what you did to those kids. Watch your back, Child Killer.

Your Worst Enemy

The sound of Royce's key in the door startled Tawatha. He stepped into the living room and raised an eyebrow at her sitting position on the sofa. He placed his keys and the Jimmy John's bag on the coffee table and sat next to her.

"I've been calling you for hours. Why haven't you answered the phone?"

Tawatha stared at the iPhone Royce purchased for her so they could communicate. He handed it to her, paying careful attention to point out the missed calls. She placed her hand on his shoulder. "Let me run to the bathroom. We can talk when I come back."

Royce noticed the pained look on her face. He leaned back and wondered what he'd gotten himself into. Maybe it was a midlife crisis. Maybe it was the fact he'd be turning sixty soon and missed having a wife and a daughter. His divorce felt like the final blow to a once perfect life. His daughter, Ramona, died in a car accident, leaving Royce and his wife strangers. Ramona, a twenty-three-year-old graduate student at Indiana University, died en route to Millicent's birthday party. She was the victim of a head-on collision by a semitrailer. Numbness set in after her funeral as Royce and his beloved Millie tried to get back on track. Sure, the sincere, empathetic clichés comforted them for a moment, but their lives were forever altered. When Tawatha walked into Hinton and Conyers, Royce's construction company, he felt alive again. She looked so much like Ramona he avoided her for the first three weeks she worked. Slowly, he got to know her, admonished her for the skimpy attire she wore each day, and encouraged her to rise up and be a young lady. Her four children became his surrogate grandchildren. He showered the children with clothes, money, and tickets to Pacer and Fever games. When she killed them in the fire, he knew he couldn't abandon her as everyone else had. He knew her temporary lapse in judgment was the result of being overwhelmed with the children. There could be no other explanation.

"Royce, how was your day today?"

Tawatha rejoined him on the sofa and grabbed the food bag from the coffee table.

"I had some business to take care of with Millie. We finally sold our last piece of property in Winona Lake."

"Does she know I'm here?"

"No, Tawatha. Only my business partner knows."

"Bet Mr. Conyers isn't happy, is he?"

"Well, he thinks I could have used better judgment, but the last time I checked, fifty-nine was old enough to handle my own business."

Tawatha stopped mid-chew, placed her sandwich back in the wrapper, and sidled next to Royce. She rubbed his leg and nibbled on his ear lobe.

"You're also old enough to handle business with me," said Tawatha.

Confused, Royce removed her hands from his thigh. "Tawatha, what are you doing?"

"Earning my keep," she said. She attempted to kiss his lips this time, but he tucked his lips inward so she'd be unsuccessful.

Royce stood. He was embarrassed his body betrayed him. He couldn't hide his erection and wondered why he hadn't anticipated this.

"See, you want me." She stood to hug him, but Royce stood his ground.

"Sit down so we can talk," said Royce. Tawatha pouted and fell back on the sofa. Royce paced until he could calm himself. "We have to establish some ground rules. I never meant to mislead you in any way, Tawatha. My generosity isn't some sick bid to have sex with you. The only regret I've had outside of losing my daughter is not helping my childhood cousin, Quenton. We grew up together, were scholars, and got full-ride scholarships to IU. Something went wrong our freshman year. Quen was arrested for theft. He never bounced back after the first arrest, and the family tagged him The Habizzle, or the habitual offender.

"We turned our backs on him, never letting him stop by for food, showers, or anything. He stopped by Hinton and Conyers one day to ask for one hundred dollars, and I treated him like gum on my shoes. I may have tossed him a ten and told him to get lost. He looked awful and smelled like he'd fallen in a hog trough. Last I heard, he walks up and down New Jersey Street panhandling people for change. People call him Lean on Me for some reason. I've never been able to find him. I vowed after our last encounter that if I could help someone, I would."

Tawatha cupped her hands over her mouth. She remembered hearing the name Lean on Me from Lasheera's crack days. "My how the tables have turned," said Tawatha.

"Excuse me?" Royce asked.

"Nothing. I know Lean on Me through a former friend. I mean, I don't *know* him, but I'm aware of his activity on the streets." Tawatha decided to tuck that golden nugget in her memory bank until the time was right.

"Small world, isn't it?"

"It gets smaller every day. Listen, I guess I owe you an apology, Royce. I've never known a man to *not* want something from a woman. Everyone has a price and I thought…" Her voice faded.

"You need a paradigm shift, Tawatha."

"A what?"

"Paradigm shift. It's a change from one way of thinking to another." Royce stood. "I have to get to the house. I have some consulting contracts to flesh out, and then I'm going to bed early. Call the main house if you need anything."

"Royce, thank you again for all you're doing. I'll find a way to repay you. I promise."

"If you want to repay me, be here when your parole officer comes around. He came by the house and did a top-to-bottom inspection last week. Since my address is your new residence, he said he'd be doing a once-a-month mandatory check on you. It could be at any time, so stay near the house."

"What if I need to get around?" Tawatha thought of the unexpired license she still possessed.

"The keys to the Ford Focus are in the main house. Millie bought the car for her nephew in high school but took the keys from him when his grades never rose above C's. You can drive it if you like."

Tawatha walked Royce to the door and gave his back a fatherly rub. She felt ashamed of how she came on to him. *I have to change my old ways. Every man isn't about sex.* "Royce, after this sandwich and the news, I think I'll turn in early, too."

Tawatha reclined again, uncertain of how she would fill her days. She'd tried with no success to reconnect with her loved ones. No one wanted to see her or believed she had changed. There would be no three musketeer action she once enjoyed with Lasheera and Jamilah. Jamilah was still in her corner, but skipped town after the trial with her new boyfriend. They wouldn't reconnect for at least two weeks.

She took one more bite of her sandwich, placed it back on the coffee table, and grabbed the remote. Since becoming a mainstay in the news, Tawatha didn't enjoy watching headlines as she did before going to jail. Tonight, however, she wanted to reacquaint herself with local events. She appreciated Royce's generosity as she aimed the remote at the huge flat-screen TV.

Andrea Morehead of WTHR-13 stood outside Easley Winery anchoring an event. She stopped individuals as they went inside the building. Tawatha noticed several faces from local publications as they milled around in black-tie finery. Tawatha turned up the volume when she spotted a tall, thin woman speaking with Andrea.

Andrea held the microphone closer to the woman as she smiled for the camera.

"Shandy, what does tonight mean to you?"

"Andrea, this is a chance to give back to the community and help the youth of the city obtain scholarships."

"What items are you auctioning off tonight at the banquet?"

Shandy motioned to a man whose hand gestures conveyed that he was the life of the party. Tawatha did a double-take when the love of her life neared the camera. Shandy whispered something in his ear as he ran his fingers through his curly mane. To Tawatha's chagrin, he had cut his locks years ago.

But looking at him now, she warmed at his model looks. He was the best lover she'd ever had, and she never got over the fact they couldn't be together. She sat back on the sectional and wondered what the child they'd created looked like. The Indiana Department of Corrections forced her to give up their daughter, Jameshia, for adoption. She wondered if Jameshia had her father's eyes, creamy skin, and beautiful smile. Did Jameshia have a mass of unruly curls, or did her new mother keep it braided or plaited with bows? Awash in memories of their past, she scooted closer to the screen to hear him speak. Her stomach flipped as he kissed Shandy on the cheek and looked at Andrea to answer the question.

"Tonight, we're auctioning off gift certificates in various denominations for services at our four salons. The smallest amount is one hundred dollars, and the largest amount is twelve hundred dollars." Shandy moved closer and wrapped her arms around him. "We want to make sure the ladies and men of Indianapolis are looking their best. Every Dixon's Hair Affair salon is equipped to do that and so much more."

"Thanks for stopping by to chat with me," said Andrea.

They strolled into the winery, smiling, and giving the impression of a perfect couple. *Why wouldn't he be with me? What didn't I do?*

Tawatha admired his drive. *Four locations.* She eyed the laptop Royce pointed out earlier and wondered why she hadn't thought of the idea that was suddenly brewing. She retrieved the device from the desk, turned it on, and waited for it to boot up. Royce typed out the user name and password for her on a slip of paper that he'd placed on the desk. She sought the answer to her questions through Bing. In less than ten seconds, she had the addresses of each of James's locations. She jotted the addresses down.

James Dixon, if you give me one more chance, I know I can make you happy.

Chapter 7

Aunjanue waited outside for her best friend, Tarsha. The stuffiness of the house and the breaking news story of her mother's release from prison sent her to the comfort of her backyard flower garden for fresh air and regrouping. *How could someone let a murderer back on the streets?* She waited for dusk to arrive and hoped a hint of darkness would keep the neighbors at bay. Aunjanue, or Onnie as she was known to friends and family, assumed the backyard would shelter her from impending commentary. Since being granted guardianship to Lake and Lasheera by her grandmother, Roberta, Onnie accepted pity heaped on her by the community as God's way of helping her breathe. Once known as "the art student who's gonna make a name for herself," she quickly became "that poor girl whose mamma up and killed three of her kids over somebody's husband." After her brothers and sisters perished in the fire during her sleepover at Tarsha's place, strangers approached her at odd moments. In Kroger, a woman gently pushed her aside in the self-checkout line and paid for Onnie's field trip snacks. "It's my way of helping you through this," insisted the woman. She slid a one hundred-dollar bill in the cash slot, waited for the change to flow in the lower receptacle, and thrust the change in Onnie's hands. She disappeared before Onnie could protest or return the change. Other times, people stared, and acknowledged her with a nod or sigh. Sometimes she could hear them say, "I hope she's okay."

Onnie removed a pair of gloves and a bag of Miracle Gro, her favorite cultivator, from the gardening table in the shed. Times like these called for turning dirt and talking with her best friend. This year, Lake suggested she plant peppers and tomatoes along with her flowers. She looked around at the burgeoning hollyhocks and azaleas in the yard. She imagined her sister, S'n'c'r'ty, sniffing the beauties and complaining they didn't smell like roses. Her brothers, Grant and Sims, would probably clip them and place them in a vase for cute girls at school. They were gone but not forgotten. They lived on in her memory. She sketched drawings of how she imagined them now.

"You doing okay, Onnie?" asked Mrs. Rosewood, her next-door neighbor.

Startled, Onnie grabbed her chest.

"I didn't mean to scare you, dear. I saw the news story earlier, and well, I was worried about you." Mrs. Rosewood, donning her after-work attire of a soft-pink velour tracksuit, matching Keds, and a bottle of sparkling water, joined Onnie near the flowers.

"I'm okay, Mrs. Rosewood. I needed to get out of the house for a few minutes. I'm waiting on Tarsha now."

"I'm so glad she's coming by. You know I'm not one to pry, but remember my doors are always open for you."

"Yes, ma'am."

They hugged and Onnie watched her amble toward her house.

Onnie knelt now, gloves hugging her trembling hands, and the bag of Miracle Gro keeping her company. She sprinkled the plant food on the dirt and willed herself to keep her evil thoughts at bay. She hated her mother and hoped she didn't try to get in touch with her. Her hate for Tawatha escalated the day she left Castleton

Square Mall. A man walking behind her said, "Damn, you are the baddest woman I've ever seen." She quickened her steps, embarrassed by the attention she received and the familiarity of his words. Men spoke the same sweet nothings to Tawatha when they went out together. She went home that day, tried on her new outfit, and quarter-turned in the mirror. Tawatha's image stared back at her. Onnie purchased a T-shirt and jeans from the mall; they fit perfectly. She looked just like her mother with her delicate, rich brown face, hefty breasts, small waist, and large derriere that garnered date offers and inappropriate conversations wherever she went. Little did those men know, Onnie hated math, but her equation about life was simple: man *plus* sex equaled children and complications. She vowed to remain a virgin until she married, *if* she ever decided to take that path. She'd be a professional student if necessary, acquiring more degrees than a thermometer if it meant not being lovesick like her mother. She dated Roger Keys, captain of the Northwest High School football team. He respected her and didn't pressure her for sex, but she suspected someone was keeping him company when she wasn't around. She pulled weeds from the peppers when a familiar voice called out. "Couldn't wait for me, could you?"

She spun around to see compassion flowing from her best friend's face. "Tarsha."

"Come join me on the swing," said Tarsha. She held up a bag of goodies from her part-time job.

Onnie ditched her gloves and headed to the pergola with Tarsha, regaining her appetite as the smell of chicken stew watered her mouth.

"I thought you didn't get off until ten," said Onnie as she grabbed the Panera Bread bag from Tarsha.

"I told my boss I had a family emergency. You are family, right?"

said Tarsha. She swatted Onnie's hands from the bag and removed chicken stew, an apple, and sweet tea. She placed a napkin on the swing, laying the food out so Onnie could eat.

"You didn't have to do that. I'm glad you did, though."

Tarsha took a deep breath. "How are you doing?"

"I don't know. I'm mad. I want to cry and scream—do something. I know if I do something crazy, I'll have to go back to therapy. I want to maintain my composure. It's just like my mother to mess things up. We were going out to dinner tonight to celebrate my college acceptances, and she gets out."

"How did that happen?"

"Some sort of jury-tampering technicality. I don't know the details and don't care. She's dead to me and I don't want to see her."

"What if she does?"

"What if she does what?"

"Onnie, you're the only child she has left. Well, the little girl, too, but you told me someone adopted her. I wouldn't be surprised if she did a drive-by through the neighborhood to stalk you from a distance."

"Auntie Sheer and Uncle Lake are two steps ahead of you. Lake contacted the police to ask them to patrol the neighborhood, and Mr. Wilson said he'd look out for me at the school."

"Mr. Wilson, your art teacher?"

"Yes. And Mrs. Rosewood stopped by before you came to let me know her doors are open. Translation: I'll be looking out for you like the new and improved Five-O."

Their laugher eased the tightness of the mood. Onnie took the top from her soup, grateful that Tarsha remembered her favorite food. Since her siblings died, other girls at school attempted to befriend her, but she questioned their motives. Tarsha remained her rock and sounding board.

"Momma said she wants to take us shopping in Cincinnati this weekend. It's a small token of her being proud of you for getting into all the colleges you applied to." Tarsha gave Onnie the sweet tea.

"I'd like to go away, but I'm finishing some canvasses this weekend with some other art students. We have the nursing home community service project. I like spending time with the elderly folks we met."

"I'll ask to be put on the schedule this weekend also. I wanted us to go shopping together, but if you're going to the nursing home, I'll work."

"Tarsha, thanks for being my friend and not judging me. I wouldn't have made it all these years without you and your family."

"That's what friends are for, sis."

Tarsha stopped short of calling Aunjanue her sister from another mother. The words *Tawatha* and *mother* didn't mix.

Chapter 8

I have a female penis, James thought. He closed his eyes, willed sensuous desires, but nothing made the captain stand at attention. *Come on, boy, not tonight. Stop being so moody and rise.* He had stalled Shandy for the past thirty minutes. Feigning banquet exhaustion, he made a beeline for the bathroom, turned water on full blast, and hummed an Usher tune. James sat fully clothed on the toilet and formulated excuses not to have sex with Shandy.

My head is woozy from all the wine.

Baby, aren't you sleepy? Let's rest for strength and get it on early in the morning.

You look tired. Get some rest, Shandy.

She knocked on the door and interrupted his cop-outs. "May I join you, James?"

"Give me a sec, Shan."

"If I give you a sec, you'll be finished showering," said Shandy. He could hear the desperation flooding her voice.

James stripped, grabbed a face cloth, and jumped in the shower. He quickly sponged his hair and body. He wrapped a towel around his body and opened the door for Shandy. He yawned and pretended not to see her naked body or the wide grin on her face. The sight of him shrouded in a towel dimmed her smile.

"Oh, I thought we would shower together," said Shandy.

"Shan, my head's a little woozy from all the wine," he said. James kissed her forehead and strung together his other excuses. "Aren't you sleepy? Let's rest and get it on early in the morning. You look tired. Get some rest, baby," said James. He gave her butt a light tap and headed to the bed.

Livid, Shandy yanked a shower cap from the caddy, angry with James for ignoring her again. They'd perfected their public façade: handholding, kissing, and finishing each other's sentences. Behind closed doors, the distance grew monthly. Lately, she found him staring at nothing, deep in thought, and short on words. She watched him mail out child support checks to his son. She caught the address shift from California to Georgia. Whenever she asked him what was wrong, he lied and said it was about the businesses. She knew that was a lie because money may as well have been falling from the sky into each salon. *If he wants his son to live with us, why doesn't he say so? Maybe he's cheating. Women throw themselves at him when we're together, so I can only imagine what they do when I'm not there.* She pushed away the thought, lathering and scrubbing her body vigorously. *It's tonight or never. He has to make up his mind.* She leaned into the massive shower heads, tears flowing and mixing with the water. She sat on the warm granite shower seat, embarrassed she'd allowed herself to fall for a man who wasn't her husband. *I moved in this house without a ring or a solid commitment. What's wrong with me?*

She stood, vowing to be a woman and settle the matter. She dried off and entered the dark bedroom. James's shoulders rose and fell in his familiar sleep pattern. *He couldn't have fallen asleep that fast.*

Shandy counted to ten and flipped on the light. "James, we need to talk."

He pulled to covers back and faced her. "Can't this wait until the morning?"

"We've been waiting long enough to have this discussion. We

may as well get it out in the open," said Shandy. She held his hand. "Do you want me?"

"You're very special to me, Shandy."

"That's not what I asked. I want to know if you want me. We don't do anything outside of business."

James's iPhone lit up. He reached for the phone on the nightstand, but Shandy took it from him, spied the 706 area code, and slipped the phone in her robe pocket.

"May I please have my phone, Shan? It could be business."

"Or it could be someone *else* calling. What kind of business discussion goes on after midnight?"

James controlled his temper by clenching and unclenching his fists. He understood her frustration and didn't want to upset her. *Reason with her.* "Shan, at least let me see if it's a supplier. I haven't checked my phone for hours. It could be an old message."

She tossed the phone at him and went downstairs to the kitchen.

He entered his passcode. He noticed a text from Aruba's number six hours ago. He also saw six missed calls from her father's number. Aruba's message simply stated, "I'm."

Panic stricken, James dialed Lance's number, choosing to listen to the voicemail later.

"Son." He answered on the first ring.

"Mr. Stanton, what's wrong? Is everything okay? Did something happen with Jeremiah?"

"How soon can you get to Georgia, James?"

"I can take the next flight out. What happened?"

Shandy reentered the bedroom sipping a cup of coffee. The shakiness in James's voice halted her.

Wanting privacy, James took the call in the bathroom.

"James, Aruba tried to commit suicide earlier today. She's been despondent for months now, and she tried to end it all today. The doctors said if I had found her ten minutes later, she would have died. Nella didn't want me to call you, but I feel you have a right to know what's going on. Divorced or not, you still have a child together. Fair is fair."

James held the phone to his ear as he headed toward the closet. He pulled out a suitcase and placed it on the bed. Shandy whispered, "What's going on?" Distressed, he ignored her.

"Where is she now?"

"We're in Augusta. She's in the emergency room at the Medical College of Georgia. She'll either be admitted here or sent to another facility. We don't know right now. She has a seventy-two-hour hold before she's released."

James pulled casual clothes and shoes from the closet.

"Should I fly into Atlanta or Augusta?"

"Augusta. I think you should get here as fast as you can. Jeremiah's gonna need you now more than ever."

"I'll call you when I get there."

James ended the call. He was still aflutter with packing.

"I heard bits and pieces. What happened to Aruba?"

"She tried to kill herself today."

Shandy folded her arms. "James, I'm sorry."

Shandy approached James to hug him, but he stopped her. Socks in hand, he tossed them in the suitcase and motioned for Shandy to sit on the bed.

"Earlier, you asked me if I wanted you. I care for you. I respect you, but I can't go on in this relationship with you. I've never stopped loving my wife—my ex-wife. We both made some dumb mistakes over the years, but that place in my heart for her remains. It always will."

Shandy sighed. "Those were the most refreshing words you've spoken since we've been together."

Puzzled, James looked at Shandy. "You're not upset with me?"

"I'm not upset with you. I'm upset with myself for thinking things would change. You haven't really been *with* me since the first year we met."

James knelt next to Shandy on the floor and held her hand. "We're so good together in business," said James.

"Not so lucky in love," said Shandy. She released his hands, stood, and headed toward the closet. She removed cologne and after-shave from his side.

"You don't have to help me pack. I know this is hard enough for you," said James.

"Business is business. You need to make sure you have everything before you leave. Who knows when you'll be coming back?"

"True. We'll have to keep in touch about the day-to-day operations. I anticipate I'll be gone about a week and a half." James sat on the bed and rocked back and forth.

Shandy spoke to break the awkwardness. "Listen, I'll log on to Delta and book your flight. How does that sound?"

James, dizzy from the shock of his ex-father-in-law's call, rubbed his temples. "I did this to her. If I'd been faithful and treated her right, she wouldn't be fighting for her life."

"She left you for someone else."

"After I dogged her out."

No verbal tennis match tonight. "Window seat or aisle?"

"Doesn't matter."

James kept his head in his hands. He wasn't sure what he'd say to Jeremiah or his former in-laws, but he knew he had to make amends—if not for himself, then for the sake of his son.

After a few mouse clicks, Shandy said, "Your flight leaves at six in the morning and arrives in Augusta at 9:26 a.m. You have one stop in Atlanta."

Shandy pulled him from the bed to the chair. She then propped her feet up on the ottoman. She felt a twinge of jealousy rise as she placed her head on his shoulder. "Someday, I want a man to love me like you love Aruba."

"You're a hell of a woman, Shan. It will happen."

"Just not with you."

He placed his arms around her, embraced her for what he knew would be the last time, and mentally prepared himself to get his family back.

Chapter 9

James landed in Augusta later than anticipated at 10:18. He exited the plane swiftly in an attempt to get away from the chatterbox who had sat next to him since the flight from Indianapolis. She seemed quiet until he slid into his window seat. Cocking her head to one side once he sat down, she uttered, "Dixon's Hair Affair! Leave your worries at the door, right?" The twenty-something petite woman extended her hand, and for the next three hours, she dominated the conversation about everything from hair care to her impending divorce. She fondled her tennis bracelet the entire time she spoke and made a point of telling James her divorce would be final by the spring. She added that she planned to marry again before turning thirty. She ran her fingers through her relaxed braids and said, "I've been thinking of going natural, but I've heard horror stories of how the relaxed and natural hair separate from each other. Mind if I ask you a few questions?"

He answered her questions as best he could, but was dismayed that she remained on the plane when they stopped in Atlanta. After they took off for Augusta, however, he went to sleep. She followed him to the luggage carousel where they waited for their suitcases.

"I did all that talking and didn't tell you my name. I'm Barbara," she said. She retrieved a hefty, floral bag from the carousel and rubbed James's arm.

The words of his mentor, Isaak Benford, came to mind. "Everyone is a potential customer, so treat the conversation as such."

"Good luck with your transition, Barbara. If I might make a suggestion, with a face as lovely as yours, you should do a big chop. Save yourself the agony of wrestling with relaxed and natural hair."

"You really think I can pull off a TWA?"

"I'm positive you can rock a teeny-weeny afro," James said.

"I sure wish I could call you and get personal assistance with this transition," Barbara said. She twirled her shiny braids around her fingers.

"You don't have to call me," said James. He pulled a postcard from his shirt pocket and gave it to her. "This is our website devoted to natural hair. Log on and click on the tabs for information about the process as well as specifics about my natural hair care line. Should you have questions, call the number on the site and our hotline team can assist you."

"May I give you my number just because? You are so sexy!"

"I'm strictly business these days, young lady," said James. He hoisted his bag from the carousel.

Barbara's countenance drooped. She turned away and rolled her bag in the opposite direction. He watched the lovely young woman walk away as she added an extra twist to her stride.

James marveled at his restraint. There was a time when Barbara would have been able to capture his attention and everything else. He eyed his watch and scanned the airport for Alamo signs. Shandy had sent him directions to the East Central Region Hospital, Aruba's current location. He needed to rent the car and get to her as quickly as possible. After checking out at Alamo, he headed toward the hospital. Aruba and James frequented Augusta when they visited relatives and friends during their marriage, and he knew the city like the back of his hand. This time, the eight-minute drive to the hospital seemed like an eternity as Aruba's face danced around in his thoughts. He wasn't sure what to say to her or if she would speak to him. Lance used the term "checked out" to describe her. Lance also said for the first seventy-two hours, she couldn't receive visitors.

James pulled into a parking space, took a few short breaths, and walked toward the facility. He approached the receptionist's desk. "I'm here to see Aruba Faulk," said James.

"What is your relationship to the patient?" asked the receptionist.

With confidence, James answered, "I'm her husband."

"Mr. Faulk, she's in room 184. She can't have visitors yet, sir. You can join your in-laws and your son. They're sitting in the lobby area down the hall." As James walked away, the receptionist called to him, "Your son is adorable. I'm sorry he has to be here under these circumstances."

James shook off the Mr. Faulk insult and endorsed her concern with a nod. "So am I."

James headed down the hallway. He saw Darnella, Lance, Jeremiah, and Maxine, Aruba's grandmother, sitting in hard chairs. Jeremiah noticed James and ran toward him.

"Daddy!" Jeremiah screamed as he ran into James's arms. His face lit up as he jumped into his father's embrace.

Darnella tossed *Good Housekeeping* back on the coffee table. "What are you doing here?" she shouted. Three other people in the lobby area turned their attention to the unfolding drama.

"I'm here to see my son and Aruba," said James.

"Nobody invited you here, so you can go back to that skinny tramp you're living with and leave us alone." Darnella jumped from her seat and stood in James's face. "You've done enough damage to her."

Lance pulled Darnella's arm to quiet her. "I called him here. There's no cause to make a scene. Let's step outside to discuss this." Lance turned to Maxine. "Watch Jeremiah while we go outside to talk."

Darnella folded her arms in defeat. She followed Lance and James outside to the parking lot. Lately, Lance had been going behind her back, disrespecting her wishes, and making things difficult between them. *Doesn't he care that our daughter almost died over all of the drama James caused?* She would have never gone after her friend's husband if he had been taking care of his family in the first place. Not to mention that nut *he* slept with and created a bastard. *"Deadbeat,"* said Darnella.

"What did you say, Mrs. Stanton?" James asked.

"I called you a deadbeat, and I didn't stutter," said Darnella.

"Enough, Nella," said Lance.

The three of them found a bench outside the facility. Neither chose to sit.

Lance turned to Darnella. "I'm not saying this more than once. You've kept this man away from his child long enough. You're walking around here all self-righteous and you're not considering Jeremiah."

"What's there to consider? James hasn't been—"

Lance put his hand up to silence Darnella. Lance faced James. In his desire to make sure his grandson had a father figure, he didn't want to appear to be against his wife. "Son, in Darnella's defense, you haven't reached out to Jeremiah. We know you're busy with your businesses, but he needs you."

"With all due respect, Mr. Lance, I call my son every week. Whenever I call, Ms. Nella says he isn't available or he's across the street with Ms. Maxie."

They faced Darnella now.

"Matter of fact, I send him a check every week, so the two of you don't have to struggle to provide for him. I know you're doing well in retirement, but I make sure to take care of him. I'm not the villain someone wants me to be," James smirked.

"Darnella, is this true?"

Darnella shifted uncomfortably and held on to the bench. She pursed her lips and said, "So what! Look how long it took him to step up to the plate and handle his business. I'm supposed to let my guard down again and let him hurt Aruba?"

Lance sat now, baffled by his wife's selfishness. He had no idea James had put forth so much effort to stay connected to Jeremiah. He wasn't sure the past could be erased, but James deserved a chance, and as long as he was around, he'd make sure he got it.

"We can't see her right now anyway. I suggest we see what the doctors say. We can stay here for a few hours and figure out what we'll do tomorrow."

Darnella ignored Lance and headed back inside the hospital. James sat near Lance. They each felt a newfound respect for the other.

"I know I messed up, but I don't want another man raising my child. Aruba might not want to be with me again, but I think it's worth a try."

"I'm no stranger to infidelity. Hell, neither is Darnella. I think she's sore because she doesn't want you to hurt Aruba again. But y'all are grown and have to work this thing out yourselves."

"I'll be here a while. I booked a hotel for a week, but after the blowup we just had, I might look into renting a house. Jerry can spend time with all of us. If I have to set up shop here to do hair, I will."

"Do what you have to do to get your woman back, James. You have my blessing."

Chapter 10

Dr. Outley Shipman met with Aruba at ten the next morning. Aruba's involuntary admission into the psychiatric facility embarrassed the family, but Dr. Shipman assured them he could get Aruba back on track. Only Lance, Darnella, and James came to the hospital; Maxine stayed behind to get Jeremiah off to school.

Darnella eyed her watch as they sat in the lobby area. "What's taking Dr. Shipman so long?" she asked.

Lance rubbed her shoulder but said nothing. He quietly stewed from yesterday's revelation of Darnella's secrets. Lance believed Darnella was past midlife crisis episodes; he wondered if she was evil, or so detached from reality she couldn't see how much her actions resembled the ones she loathed from James. "Speck and logs."

"Did you say something, Lance?" she asked.

"Nope." His gaze returned to the window.

"For the record, James, I let you come today because Lance thinks this is the right thing to do. If I had my way, you wouldn't be here at all."

"Yes, ma'am."

"Oh, so you're patronizing me now?"

"No, ma'am."

James leaned forward and pulled his iPhone from his pocket. He saw a few missed calls from Shandy. He said to no one in particular, "I'm going to make a few business calls outside. I'll be back."

"Go ahead and call your women. I'm sure you have a slew of messages from them," Darnella hissed.

"I..." James waved his hand and walked away, leaving her venom in the lobby.

Lance faced her. "I'm telling you again, Nella, I'm not putting up with this nonsense. Leave the man alone and drop the attitude. Can you try to be civil for our daughter?"

"I am being civil. Can't I speak my mind?"

Dr. Shipman interrupted Lance's response. "Hello, Mr. and Mrs. Stanton. Would you please come this way?" he asked. He pointed to an office.

They followed him and sat next to each other, both nervous about Dr. Shipman's findings. He placed a manila folder on the desk and clasped his hands together.

"Aruba is not as despondent as yesterday, but she has a long journey. I am recommending outpatient therapy once she's released." He removed a sheet of paper from his folder and slid it to Lance and Darnella. "Here is a list of excellent therapists in this area. She'll need counseling. She's unrestrained but medicated right now. It is crucial that she have family participation to get better. How much time are you willing to invest in her recovery?"

"Neither of us work now, so that shouldn't be a concern," said Lance. "We'll do what it takes to help her."

"She asked to see someone named James. Who is he?"

Darnella shifted in her seat and pursed her lips. "My *ex* son-in-law."

"He's actually outside right now. I'll go get him," said Lance.

"Please do. I shouldn't, but I'll allow each of you to go in, but only for increments of ten minutes. Too much visitation is not good for her right now."

Darnella waited for Lance to leave the room. She leaned forward, clutching her strand of pearls. "Is there a way I can stop James from seeing her? I don't want him to upset her any more than he has. He wasn't the best husband to her, Dr. Shipman."

"I'm afraid I can't make that call, Mrs. Stanton."

Lance and James returned to the room before Darnella could further protest.

"Dr. Shipman, you said Aruba asked to see me," said James.

"Yes, she did. I'll take you to her room." James walked in stride with Dr. Shipman to room 184. Without asking, Darnella's reaction let him know the divorce had been ugly. Still, he hoped they could be amicable for the sake of their child. He opened the door and pointed to his watch. He whispered, "Ten minutes." Dr. Shipman walked out and left James alone with Aruba.

James neared the bed slowly, not sure if he had the right room. He willed himself to face Aruba but found it difficult. His heart sank at the sight of her. He pulled up a chair next to the bed and sat down. She hadn't noticed him come in. He grabbed her right hand. Her ghastly appearance crushed him. Aruba's claim to fame was being a Kenya Moore lookalike. James looked at her ashen face, chapped lips, and dull skin. He couldn't stop wondering how long she'd been in this state. He ran his hands over her brittle, matted hair, which was once a healthy mane of bouncing curls. Acne dotted her face. Her nails, chipped with old polish, were varying lengths of neglect. Aruba always kept her hair and nails done.

"Aruba?"

She slowly turned to face James. Their eyes locked; she quickly turned away.

"Don't be afraid. I'm here now."

After a long pause, she faced him again and said, "You...feel sorry for me." Her dull monotone was a reminder of the medication her father mentioned.

"How can you say that? I never stopped caring for you. I'm here and I'm not leaving until you get better."

She wept at the sound of his words. He sat on the bed this time and cradled her in his arms. Too weak to return his embrace, she let him hold her and rock her back and forth.

Chapter 10

Nicolette washed clothes for a sleepover as Victoria contemplated ignoring her mother's call for the seventh time. She knew the penalty for ignoring the call would be a personal visit, and *that* she couldn't endure. Victoria grimaced at the sight of her mother's name. *Dammit!*

Three weeks had passed since The Capital Grille debacle. Emory kept his distance, and her mother was a tad too gleeful about their breakup. When Lillith called, it wasn't to comfort her or ask how things were going. It was simply to say, "You did the right thing. The man would have been more trouble than he was worth."

Victoria sighed before answering the call. "Hello, Lillith."

"Don't sound so enthused to hear my voice, darling. I called to check on you."

Is that what you call it? "I appreciate the call, Lillith, but you shouldn't have. Really."

"Nonsense. Mothers are supposed to nurse their lovesick daughters back to a state of common sense. Now tell me you don't feel better now that *he's* not around."

"I miss Emory, Lillith. I miss his voice, his laughter, and the way we cooked together."

"Are you serious? You put on quite a few pounds being with him, in case you didn't notice. If he had stuck around, you two would have been twins, wobbling around, looking like candidates for *The Biggest Loser.*" Lillith giggled into the phone and said, "Stop!"

Victoria knew the giggling meant one thing: Lillith was entertaining one of her cubs. She marveled at her mother's ability to attract younger men, even after a stroke left her mouth slightly crooked and partial paralysis on her right side. Lillith's clothing left little to the imagination, and she pretended her small pot belly didn't exist. She stuffed her size fourteen body into size eight clothing and dared anyone to challenge her style of dress. Victoria wanted so badly to call Lillith *mom*, but that wasn't a possibility. Lillith ripped a page from the Joe Jackson School of Parenting and insisted Victoria call her by her first name. Not Mom. Not Momma. Not Mother. Before she left Victoria in Marguerite's care, Lillith told people Victoria was her niece. Victoria often wondered if Leland, her father, would ever come back into her life, or if Lillith's overbearing ways made him disinterested in having a relationship with her. A weird, clicking noise captured Victoria's attention.

"Lillith, what is that sound?"

Lillith giggled again. "It's Bobby clipping my toenails. He's giving me a pedicure. Afterwards, we're going out for drinks and dinner at the Mardi Gras Café tonight. Isn't that sweet?"

Victoria dry heaved. Bobby Yoder, a twenty-six-year-old valet, had been dating her mother the last six months. When he wasn't driving Lillith's car to run errands, he was propped up on her sofa eating chicken poppers, guzzling beer, and commentating with Reece Davis as if he deserved a seat at an ESPN desk. Lillith didn't want to hear that Bobby needed and had found a mother figure in her. The thought of Lillith being intimate with Bobby churned her stomach.

"How is my granddaughter doing?" Lillith asked.

"Nicolette is doing laundry for a sleepover."

"A nine-year-old washing her clothes. I bet the two of you miss Alva, don't you? A nanny is a treasure in this day and time."

Victoria cleared her throat. "I speak with her often. She returned to Antigua. We miss her and enjoyed the time she shared with us."

"Humph, if I had a nanny, you couldn't tell me anything."

Victoria heard Bobby say, "I gotcha back, Lill," as he continued clipping her toenails.

"I bet you do," said Lillith.

Victoria's doorbell rang, saving her from the smart quip she had ready for Bobby and Lillith. *Saved by the bell.* "I have to go, Lillith. Someone is at the door."

"We might stop by on our way out tonight," said Lillith.

"I won't be here. I'm taking Nicolette to her sleepover, and then I have a few things to do. Enjoy your night out with Bobby," said Victoria. She ended the call, disgusted by Bobby clipping her mother's toenails.

Victoria sped to the front door. She hoped Emory was ready to talk face-to-face. She peeked through the side panel curtain and saw Yvette and Marguerite's smiling faces. Yvette held up a pink box from Cami Cakes; Marguerite held up a Publix box. She wasn't ready for visitors and had held Marguerite and Yvette at bay with phone calls. She knew they'd eventually get tired of talking on the phone. She opened the door.

"What do I owe the pleasure of this visit?" she asked.

"You thought you were slick with the phone calls. We had to make a personal visit to make sure everything is okay with you. Besides, Foster told me to tell you if you can go to work, you can come to church," said Marguerite. She placed the boxes on a hallway console table and removed her jacket. Yvette followed suit and gave her jacket to Marguerite to hang in the hall closet.

"Let's go in the kitchen. I'll make some coffee and watch the two of you eat these goodies. You both know I'm trying to lose weight," said Victoria.

"You have a seat with Yvette while I make the coffee," said Marguerite.

"This is confessional, so you're allowed a tiny treat. You look like you're down a few pounds already," said Yvette.

"Stress and more stress," said Victoria. "If I've lost weight, it's because I can't sleep or eat. I'm embarrassed about the way I acted at the party."

Marguerite busied herself making coffee while Yvette and Victoria sat at the island. Marguerite worked Victoria's kitchen like an old pro, removing dessert plates, forks, and napkins from cabinets.

"We bought a dozen goodies from Cami Cakes and a cake from Publix. We'll all share these treats," said Yvette.

"I'm not hungry, but I'm glad you're here. I just hung up with Lillith, and she's going out again with Bobby tonight."

"Marguerite poured coffee and joined them at the island. "I will not talk about my crazy sister today and her love interests. This visit is all about you, Victoria. How have you been?"

"I'm not sure. I think I did the right thing. I can't express what I feel. Emory is the nicest man I've met in years, but for some reason, I can't trust him or anyone." She looked at Yvette. She dropped her head and took a chocolate coconut pecan cupcake from the box.

Yvette hoped Victoria would open up about her past hurts. She refused to share things with her, leaving Yvette thinking she may have offended Victoria in some way.

"Is it because of Aruba?" asked Marguerite.

Victoria's side-eye look to Marguerite clued Yvette that a woman was involved in the standoffish treatment she'd received over the years. Yvette sat back and waited for the conversation to proceed.

"She's a factor," said Victoria.

"Who is Aruba?" asked Yvette.

"I'll let her tell you," said Marguerite. "I don't think it's my place to share what happened in her marriage."

Victoria charged full speed ahead. "Yvette, I always told you my ex-husband died, but we broke up after a friend of mine…stole him."

"Oh my. I'm so sorry to hear that," said Yvette.

"Just to clear the air here, a man can't be stolen. People go where they want to go, but Aruba had a plan to take him," said Marguerite. "She skinned and grinned in my niece's face until she had him. She moved on to California with him, but the joke was on her in the end when she discovered he had ALS."

"That's payback and then some," said Yvette. She turned to Victoria. "Is that why you never share anything with me? There has always been an aloofness there, but I thought I'd done something personally to you."

"I don't trust people, especially other women. When I think about getting close to someone, I think of how she wore my clothes, drove my car, and spent time in my home. I'll never put myself in that position again with someone."

Her words settled around the island as they ate their treats and drank their coffee in silence. Yvette rubbed Victoria's shoulder. Softened by the revelation, she realized crossing paths with Victoria wasn't about friendship; it was an assignment.

Chapter 11

Tawatha pulled the floppy hat over her head, adjusted the oversized sunglasses on her face, and waved to Royce as she backed out of the main house garage. She'd marked this day on her calendar to follow up on job leads—or so she told Royce. Next to her were indeed appointment times for interviews at Marsh, Kroger, Burger King, and Federal Express. She'd spent several nights filling out online applications and printing out interview dates. The true nature of her outing was nestled beneath the printed sheets—addresses and directions to the homes for Roberta, Lasheera, and James—compliments of Switchboard, Spokeo, and Intelius. She'd grown tired of being ignored by her family and friends. Since they all purported to be Christians, she couldn't understand why they didn't want a decent relationship with her. She understood James's stance, but Roberta and Lasheera were a different matter. She'd learned from Jamilah that her mother decided to let Aunjanue stay with Lasheera and her husband, Lake, so she'd have the benefits of a younger, more vibrant family. Roberta and JB were capable of raising Aunjanue. She wondered how often Aunjanue visited her grandmother and what type of things she did for fun. Did she have a boyfriend? Was she sexually active? She'd searched her name online and found that Aunjanue's academic life hadn't suffered. A senior at North Central High School, she participated in lots of activities that fostered her love of art. She'd also been accepted to numerous colleges and universities. She checked for Facebook and Twitter profiles but found nothing. If no one else bonded with her, she'd make sure to re-establish a relationship with Aunjanue.

She pulled the first map from her printed directions and looked at Lasheera's name at the top of the paper. As she navigated the I-465 S traffic, her envy intensified when she looked at the address. "How does a former crackhead find a husband and move into such a nice neighborhood? She got Lake, but I couldn't keep James," Tawatha said. She didn't care what anyone said, James still loved her. He just didn't know it yet. He bided his time with the skinny woman on television until she got out of jail. Of this, Tawatha was sure. "If Lake can overlook 'Sheer's past, James can overlook the house fire. After all, I did it for him. We can get our daughter back and raise her together." Tawatha's anger rose now; she turned up the oldies station and sang along with Marvin Gaye and Tammi Terrell as they belted out "Ain't Nothing Like the Real Thing." This tune accompanied many Saturday morning cleanings when she lived in California with her mother and twin sister, Teresa. Even now, Tawatha remembered sweeping floors and waxing windows with crumpled newspapers. "Yeah, I'll show Jameshia how to clean and cook." Her solo conversation continued until she turned into the entrance of Lasheera's subdivision. For an extra fee, she received a birds-eye view of Lasheera's house. She parked three houses down and waited. She knew nothing of Lasheera's work schedule, but she figured Lasheera worked Monday through Friday. *Maybe she's out shopping this Saturday morning.*

The oldies radio tunes mocked her as "Games People Play" by The Spinners began. She looked at the children playing in their yards, riding bicycles, and selling lemonade at colorful stands.

Mothers and fathers clustered in each other's yards were laughing and swapping stories. She hated their suburban souls with all her heart. "James and I can have this someday. I know we can." A stray ball rolled in front of her car and Tawatha watched its owner retrieve it. The little boy waved to her and ran back to the game he played with four other boys. She thought of Sims and Grant then. She opened her purse to get her children's photos when she saw Lasheera's garage door open. Tawatha snatched her sunglasses off to get a closer look at Lasheera. She looked good from where Tawatha sat. Lasheera and Lake held hands as Lake walked her to a car parked in the driveway. Lasheera looked well. She had filled out in a womanly way; she didn't have to same body Tawatha had grown accustomed to seeing when she did drugs. Her hair had grown past her shoulders; she wore stylish jeans and a soft, green cashmere sweater with a decorative scarf tied in a triple loop. The September weather didn't warrant a heavy coat, so the sweater and scarf did the trick for the day. Lake leaned into her face, caressed her light-brown skin, and kissed her lips. He whispered something in her ear, causing them both to laugh and fall into each other's arms. She playfully pushed him away. They advanced a few steps, and Lake opened Lasheera's door. Once Lasheera was seated, they kissed again and Lake waved goodbye as Lasheera backed out the driveway. Tawatha scooted down in the seat and waited until Lasheera passed. She set her iPhone alarm for five minutes and sat back up to watch the neighborhood happenings. Lake reappeared from the garage with a weed eater. He trimmed shrubs and bushes. "He is fine!" Tawatha said.

Lake wore a fitted muscle shirt, jeans, and boots as he manicured the lawn. Tawatha remembered a cute, chunky guy with a boyish face and an easygoing personality. The man doing yard work made Tawatha swoon. Everything about him, from his sexy glide to teak wood skin glistening in the September sun, made her angrier that Lasheera had landed such a great catch. Tawatha remembered how much Aunjanue admired him as her art teacher. Jamilah mentioned he'd gone back to school to obtain his Ph.D. Tawatha surmised he was making more money and probably heading the household like a man should. Tawatha pulled a pack of Marlboro Lights from her purse, lit one up, and cracked her window. She continued to enjoy the view of Lake as his arms spanned the reach of the higher bushes. Zion joined him, making Tawatha sit higher.

Zion, Lasheera's son whom she created with a married man while doing drugs, followed Lake around the yard picking up discarded leaves. They set trash bags in the garage and began horseplay on the lawn. Zion's growth astounded her. He was almost ten and tall like his biological father, Marvin. His jeans and T-shirt were ironed so hard she saw the crease in the pants three houses down. His cotton candy Afro sat high and proud. He'd been a crack baby who had spent months in the neonatal intensive care unit before Lasheera was able to bring him home. Tawatha teared up at the memory of holding his frail hands through the glass incubator at St. Vincent's Hospital. "Life is moving on for everyone except me."

She took another drag of her cigarette and continued to watch Lake and Zion in the yard. She had become so engrossed with their family time she jumped at the tapping of a black baseball bat on her window. She smashed the Marlboro in the ashtray. Readjusting her shades, she let the window down to address the woman wielding the baseball bat.

"May I help you, ma'am?" Tawatha asked.

The woman extended her free hand. "Belinda Rosewood. Your name?"

"T... Tina Lewis."

"What are you doing sitting out here in the neighborhood? Looking for someone in particular, Ms. Lewis?"

"I'm out searching for houses. My realtor told me it's best to check out a neighborhood on a Saturday. I get to see how vibrant the neighborhood is," said Tawatha. She gripped her trembling hands together.

Belinda made Tawatha's flesh crawl. She may have been decked out in pink, but there was nothing soft about her. Tawatha could tell she was a one-woman neighborhood watch, and she didn't like being the target of her vigilance. Belinda's small hands grazed the bat before she tucked it underneath her left arm. She pointed a pink, manicured finger in Tawatha's face.

"Are you looking to occupy the house or burn it down?"

"What are you talking about?"

"I know exactly who you are, Tawatha Gipson," said Belinda. She snatched the shades and floppy hat from Tawatha and tossed them on the ground. She cracked the bat in her hands and raised her voice.

"I will let Lasheera and Lake know you've been spying on them. If I see you in this vicinity again, Slugger and I make you regret you ever got out of jail!" Belinda pointed the bat at Tawatha's face. "You're not welcome here. Do I make myself clear?" Belinda picked up the hat and sunglasses and tossed them in Tawatha's backseat.

"Yes...ma'am," said Tawatha.

Tawatha's trembling hands shook more as she wrestled with the keys. She started the car and sped from the subdivision, checking her rearview mirror as Belinda stood, caressing the bat and flashing a sinister smile.

Chapter 12

Lasheera turned the blue envelope over again in the Walgreens parking lot. The huge envelope contained bills, clipped coupons, and a summons to appear in court from Zion's father, Marvin. She removed the summons from the blue envelope, wondering how Marvin had found her. He'd relinquished all parental rights four years ago when his wife said, "Not another dime is leaking out my house for your bastard son." Like magic, Marvin signed the necessary paperwork, granting Lasheera sole custody of Zion. Lake's love and understanding helped smooth the transition from newlyweds to new parents. Shortly after Zion graced their presence with his boyish laughter and wide-eyed enthusiasm, Roberta approached them about taking temporary custody of Aunjanue. Roberta's arthritis and Johnny's migraines made them poor candidates for parenting a fourteen-year-old girl. Roberta loved her granddaughter, but her old bones were no match for the evolution of modern teens. She didn't know an iPad from an iGate, and she wasn't interested in learning the difference. Seeing Onnie on the weekends and at special school events satisfied her.

Lasheera knew Marvin's motive for visitation had everything to do with his wife's passing. Lake had slid the *Star News* obituaries to her over coffee and cereal four months ago. They were shocked that Marvin's wife had succumbed to a heart attack; forty-five seemed too young to die. The obituary referenced her cause of death and the American Heart Association's "Go Red For Women" website for donations in her memory. Lasheera, stunned to learn Zion was listed as their son in the paper, offered her assistance for the funeral. Marvin rebuffed her, telling her their affair and Zion's birth played a part in his wife's death. So, she was shocked to receive the letter seeking visitation. *What is he up to?*

Lasheera shook off the thoughts of Marvin and entered the pharmacy. She forgot to check up on Onnie and stepped to the end of the cosmetics aisle to call her. Onnie answered on the first ring.

"Did you make it to the location with the other students?" Lasheera asked.

"Yes, we're here. I think today will be a good day since Mrs. Maggie is quiet. Tarsha and I are going skating tonight, so I'll be home later."

"We have church in the morning, so don't stay out too late," said Lasheera.

"I'll be home by twelve. Roger is out of town with his parents, so no date tonight. Only skating."

"Is he coming back in time for dinner with us tomorrow night?"

"I'm not sure. He texted me earlier, but I didn't respond yet. I'm getting the drawings together with the other students right now. I'll call him when I leave."

"Be careful and mind your manners. Oh, and tell Caleb we have a double date soon with him and Stephanie. Lake will call him about the exact night."

"Yes, ma'am. I'll tell him."

"Don't call me *ma'am*. I'm not that old. Auntie Sheer is fine."

"I will, Auntie Sheer."

Lasheera ended the call feeling more at ease. Since Tawatha's release, she called Onnie frequently to make sure she was safe. Caleb Wilson, her new art teacher and protégé of Lake's, looked out for Onnie's academic and social well-being. He didn't show favoritism, and he kept her in line when she seemed disinterested in class. She'd been an active participant in class since Tawatha's release. He promised he'd make sure to keep her on task in class, especially since he had caught her daydreaming several times the past few days.

Lasheera tucked her cell phone in her purse and combed the aisles for clipped coupon items. The coupons were her grocery list since she never veered from planned purchases. Lake was a stickler for saving money. He'd influenced her in more ways than he knew, and she wanted him to know just how much she appreciated him. She planned on going to the pharmacy on the way out for their meds.

"Excuse me, Ms. Lady," someone called from behind.

"Yes?" Lasheera spun around, hesitant at first but not wanting to appear snobby. She stood her ground but was alarmed by the woman's disheveled appearance.

"My car broke down a few miles up the road, and I need some gas money. Can you help a sista out?"

If she has a car, I have a jet, Lasheera thought as she looked her up and down. The stout woman's eyes bugged as she held her hands out for the money. She shifted back and forth as if she had to use the bathroom, but stopped abruptly when another patron walked down the aisle. The holey, New York Knicks T-shirt she donned hadn't been washed in weeks; neither had she. Her cargo pants, equally dingy and sliced with a knife or scissors, offered a peek-a-boo effect to legs filled with scrapes and cuts. She scratched underneath the baseball cap she wore, stopping only to look at the grime beneath her nails. When she opened her mouth to speak again, Lasheera winced at the jagged remains that were once teeth.

"You looking at me like you don't believe me. Tell you what, you can take me up the road and I'll show you my car. Matter of fact, Raymond is waiting in the car for me," she said. She eased closer to Lasheera. "If you could help me out with some gas and something to eat, I'll be so appreciative."

"I'm sorry, but I don't have any money to help you." Lasheera scrounged around in her purse, remembering the Popeye's gift card Lake received from one of his former student's parents. Filled with angst, she gave the card to the woman.

"This card contains fifty dollars. This should get you something to eat. I hope that someone else can help you with some gas. Have a good day," said Lasheera.

Lasheera turned too slowly before the woman swept her up in a hug. Nauseated now, Lasheera held her breath as the woman's rank body odor filled her nostrils.

"Thank you. You just made my week. I'll go out here and find somebody else to help us, but at least I'll have something to eat," said the woman. Satisfied, she clutched the gift card and disappeared through the magnetic entryway.

Lasheera sat in a seat near the pharmacy now. She had to process the encounter. Homeless or not, the woman struck a chord with her. *Did I ever do that to anyone?* Lasheera shook off the guilt of her crack days and steadied herself at the pharmacy counter. Her favorite pharmacy technician waved to her.

"Picking up today, Mrs. Carvin?" the young lady asked.

"Yes, there should be one prescription for me and two items for my husband, Lake."

The technician punched away at the computer and took Lasheera's payment for the items. Too shaken up by the chance meeting with the homeless woman, Lasheera declined the post-purchase consultation.

The woman's smell saturated her scarf and sweater. Memories of Tawatha and the smell of the woman ignited a feeling that was becoming familiar. She wanted a hit of crack so badly she could taste it. She'd staved off the feelings lately because Lake, Aunjanue, and Zion needed her. They would never forgive her if she traveled down that road again. She made her way to the car in a haze, drove off, and stopped at the KFC drive-through for a Coke. She needed something to wash down her Extra Strength Tylenol. She pulled into an empty space in the lot and removed her pharmacy bag. She opened the bag, removed the bottle of pills, and noticed an error. The bag read *Lajuana Carvel*, not *Lasheera Carvin*. She eyed the bottle, fancying it a hush-hush miracle: Lajuana Carvel took Ambien.

Lasheera remembered Roberta needing a sleep aid after the children's deaths. Ambien calmed her down like no other drug. Lasheera couldn't sleep, wasn't eating as much, and found it difficult to keep her mind off drugs. *I'll take a few until things calm down.*

She placed the white bags back in the glove compartment and crept out of the KFC drive-thru. "Thank you, Walgreens, and thank you, Lajuana Carvel."

Chapter 13

The art students met in the Majestic Acres Retirement Community's recreation room per Onnie's request. Mr. Wilson encouraged her drawing idea, and the Recreation Director green-lighted her Sunset Canvas Project. Onnie's desire to spend more time with senior citizens grew stronger after Roberta isolated herself from family and friends. Gone was the vibrant, spunky grandmother who enjoyed watching her stories, frequenting riverboat casinos, and making batches of homemade peanut brittle. Onnie reasoned that if a life-altering incident like the fire could change a woman with a good support system, then how do elderly men and women with no relatives handle day-to-day living? Roberta's father-in-law, Herman, spent four years at the Majestic Acres Retirement Community before moving on to a different facility. Onnie enjoyed visiting him with Roberta and Johnny after church. She loved sitting with him, brushing his shock of white hair, and sharing endless bags of orange slices and circus peanuts. A natural-born storyteller, Herman spun yarns about his segregated childhood, leaving Onnie in awe about how much times had changed. During one visit, Herman lamented the only picture he'd taken as a child was stolen in a home invasion. Onnie sketched a charcoal drawing of how she visualized Herman as a boy. He adored the drawing so much he carried it from room to room to other residents. Soon, they requested she do charcoals of family members, pets, and homes. She enlisted the help of her classmates, and the Sunset Canvas Project was born.

Today, she handed out assignments to each student. She waved to Mr. Wilson, who joined them in the recreation room later than expected.

"Onnie, thanks for getting everyone started. Flat tire. I had to get a new one before I could get here," he said.

Aunjanue smiled at him, glad he'd ditched his suit and tie for casual attire. If she could have a big brother, it would be Caleb Wilson. His vast knowledge of art captivated her and made her want to succeed in her endeavors. Her classmates giggled like little girls when he came near. He channeled his artsy side today with a crocheted skullcap pulled close to his ears. When he smiled back at her, his five o'clock shadow framed his angular cheeks perfectly. His chocolate skin, medium build, and easy stride fit his six-three build. His tie-dyed T-shirt and khaki pants made him look more like a student than a teacher. Her classmate, Wendy, had the nerve to say that he was sexy. The statement made her recoil. Aunjanue saw him as an old man, and wondered what teenage girl would think a thirty-two-year-old man was sexy.

"You're welcome. Everyone knows the person they'll be drawing. Of course, I'm with Ms. Maggie. She's calm today, so I should have her chalks completed before we leave."

Mr. Wilson faced the students and said, "Thanks for giving up this Saturday. You have no idea how much this means to the senior citizens in this facility. Some of them have no relatives or friends, so spending time with them is community service for you and a great gift to them."

They nodded and looked at the room numbers and names they'd been given.

Aunjanue addressed her classmates. "The seniors are expecting us, but we don't want to wear them out. Let's plan to be back here within two hours," she said. "Will anyone else need more than two hours to finish their drawings?"

No one protested, and they filed out of the room to their respective adoptees. Mr. Wilson fell in stride with Aunjanue as she headed to Mrs. Ransom's room.

Mrs. Maggie Ransom, Majestic's most colorful resident, spent her mornings and most evenings in the TV room of the facility. She told anyone who would listen that her children lived in Detroit, but they were coming to get her soon and take her home. She called their names intermittently, the sons first, followed by her daughters. She chose Aunjanue to do her drawings. Ravaged by the onset of Alzheimer's, Ms. Mag, as the staff nicknamed her, called out to Aunjanue the first time she saw her. "Come here, Felicia, and bring me a cookie!" Soon, Aunjanue learned Ms. Mag had a daughter named Felicia. Ms. Mag had twelve children, in fact. Some were deceased; others chose to keep their distance. The first conversation they shared was a hodgepodge of Ms. Mag singing, reminiscing about the past, and chiding Aunjanue to look in the shoebox beneath her bed. Majestic Acres encouraged interaction between the students and patients, but they were neither to accept gifts from the residents nor to bring items to them. Aunjanue always managed to stave off the shoebox request, afraid Ms. Mag might offer something family members wanted to remain with relatives.

She stood at Ms. Mag's doorway with Mr. Wilson. Ms. Mag sat in a green leather chair, the embodiment of the old adage: "Good black don't crack." Her blemish free, rich, dark skin could put an African mask to shame. Her housecoat and comfy slippers were covered by a quilt draped across her lap. She'd received her weekly hairdo from one of the CNAs. Her salt-and-pepper plaits hung past her shoulders and had colored rubber bands tied at the ends. She leaned over to place a jar of peppermints on her nightstand. She focused her attention on the doorway and said, "Felicia, what are you and your husband doing here?"

Aunjanue looked at Mr. Wilson and winked. He bowed his head in agreement. "We came to see you today to draw your picture. Don't you remember I told you I was coming back to capture your beauty?"

She took a seat across from Ms. Mag as Mr. Wilson sat on the bed.

"Felicia, you're going to have to do more than draw a picture to capture my beauty, fine as I am," said Ms. Mag.

She focused her gaze on Mr. Wilson. "I'm finer than cat hair and cleaner than the board of health," said Ms. Mag.

Mr. Wilson laughed before regaining his composure.

"Are you laughing at me, Henry?"

"No, ma'am. I didn't expect you to be in a joking mood today," said Mr. Wilson.

"I never liked your husband, Felicia. He's handsome as all get out, but he's not the one for you. You're gonna see what I mean one day," said Ms. Mag. She folded the quilt and placed it at the foot of her bed. Her private room was a luxury her children gifted her when she moved in.

Aunjanue averted her eyes from her teacher, afraid looking at him would make her laugh also. She pulled up the matching green leather chair and removed items from her sketch bag. She flipped the pad to the drawing she started the last time she visited Ms. Mag.

"When do you all leave for Detroit?" Ms. Mag asked.

"We go back on Monday," said Aunjanue. She sketched Ms.

Mag's face with care, paying careful attention to her hooked nose and glassy eyes. She wanted to make sure she captured her as she was in that moment. She also planned to sketch a younger version of Ms. Mag. She would ask the director of the facility for help with that feat.

"When do you plan on giving Felicia some children, Henry? I'll be too old to hold my grandbabies soon," Ms. Mag said to Mr. Wilson. She laced her arthritic fingers together and waited for an answer.

"Ms. Mag, I've been working so much that we haven't had time to make children," he said.

"Well, it's good you're working. You have to hold on to a job in this day and time," said Ms. Mag. She yawned, drifting off to sleep as Aunjanue framed her eyebrows.

"Does she always call you Felicia?" he whispered.

"Most times. I come to visit her often, and she shares so many stories about her childhood and her children. I wish they'd visit her sometimes."

"She has you, so that's what matters," he said in a low tone.

They sat quietly, watching Ms. Mag's chest rise and fall. Aunjanue sketched the photo of her, pleased Ms. Mag would have a replica of herself, even if she didn't know it. As she framed Ms. Mag's lips, the elderly woman roused, looked at Aunjanue and said, "Don't you trust Henry, Felicia."

Chapter 14

James circled the street once more to make sure he had the right address. He dedicated this Saturday to spend time with Jeremiah and to check out the property his mentor, Isaak Benford, allowed him to live in during his stint in Georgia. Isaak, the catalyst for James's business success, offered the property when he found out he'd returned to Georgia to reconcile with his ex-wife. James's chance meeting with Isaak's wife, Katrina, started a partnership surpassing mentor-mentee status. James considered Isaak a friend, and he appreciated his support. Isaak, owner of the real estate investment company, Benford and Associates, owned and rehabbed properties around the country. When James told him he was staying in the central Georgia area, Isaak had his cleaning team prepare a house he'd recently purchased in Augusta. His corporate partnership with Cort Furniture enabled him to fully furnish the house. James looked at the address he'd received from Isaak's text again and pulled into the driveway.

"This house is nice," Jeremiah said. This was the most enthusiasm he'd shown since James's return to Georgia.

James dialed Isaak's number. Isaak answered on the first ring.

"Did you find the property, Boss Man?"

"Found it. We haven't gone in yet, but I had no idea the house would be this huge. I don't know if I can repay you for this one, Ike. I'm speechless," said James.

"I'm waiting on a call from Mitch about some of his friends who own barbershops on Wrightsboro Road. I know you're used to having your own barbering space, but he'll hook you up so you can push your products and do some hair. If he doesn't contact me, I'm sure he'll reach out to you." Isaak paused. "How is Aruba doing?"

James looked at Jeremiah. "Sit here while I go around back, Lil Man." Jeremiah frowned and crossed his arms. "I'll be right back."

James stepped out the car and walked around back. He loved Georgia weather; it never got Midwest cold and remained in the high 70s throughout the early fall. James ran his fingers through his hair and stood near the grill on the deck.

"It's one day at a time, Ike. She's under psychiatric care and taking Lexapro. She's not talking much, but the fact that she's talking is progress."

"Has your mother-out-law gotten better?"

"Outlaw sums it up! Man, this is a short conversation. It would take all day to discuss that foolishness. She's softened enough that we're taking turns getting Aruba to the doctor, but she's still not happy I'm here."

"Keep me posted and let me know if you need anything else." Background noise interrupted the conversation. "Katrina said hello."

"Tell her I said hi," said James. Jeremiah joined James on the deck with Edmund's Barbecue and Catering bags and a drink holder.

"I'm hungry," Jeremiah whispered.

"Ike, I've got to go. I'll call you once I inspect the house."

"Please do. And James, I mean it when I say that you're in our thoughts and prayers."

"Thanks, Ike."

James ended the call. He gave Jeremiah the key and instructed him to open the front door as well as the patio door once inside. He appreciated his in-laws for raising his son since the divorce, but James felt a stronger sense of responsibility in raising his son. Winston Faulk, Jeremiah's stepfather, didn't live long enough to make an impact in his life, and he'd be damned if another man would step in and raise his son. He'd opened up to Shandy about leaving Jeremiah at the daycare and home alone, but he was a changed man. He would show Darnella, Lance, and Jeremiah he could lead his family. He'd gotten his financial house in order, curbed his appetite for women, and he was committed to being a visible presence in his son's life.

"Come sit at the table with me," said Jeremiah, slicing through James's thoughts. He stood at the patio door gesturing for his father to join him for barbecue.

James walked into the kitchen area. In his wildest dreams, he would have never imagined making the connections he'd made over the last five years. Not only had Isaak provided a place for him to stay, Mitchell Coleman, his salon contact, texted several numbers of other salon owners in the area. He sat down across from Jeremiah, removed food from the bags, and said, "Lil Man, check the fridge to see if we have any ice."

Jeremiah sat, his wooden stance apparent to James. "Son, did you hear me?"

"My name is Jeremiah, not Lil Man. Grandma Nella and Great-grandma Maxie call me Jerry. No one calls me Lil Man, though. That's a baby name, and I'll be ten soon. Besides, Great-grandma Maxie said it's thuggish."

"Jerry it is, Son. I was so used to calling you that when you were younger. It's a force of habit. Sorry."

Jeremiah checked the freezer for ice. Surprised that food filled both sides of the double doors in abundance, he turned to James. "I thought no one lived here."

"This is my place for a while, Son. I moved back to help out with your mom until she gets better."

"What happened to the lady you lived with in Indiana? Grandma Nella said that Mom did all the hard work and Shan reaped the benefits."

James hadn't anticipated blows so early. He planned to ease back into the relationship with his son little by little. He wasn't prepared to answer adult questions with a nine-year-old, but now was better than later.

"What else did your grandmother say?"

"I'm not supposed to share this because I overheard her talking to her friend, Ms. Ann, but she said Mom would have never been in California with Dr. Faulk if it wasn't for you."

James's jaw tightened. He watched Jeremiah rip open a packet of hot sauce and pour it on his pulled pork sandwich. He let Jeremiah chew his food and have a swig of lemonade before he resumed his questions.

"How do you feel about things, Jerry?"

Jeremiah shrugged . He looked James in the eye for the first time. He'd avoided contact with his father since he arrived from Indiana. Looking at him now, he missed the times they'd play in the front yard, or when James took him for ice cream or to the park. His grandmother said he imagined those incidents, but he remembered them as if they had happened yesterday.

"I wish you and Mom could get back together now, but it's too late. She's sick. You have another woman, and she lost everything after Dr. Faulk died."

"What do you mean by that?"

"We had a big house when we first moved to California. But Dr. Faulk got sicker, and Mom and the nurses had to bathe him and take care of him. We wound up in an apartment and had to put our stuff in storage. I don't want her to be hurt by another man. She should stay single."

"Oh," said James.

"And another thing, divorce takes people away."

"I'm sorry about Dr. Faulk's death."

"I don't mean that. I used to play with Nicolette all the time, but after Mom married her Dad, we couldn't talk anymore. Even though she's a girl, I liked her."

"Son, I made a lot of mistakes. If your mom and I don't get together again, I plan to be here for you. I love you, Jerry, and I'm not going anywhere."

"What about Ms. Shan?"

"We had a long talk, and she knows I'd rather be with you and your mom."

"Is she going to do something crazy like the other lady Grandma told Ms. Ann about?"

If James lived to be two-hundred years old, he'd always regret hooking up with Tawatha Gipson. She was more than a thorn in his side; the thought of her made his stomach flip. He should have known Darnella would mention Tawatha whenever she disparaged him to her friends.

"That's in the past, and I'd rather not talk about it, Jerry."

"Did she really kill her kids to be with you?"

"Jerry, I won't discuss that with you. Now wipe the sauce off your mouth and finish your food."

"But Dad—"

James gave Jeremiah a stern look and he backed down. They ate in silence as both checked out the surroundings of the home. Across from them was a beautiful living room filled with stylish, mahogany furniture, a huge flat screen, and a decorative layout resembling Aruba's style. James refocused his attention back to the kitchen and marveled at the granite countertops buffed to a high sheen.

"May I watch television when I'm done eating?"

"After we clean up our mess. I'll even join you. How 'bout some sports?"

"That's fine, but I can only watch an hour of TV. Great-Grandma Maxie makes sure I do my homework on Saturdays so I'm not behind or rushing on Sundays."

"What else does she make you do?"

"She taught me how to cook a few things. I know how to wash and fold clothes, and I get paid to cut the grass. She said that lean time is clean time, and I can't be lazy around her."

"Wow, that's a lot!"

"Yea, she said a man needs to be independent."

"She's right."

"I'm gonna be independent because I never want to get married."

"You say that now, but your mind will change when you get older."

"No way! All I want is a little sister to play with."

James looked at his son, realizing the odds of having another baby with Aruba were slim to none. He didn't want to disappoint him, so he offered, "Jerry, I'll see what I can do about that, okay?"

Chapter 15

The cupcakes two weeks ago were an epic fail, thought Yvette. She joined Victoria in the last phase of the thirty-minute circuit at their neighborhood Planet Fitness. Victoria ditched her guest pass at the CNN fitness center after breaking up with Emory. Yvette had a better understanding of Victoria's pain, so she decided to *show* her friendliness instead of *telling* her what it meant. Victoria acted as if she'd been the only woman who'd been betrayed by another woman. *Everyone gets war wounds on the friendship path; learn the lesson and keep going*, Yvette thought. Still, Yvette couldn't imagine sharing clothes, secrets, playdates, or contacts with someone who actually had the nerve to run off with the man. It was one thing to genuinely admire someone else's relationship, but to actually end up with a Tiffany ring? Well, that was something else.

"So, what do you want to do now?" Yvette asked. She sipped water and waited for Victoria to get up from the workout bench.

"I can't do anything until you help me up," said Victoria. Exhausted, she strained to sit up but couldn't move.

Yvette pulled her up from the bench and helped Victoria stand. Victoria's face looked like boiled ham, and she struggled to breathe. She wouldn't mention the noticeable weight gain since the night of the party.

"I was about to suggest the treadmill, but I think we've done enough for the day."

"I need to walk."

"Are you sure?"

"Look at me. What do you think?" Victoria pinched her rolls of fat together. "Something has to give."

"Okay. Let's give nature a shot. I have a little business to do later in Hampton, so let's walk at McCurry State Park. Afterward, we can have smoothies—no fattening foods, only cool drinks."

"Sounds good. I haven't walked outside since..." Victoria turned away from Yvette.

"Since when?" Yvette asked.

"Aruba and I used to walk in the park all the time in Indianapolis."

"So you're mourning Winston, Emory, and Aruba?"

"That's not fair, Yvette. I've been through a lot."

"Join the hurt club! Everyone's experienced *something* painful. It pains me right now to see you giving Aruba so much power over your life and emotions. She doesn't deserve that much energy," Yvette snapped. She didn't mean to give such a terse response, but Aruba was renting too much space in Victoria's head, and someone needed to tell her. If she had to be the designated informant, so be it.

Victoria's chest heaved and tears streamed. "You didn't have to be so direct!"

"Yes, I did. You can hate me all you want, but friends don't let friends go around looking like Negro spirituals." Yvette pretended to hold a microphone. She deepened her voice and sang, "Nobody knows the trouble I seen ..."

"Stop it, Yvette!"

She switched to an English timbre. "Nobody knows my sorrows."

"You win! I'll go walking with you. Anything. Just stop embarrassing us!"

Yvette exited Planet Fitness, her voice rising as she sang, "Sometimes I'm up, sometimes I'm down, sometimes I'm almost to the ground."

Yvette drew attention now, and Victoria pushed her back playfully. Victoria laughed. It was deep-in-the-belly guffaw Yvette had never heard.

"Is my singing what you needed to break your funky spell?" Yvette asked.

Victoria continued to laugh as they sat in Yvette's car. Pleased her plan was working, Yvette enjoyed seeing her friend smile. Even if Victoria didn't accept the olive branch she extended, she'd walk away knowing she had put forth the effort of genuine friendship with her.

"So how far are we riding?" Victoria asked after catching her breath.

"Sit back and enjoy the ride."

Yvette hit I-75 and turned off her music. She wanted no distractions as they rode to the park.

"I was too abrasive earlier. I feel you're trapped by all the sadness you've experienced. Life gets better—if you're open to it."

"What makes you think I'm not open?"

Yvette pursed her lips and gave Victoria a quick glance. She didn't want to veer off the road, but part of her wanted to pull alongside the road and recite the list of slights she'd endured. She kept driving.

"Let's see. You're Ft. Knox secretive about your life."

"It's not good to tell people your personal business."

"You clam up when anyone mentions, well, mentioned, your relationship with Emory."

"I wanted to keep things between us sacred."

"You *really* don't like women, except your Aunt Marguerite. I'm still trying to figure out how you feel about your mother." *I'm being too forward. Let me soften up.*

"I wouldn't say I don't like women. It's like I told you when you stopped by with Marguerite, the betrayal with Aruba was so strong I haven't recovered. My whole life was turned upside down because of one person."

"Turned upside down, yes, but not over. Are you telling me you plan to stop living because of Aruba…" Yvette snapped her finger. "What's her last name?"

"Dixon. Aruba Dixon. Wow, I guess I should say Faulk since she married my ex."

"Her last name doesn't matter. I wanted you to say her full name to make her real. If you could see her right now, what would you say to her?"

"I wouldn't say a word. I'd punch her in her face and beat her within an inch of her life."

"Really? You're so sensitive that you don't kill bugs, so I know that's not true." Yvette thought of another way to broach the subject. "Pretend I'm her. What would you say to me if I were Aruba?"

Victoria recalled her rehearsed speech. "Why? Why did you take the time to befriend me if you knew you were up to no good?"

"If I said I'm sorry, would you forgive me?"

"I don't know. That's a tall order."

"At least you didn't say no. We're making progress."

"Why is this so important to you anyway? You have a wonderful husband and a good marriage, so why do I matter to you?"

"Because I *was* you some years ago."

"Not Carl?"

Yvette shook her head vigorously. "No, Carl Hankerson is the love of my life! I wouldn't have been with him, though, if I'd allowed bitterness to get the best of me."

"What happened?"

Yvette veered to the right and got off on Exit 235 toward Griffin, Georgia. She stayed in the right lane and clutched the wheel tighter. "I was a senior in college planning my wedding. I am not minimizing what happened to you, and I know a dating relationship is different than marriage, but back then, I couldn't imagine my life without David Rinks. We grew up together. He was my high school sweetheart, and all I could see was him."

"David Rinks that attends our church?"

"The one and only. We were set to wed in July, my senior year. He graduated a year before I did and moved to New York for a job with IBM. I didn't think twice when he thwarted my attempts to visit him. He told me to concentrate on getting out of school so we could be together. His mother and sister visited me at my dorm in Fort Valley, Georgia, and every Sunday, I enjoyed a soul food feast at their house.

"One Tuesday, I stopped by midweek, unannounced, to see my A-M-I-L—"

"A-M-I-L?"

"Almost mother-in-law. She stood at the door, acting as if we were strangers. I had photos of mother-in-law dresses for her; my mother insisted she finalize her choice so they'd match. Before I knew it, a small child who was the spitting image of David ran past his mother and said 'Mommy,' then shrank back when he realized I wasn't his mother."

"Jared?"

"Yes. He was two, almost three at the time, and they'd hidden the child from me since his mom, Cynthia, birthed him. Of course,

David called, begged, pled, and everything, but I knew I couldn't walk down any aisle with him. How could I trust a man who looked me in my face and carried on a three-year betrayal? He said he'd made a mistake by having a one-night stand with Cynthia. He eventually stopped trying to get me back, married Cynthia, and somehow, our lives continued to intersect.

"Cynthia isn't too thrilled to be around me, but we've built a cordial bridge over the years. Carl and I even gave Jared an awesome graduation hook-up this year. We promised not to share what it is, but let's say he won't have problems going back and forth to college."

"Yvette, I had no idea you've gone through so much pain."

"Hey, every smiling face isn't happy. People mask a lot," said Yvette. She swung a right on Lovejoy Road and allowed her truth to soak in.

Victoria looked at her flawless associate. Even in sweats, Minimus shoes, and standing at five feet eleven inches, she exuded confidence. Yvette's volleyball days were over, but men still approached her and asked if she modeled. Yvette's sandy-brown, shoulder-length hair was pulled back in a ponytail. Yvette lived for Smashbox Camera Ready BB Cream, but today, Victoria admired her blemish-free, caramel skin. Beautiful inside and out, Yvette didn't deserve to be treated the way Victoria had treated her. *I've got to do better*, Victoria thought.

They arrived at McCurry Park, coasting into a space near the baseball field.

"Yvette, did I keep you from doing your business run?"

"You're my business run. Let's go walk off these pounds."

Chapter 16

Jamilah unlocked the side entrance to her home office. The meeting with Roberta and Lasheera was set after Belinda spotted Tawatha crouched down in sunglasses and a gardening hat across the street. Although Tawatha wasn't ordered to stay a certain distance from Lasheera or Aunjanue, Jamilah gave her specific instructions not to bother them. Societal reintroduction took time, and Tawatha should have known better than anyone she wouldn't be welcomed with open arms—not this soon, and maybe never. Still, Jamilah felt a civic duty to help Tawatha after rumblings of inappropriate behavior by jurors surfaced.

Jamilah checked the coffee machine and the food tray, careful to include Roberta's favorite creamers, pastries, and coffee flavors. She'd only spoken to Roberta by phone since Tawatha's release two months ago, and each tense conversation ended with Roberta vowing not to speak to her daughter. Stalking was a serious crime, and Jamilah wanted to address Tawatha's actions before they got out of hand.

Jamilah placed the elementary playground photo of herself, Lasheera, and Tawatha on her desk. She angled the photo so Roberta could see how much her friendship with Tawatha and Lasheera meant. The three of them wore matching green corduroy jumpers, paisley green-and-white turtlenecks, and green Keds.

Tawatha had tied the jump rope around her waist in a bowtie as they hugged each other; she flashed a missing-front-tooth grin in the center of the girls. "It's easy to love someone when they dot all their i's and cross all their t's," Jamilah said, repeating a saying her late mother used when reprimanding her for being unsympathetic toward others.

Jamilah missed her parents but was glad they'd both passed away before Tawatha committed the horrible act. Her solidarity with Tawatha would have strained their relationship. After they died—her mother from breast cancer, her father from a massive heart attack—she inherited her childhood home. The insurance money enabled her to finish her undergrad degree and attend law school at Indiana University. She modeled her mother and Roberta's frugality by negotiating with a contractor to have the basement transformed to a home office. The space enabled her to see clients as well as keep people away from her living space. The separate entrance allowed no access to her dwelling.

She looked up from the photo and spotted Roberta walking past the old-fashioned, ornamental light pole installed a month ago. Taken aback by Roberta's appearance, she stood to open the door for her. A palsied gait replaced Roberta's fast, hip-switching stroll. Roberta's hairdo, usually a healthy mane of fire-engine red or honey-blonde, roller-set curls, sat limp on her shoulders—gray, dull, and frizzy. Not only was her hair uncharacteristic, but her throwback outfit shocked Jamilah. She wore a horrid floral, long-sleeved dress, riding boots, and no coat. The forty-degree weather at least warranted a decent jacket. She opened the door and attempted to hug Roberta, but she stood, arms glued to her sides, and gave Jamilah a *let's-get-this-over* look.

Jamilah moved aside to let Roberta into her office. She waited until Roberta sat to speak.

"Thank you so much for coming today, Ms. Roberta. Lasheera should be here soon. May I offer you some coffee?"

"Actually, that would be nice. I can't stay too long because Johnny is taking us shopping. After that, we're dropping some items off at Gleaners Food Bank for Thanksgiving. The holiday is around the corner and we make a contribution every year."

"I remember when you'd get us all together and take food to Gleaners when we were younger. It's good to know the tradition is still going," said Jamilah. She poured Roberta a cup of coffee and added her favorite creamer. She placed a blueberry cheese-cake Danish on a dessert plate and set it before her.

"Thank you, Jamilah."

Roberta sat back in her seat and enjoyed the treats. The coffee provided a much-needed boost. She dreaded facing Jamilah but felt she had to get some things off her chest. She finished her food and placed the items on the side of the desk.

Jamilah looked at Roberta and regarded how much she'd aged since the children died. Her puffy, red eyes hadn't seen sleep in a long time. The hard creases across her forehead sat defiant, refusing to slacken. Wrinkles set in her face, making her look older than her fifty-six years. *She's given up on life.*

Jamilah cleared her throat and eyed her watch. "It's ten minutes after ten. I wonder why Lasheera's running behind this morning. She's generally the first one here."

"I can say what I have to say and be on my way. I understand your friendship with Tawatha goes back a long way. I'm not in agreement with you getting her out of jail, though. Shouldn't that have been some kind of conflict of interest?"

"Not necessarily. I've read of people going to law school with the specific purpose of helping their imprisoned relatives go free. She needed someone to help her."

"That's your opinion. I think she would have been better off thinking about her actions day in, day out. Let's say, for the rest of her life."

"Ms. Roberta, she'll have to face her actions the rest of life—in or out of jail."

Roberta pulled her stringy hair off her shoulder. "This is Onnie's senior year in high school. I wanted to keep her, but looking at her brought back so many sad memories. Lake and Lasheera stepped up to the plate to help do what I couldn't do. Tawatha coming home is going to disturb the balance they've created for Onnie."

"I'm sorry Tawatha went to their neighborhood. I will speak to her when I meet with her later today about staying completely away from the family. I called you and Lasheera here today to simply ask if you'd reconsider seeing Tawatha. She misses everyone and wants some type of connection."

"'Milah, I understand what you're trying to do. I can't see my child right now. I still love my daughter—I really do—but I didn't raise her to do what she did. Do you know how embarrassing it is knowing your child is a murderer of children? I know I made a bad decision when I got involved with her father; he was a married man at the time, but I didn't know it. I lost Tawatha's twin sister, Teresa, to pneumonia, so Tawatha knows what it's like to lose someone close."

"No one is accusing you of the crime," said Jamilah.

"They are. Family members accuse me when they won't let me visit. Strangers accuse me by shunning me once they find out I'm *her* mother."

"Ms. Rober—" Jamilah was interrupted by her cell phone. Lake's name flashed across the screen. She held up one finger to Roberta and answered the call.

"Jamilah, how are you?" asked Lake.

"Doing well. Just chatting with Ms. Roberta. What's up?"

"Will you ask Lasheera to stop by the FedEx office near our house when she leaves you? I'm positive I left my jump drive in her purse."

"Lake, Lasheera isn't here. We've been waiting for her to arrive."

"What do you mean, she isn't there? She talked about the meeting, well, ranted about it, up until she went to bed around eleven last night."

"Oh, I didn't know she wasn't onboard for the meeting."

"Trust me, she was onboard. She had a few things she wanted to tell you about Tawatha's stalking. She should have been there at least an hour ago."

"I'm worried now. What do you want me to do?"

"Don't sweat it. I'll run by the house to see what's going on. Worst-case scenario, she got a wild hair up her butt and decided she couldn't do it."

"Please call me when you find out what's going on, okay, Lake?"

"I'll call you ASAP."

Jamilah ended the call and resumed her conversation with Roberta.

"Is something wrong with Lasheera?" asked Roberta.

"I'm not sure. Lake said she talked about our meeting last night."

A light tap on the door startled them. Jamilah went to the door, opened it, and hugged Johnny. Unlike his wife, he welcomed Jamilah with open arms. Jamilah took in the fresh scent of Irish Spring.

"Is everything alright in here?" he asked. Jamilah noticed his weather-appropriate attire and imagined he'd tried to make Roberta wear a coat. His London Fog trench coat clung to his strapping frame. She glanced at his polished black boots. When the three of them were closer, and before Johnny married Roberta, she, Lasheera, and Tawatha playfully called him the Black Falcon behind his back because of his polished shoes. His gentle ways and dignified manner were no match for his rugged good looks. Retired from Chrysler Foundry, he was a salt-of-the-earth man whose calloused hands slipped in his pockets to give Tawatha's children five- and ten-dollar bills. Totally gray, he kept his beard and hair groomed to perfection and his dusky skin glistening with almond oil.

"How are you doing, Mr. J.B.?"

"I'll be better when Roberta's better." He turned his attention to his wife. "Is everything okay in here?" He removed his fedora and sat next to Roberta. He massaged her left hand and held it tight. The worry lines on her face gave away her distress.

"I was telling 'Milah I'm not ready to reconnect with Tawatha right now. I may do it later, but whenever I think of that urn holding those babies …" She choked back tears.

"Darling, let's go on back home. We can do the food bank later. Go on to the car, darling. I'll be out in a minute," he said to Roberta.

Roberta hugged Jamilah this time. She slumped her shoulders and exited the office.

"Mr. J.B., I didn't mean to upset her. I promised Tawatha I'd at least ask Ms. Roberta if she would see her."

"Thank you for the attempt. I want her to reunite with Tawatha, but I want it to be in her own time, in her own way."

"I understand. I'll let Tawatha know when I see her later."

"Congratulations on finishing college and law school, Jamilah. I know your parents are smiling down from heaven at you."

"Thank you, Mr. J.B."

He tipped his fedora to her. He saw the photo of the girls on desk and picked it up for a closer look of what used to be. He smiled at Jamilah and said, "One day, it might be this way again."

Chapter 17

Lake rushed home from FedEx, dropped his messenger bag at the door, and walked toward the stairs. Sounds from the family room halted him. "Lasheera, what happened? Ms. Roberta and Jamil—" The sight of Zion playing a video game infuriated him.

"Z, what are you doing home from school?"

"I missed the bus and Mom said not to disturb her. She said she'd take me when she woke up."

"Where's Onnie?"

"Roger picked her up and took her to school. I should've rode with them."

Zion's words fully registered. "When she woke up? You mean she's still in bed?"

"*Mmm-hmmm.* I'm hungry, too. You both told me not to make pancakes, waffles, or bacon without adult supervision. We're out of cereal, and we have Pop-Tarts, but no juice. I can't eat Pop Tarts without juice."

"Wait here, Z."

Lake tossed his coat across the back of the dining room table. He rushed up the stairs, heart pounding and hands clammy. Lasheera's strange behavior didn't worry him because he knew Tawatha's release strained everyone. Still, he wouldn't accept any excuse for her not taking Zion to school. Long deliberations and candlelit dinners brought them to where they were. They mutually decided she would quit her job at State Farm after learning Zion would join the family. Guardianship of Aunjanue sealed the deal. Lasheera's drug addiction robbed her of enormous chunks of time with her son. On the cusp of becoming a teenager, the twelve-year-old wore the scars of his mother's addiction in small ways. With tutoring from the family and a private tutor at school, Zion tested out of special education classes. Still, there were moments when he acted as if his new life would end tomorrow. Lake's patience with Zion made him calm down when he'd have temper tantrums or come undone at the slightest chore request. Lake and Lasheera revoked Zion's cooking privileges after a "surprise" deep-fried turkey dinner attempt ignited a fire in the garage.

Lake opened the bedroom door, rushing to Lasheera's side. He felt her pulse, sighing with relief when her chest moved.

"Sheer, get up! Wake up."

She felt around the bed, grasping for covers. She pulled them over her head again and turned toward the window. Lake opened the curtains and blinds.

"What do you want?" she shouted. She sat up this time, scanning the room for the culprit who kept her from getting precious rest.

"I want to know why Zion hasn't been fed, why you didn't go to the meeting with Jamilah, and why our son is downstairs playing video games instead of studying Geography with his classmates!"

Her rapid eye blinks angered Lake. He ripped the covers from her body and tossed them on the floor.

"I race home thinking something's wrong with you and you're yelling at me?"

Lake calmed himself. He didn't want to jump to conclusions,

and he didn't want to accuse her of using again. The allegation would cause a fissure in the trust they'd spent so many years building. He tried a different approach. He lowered his voice.

"I didn't mean to yell. I got worried when Jamilah said you never made it to the meeting."

"That was today?"

"We talked about the meeting last night. You went on and on about how you would give Jamilah a piece of your mind about setting Tawatha free."

"We talked last night?"

"Right here on the bed." Lake pounced up and down on the mattress for dramatic effect.

She hid her face in her hands, embarrassed.

"Z said you told him you'd take him to school when you woke up. Do you remember talking to him?"

She shook her head.

"What did you take last night? You said you had a headache, but whatever you took knocked you completely out."

She glanced at the Advil P.M. bottle on the nightstand. She had flushed the pills down the toilet and replaced them with Ambien. *Blue is blue*, she reasoned. "Only two Advil PMs. I haven't been well with the Tawatha situation and all. You understand, don't you?"

Lake snatched the bottle from the nightstand. "Let me get rid of these."

Lasheera plucked them from his hands. "I promise I won't take them before I go to bed again. You're treating me like an addict, and you said you wouldn't do that to me."

Lake threw up his hands. If he took the pills, he'd be labeled a villain. If he let her keep them, he'd give her sidelong glances each night to make sure she wasn't taking them. Sidelong glances trumped being a villain.

"Did you really dread the meeting?"

"It had nothing to do with the meeting."

"What is this about, 'Sheer?"

"I can't put it into words. I don't know. Something is missing."
Make him think it's him.

"What's missing?"

"I know you're working on your doctorate and the journey is almost done, but I miss seeing you. We don't do dinner as much, and I miss going to the park and walking with you."

"Why didn't you say anything?"

"I didn't want to say something and sound selfish."

"We said we'd communicate about everything. Everything includes the good, bad, and the ugly. If you're feeling neglected, I can't read your mind. You have to let me know, baby."

"I'm sorry, Lake. I won't let it happen again." She blew her breath into her hands and dry heaved.

"Somebody needs to slay the dragon," Lake joked.

"If you go fix Zion something to eat, I'll shower and get dressed. It's too late for him to go to school, so I'll log on to Skyward and find out what he missed today. I'll pull myself together so I can help him with his homework."

"What do I get in return for slaving over a hot stove?"

"Depends on how satisfied he is after he eats."

She stood, feigning shyness. Lake looked at her Wonder Woman lingerie set and wished they were home alone.

Zion yelled upstairs, "Would someone please help me with the pancakes?"

"Coming down in a minute, Z," Lake yelled.

She blew Lake a kiss and jumped in the shower. She turned on the showerheads full steam. Somehow, she needed to find a way to get more Ambien.

Chapter 18

P aul Gauguin, today's featured artist, flashed before the students as Mr. Wilson shared the origin of his paintings. Aunjanue blocked Mr. Wilson's lesson on Gauguin because Van Gogh occupied her thoughts. Aunjanue removed the postcard she had received at the front office from her purse and flipped it back and forth. No one saw who left it for her, but the act had Tawatha written all over it. Who else would know her favorite artist was Vincent van Gogh? Who else would select the *Red Poppies and Daisies* postcard? *Momma must have the holiday blues.*

Thanksgiving was the only time of year Tawatha displayed motherly traits. She busied herself in the kitchen making Roberta's turkey, dressing, potato salad, and collard greens. Tawatha always made Aunjanue and her siblings prepare cakes, pies, and drinks. Aunjanue imagined her little sister, S'n'c'r'ty, pulling up a chair from the kitchen table, spreading Kool-Aid packets on the counter, and dumping too much sugar in their favorite pitcher. Her brothers, Grant and Sims, used Roberta's secret pecan pie trick: They substituted corn syrup with a large jar of caramel ice cream topping. Their pies were always a hit and requested at school raffles. The memories overwhelmed Aunjanue. She raised her hand.

"Mr. Wilson, may I be excused? I don't feel well."

Mr. Wilson paused the Gauguin slides. "Yes, Aunjanue, you may be excused."

Aunjanue grabbed her things and made it to the bathroom in time. She locked the stall door and dropped to the toilet fully clothed. She wept silently about the few positive moments she had with her mother. The memories created a chest-heaving sob. She grabbed tissue and wiped her eyes. She flipped the postcard over and read the words of the typed note again: *I want us to be closer. I can imagine life for you is difficult with all you've been through. I want to make it better. Please give me a chance. Love, T.*

Her cowardly mother didn't even think enough of her to write the note out. Lasheera said her mother currently lived with her former boss, Mr. Royce Hinton. *He probably dropped this off for her.*

Aunjanue and Tarsha talked about what she'd do if Tawatha showed up at the school or at her house. Surprised she still had love for her mother, she wiped the fresh tears away. *How on earth could I love such a monster? Pull yourself together, Onnie.*

She stood, gathered up her things, and walked to the sink. She washed her face with cool water, her red eyes swelling by the moment. The bell rang, and she readied herself for Calculus. When she walked out of the bathroom, Mr. Wilson stood with his hands in his pockets. He approached her as she pulled her backpack up.

"Is everything okay?" he asked.

Aunjanue pondered telling him about the postcard, but telling him was like telling Lake and Lasheera, and she wasn't ready for them to know yet. She didn't want to lie to him.

"I'm a little blue over the holiday season. I was thinking of my brothers and sister in class earlier, and I got full. I miss them so much."

"Aunjanue, I can't bring them back, but I will keep you in my prayers. Stephanie and I will be over for Thanksgiving dinner at your house. Are you in the mood to celebrate?"

She shrugged. "Not now. Not while my mother is free."

"Lake told me about her stopping by the neighborhood." He closed the space between them. "Has she bothered you here at school? I've been looking out for suspicious activity."

"No. Like I said, I got full thinking about my siblings. I'll be alright."

"Please talk to Lake and Lasheera about your feelings."

"They have a lot on their plates, and I don't want to worry them with my problems."

"I understand. I'm sure they wouldn't mind."

The bell rang again. "I need to get to class. I'm late."

"I'll let Mrs. Philips know we were talking. "

"Thank you, Mr. Wilson."

"My name is Henry, remember?"

She laughed at Ms. Mag's name for him and headed to class. He'd made her comfortable without even trying. Each day an action unfolded, making her admire him more.

Chapter 19

Jamilah calmed herself before heading to Tawatha's place. She couldn't believe, after all their talks and her instructions, Tawatha defied her by stalking everyone. *She wants to go back to jail.* Ms. Roberta's claims couldn't be refuted; Tawatha routinely stalked each of them when they were either leaving the house or getting in from errands. She had learned their routines and waited until they arrived. Lasheera and Roberta were blessed to live in communities with a strong neighborhood watch presence. Each similar sighting of Tawatha tagged her in a Ford Focus, floppy hat, and sunglasses. She never got out of the car; she scrunched down in her seat and watched random movement. According to Roberta, she hadn't returned to either area in a few days, but no one knew when she'd slither her way amongst them again.

Jamilah's meeting with Roberta resurfaced in her mind. Roberta was a second mother to the group; Jamilah felt a sense of sadness about the meeting because they never got to the crux of why she'd called her there. Lasheera's absence proved to be a blessing in disguise. Jamilah planned to suggest Roberta welcome Tawatha with open arms so she could begin the process of getting her psychiatric help. No one dared speak the obvious truth: Tawatha's elevator went to the top floor, but the door didn't open. Since elementary school, the three of them were, in fact, the Three

Musketeers. They jockeyed for monkey bar space, twirled each other in playground swings, and occasionally, they dared each other to slope like surfers on the slides. Mammoth trees, fresh air, and secret trails populated their school playground. Without fail, Tawatha disappeared in back of the school as the three of them hopscotched or played jump rope. She would slip away, undetected most times, causing the two to end their fun in search of their friend. They found her sitting on a rock or mindlessly pulling weeds from plants. Sometimes, she sang to herself; other times, she entertained a slew of imaginary friends. The most frightening act she committed was peeping in homes behind the school. Luckily, no one was home during her peeping Thomasina moments, but the girls were scared nonetheless. They coaxed her back to the playground and class, pretending nothing happened. As she aged, her actions were explained away with familiar phrases: "She's different…you know she's a free spirit." Jamilah hoped time would stabilize her, but after the fire, she reasoned the issue had nothing to do with spirits and everything to do with illness. If only Roberta agreed to see her, the first visit would be the catalyst for helping Tawatha.

Her cell phone rang, bringing her back to the present. She saw Lasheera's name and answered, bracing herself for a showdown.

"Hi, Lasheera, how are you? Ms. Roberta and I missed seeing you."

"Girl, I apologize for not coming. I overslept and couldn't get up on time."

"The time-stickler Musketeer overslept, huh? There's a first time for everything."

"I know it sounds absurd, but I've been having a hard time since you started your Good Samaritan *act!*" said Lasheera.

"Progress! The meeting was for you to get your feelings out, so please be candid about them. The tension between us keeps growing, and we're acting like children by not talking."

Jamilah's peaceful tone knocked Lasheera down a few pegs. She'd called to yell and scream, but Jamilah, always the peacekeeper of the group, diminished her need to speak her mind in rudeness.

"'Milah, three children are dead because of Tawatha."

"Let's not forget, *one* child might be dead had someone not pulled Zion from the street after he wandered into oncoming traffic after one of your many crack-smoking binges. Your son was taken away, but you've been fortunate enough to have a second chance with him."

"Don't throw my past in my face. You know I was…" Lasheera paused as she recovered from the sucker punch.

"You were what?"

Lasheera blew an exaggerated sigh into the phone. She sat silent, unsure of what else to say.

"Let's try *in a bad place*. In need of love. In need of grace. Accurate assessment?" Jamilah asked.

"Jamilah, murder and drug use are two different things."

"Since when?"

Lasheera's argument turned to dust in her mouth. Though she'd found love with Lake and had gotten Zion back, she longed for a better relationship with her parents. Currently, their communication was touch and go. They indulged her in cordial conversation, but no longer allowed her in their home. When family events occurred, they would call with the news and hang up, never allowing her a chance to ask questions. She knew this was her penance for all she had stolen from them. Moreover, it was the fallout of having pushed her mother's chest so hard after stealing money from the family's beloved clown cookie jar. During the assault, her mother suffered a mild heart attack. The extended Atkins clan wished Lasheera had died for the way she'd treated her mom; they discouraged her from coming around.

"I get your point, Jamilah. I never said I was perfect or hadn't made any mistakes. I can't see her yet."

"I'm headed to see her right now. Do you want to send her a message?"

"Not now."

"Please consider what I said. She doesn't have to move in with you and Lake, but at least consider having a conversation with her."

Jamilah ended their call and pulled around to the back of Royce's house. She'd called Tawatha for most of the day after the meeting; she never answered. *I bet Tawatha's asleep or watching television,* Jamilah thought as she parked in an empty space near the carriage house. She walked the beautiful path of burgundy mums and rang the doorbell. After the fourth ring, she headed toward the main house. Jamilah figured Tawatha had joined Mr. Hinton for dinner. The carriage house was nice, but it paled in comparison to his stately home. She rang the bell, surprised he opened the door on the first ring.

"Jamilah," his booming voice sang. He gave her a fatherly hug and invited her inside. "Was Tawatha expecting you? She's been gone a few hours now."

"Yes, we were actually supposed to talk. I've been calling her for hours and she won't answer."

"She rarely uses her phone. I think I need to give her another tutorial. Won't you come in and have a seat?"

"Thank you, sir, but I need to get going. I'll try her another time. Please tell her I stopped by," Jamilah said.

"I'm sure she'll be back soon. I will tell her you stopped by."

Jamilah walked away as Mr. Hinton called to her. "Thank you for giving her the job-hunting leads. If she doesn't find something soon, I assured her she could do some administrative work with me."

Jamilah stammered, "You're welcome." She closed the door behind her and walked down the steps.

Disquieted by his words, she turned around on step four, climbed Royce's steps again, and rang the doorbell. He answered immediately.

"Mr. Hinton, may I come in a minute?"

"Yes. Is something wrong?"

"I need your help figuring that out. May I chat with you?"

Royce led Jamilah to the living room. Jamilah looked around and felt uncomfortable. She hated museum homes, houses with décor so immaculate she didn't want to sit.

"Does anyone ever come in here?" she asked.

"This is a livable home. Millie made this her showplace, the home of her dreams, before we broke up. I'm not materialistic at all, so if you spill, drop, or break anything, I won't be bothered."

Now that she could relax, she and Royce sat together on an elegant sofa. She dropped her attorney interrogation tone, fearing he might shut down. She needed to pick his brain in order to help Tawatha.

"I met with her mother, and Ms. Roberta said that Tawatha's been stalking her and Lasheera. She doesn't approach their homes, but she sits in the neighborhood watching them. Were you aware of her actions?"

"She told me she's been job hunting, and I believed her."

"Mr. Hinton, I don't need to tell you how hard it is for a felon to find gainful employment. Couple that fact with the nature of her crime, and let's say Tawatha won't be saying, 'Welcome to Walmart,' anytime soon."

"Every day, she shows me application confirmations from different companies. She dresses up, leaves here, and says that she's going for interviews."

"Mr. Hinton, would you mind opening up the carriage house for me? I have a feeling she is applying for jobs, but she's also using technology to stalk her relatives and friends."

Royce beckoned Jamilah to follow him through the kitchen and the patio. He walked down the back stairs past the pool to get to the carriage house. He opened the door to the carriage house as he and Jamilah scanned the room. Tawatha had reverted to her old ways, though not as severe. A few shirts, pants, and dresses hung over the backs of chairs and on the sofa. Her trash cans were full, not overflowing. She'd left her laptop open, and Royce typed in the username and password, surprised she hadn't changed it.

Jamilah sat at the desk and scrolled Tawatha's browsing history. Among hits on CVS pharmacy, Eli Lilly and Company, and UPS, several identity sites were saved. Jamilah clicked on Switchboard. com and scanned the names of the people Tawatha searched. Royce and Jamilah read the names in unison: Roberta Boston, Lasheera Carvin, and James Dixon.

Chapter 20

*I*f the universe had thumbs, they'd both be up in the air right now! Tawatha found a parking space in front of James's house, excited to see the "for rent" sign in the front yard. Since Belinda Rosewood threw a wrench in her look-see game, she stepped up her appearance. She eyed her new, shoulder-length layered wig in the side mirror. Her new Juicy Couture glasses gave her a studious look. Tawatha inspected both sides of the street. Every neighborhood had a Belinda Rosewood, and today, she refused to run scared. She pulled alongside the real estate brochure box, got out of the car, and grabbed a description of the house. She smoothed out the tweed pantsuit she'd found among Millicent's pre-Weight Watchers clothing in the carriage house. Scanned photos on the brochure showed someone altered the house since the last time she visited. The tan, chocolate, and cream décor had been replaced by soft-blue and green shades. *James probably doesn't live here anymore.*

The steep, fifteen-hundred-dollar rent was well worth the price for the neighborhood. James's immaculate house made her want to have a house of her own. Mr. J.B. fulfilled her dream, if only momentarily, when he allowed her to rent one of his properties. *Why do I always ruin everything?*

"Excuse me, ma'am, are you interested in renting the house?" A voice called from the front door.

Tawatha saw no car in the driveway, so she presumed the house was empty. She squinted to see whose voice it was. Shocked, she watched as the thin woman next to James on the newscast came toward her. She wore a winter-white swing coat, black boots, and ran her fingers through a head full of bouncing curls. She extended her hand to Tawatha.

"Hi, my name is Shandy Fulton. And you are?"

"Dana Marin." *No more names close to my own.*

"I'm the owner of this house, and I'm renting it out. Would you like to come inside to take a look?"

"I didn't think anyone was home. I don't want to disturb you."

"No trouble at all. I'm trying to get this place off my hands ASAP. You happened to catch me while I stopped in for a few things. Come inside."

Tawatha followed Shandy inside, amazed at the easy access. If James spotted her, she would rush into his arms, ask his forgiveness, and they could finally have the life they deserved. Barren, the home didn't look as it had on listing service. Furniture had been removed from most of the rooms, as had the accent pieces and paintings she remembered. The home smelled of apples and cinnamon. The floors, which were hardwood and vinyl, gleamed.

Shandy toured the home with Tawatha like a realtor.

"Dana, this is a four-bedroom, two-and-a-half bath home. The master is on the main, and there are three bedrooms upstairs. Do you have children?"

"I'd be living with my boyfriend. We don't have kids, but I like hosting parties."

"Well, you'll love the basement. James and I had it redone two years ago."

"I thought you lived by yourself. Is James your husband?"

Shandy shook her head. "He's my business partner. We've branched out into different areas, and it's best to rent the house at this time."

"So he's not here?" Tawatha asked, desperation filling her voice.

Shandy found the statement odd, but didn't press the matter.

Tawatha backpedaled. "No, I asked the question because my boyfriend, Travis, goes on and on about having a man cave, and I wanted to get a male perspective on the house."

"Oh, I see. James is traveling for business right now, so I'm sorry he can't give you the lowdown. Trust me, he would give you an earful about being in the man cave."

Shandy looked at her again. She thought Tawatha had a familiar look, as if she'd seen her either in passing or a familiar setting. Then again, she remembered that she ran into so many women at their salons that everyone melded together after a while. Beauty shops were filled to capacity with women in the get-sexy-or-die-trying mode. "Let's go downstairs."

Tawatha followed Shandy down to the basement. Everything inside of her wanted to push her down the stairs, but neighbors saw her go inside; she couldn't explain a mysterious accident. Tawatha noted this room contained furniture.

Reading her mind, Shandy said, "This is the last room that needs to be packed. Everything else is in storage until…" Shandy stopped herself. *You're entertaining a stranger. Be quiet.*

"Until what?"

"Until I find a less expensive unit. I'm about to switch from the beauty business to storage if this keeps up."

Tawatha walked in the open door Shandy provided. "Wait a minute. Didn't I see you on TV recently? You were at Easley Winery with this tall guy. He looked like a model."

"You saw us! Yes, that's my business partner, James."

"Hold up! The kiss he planted on your cheek did not say business partner. The two of you looked like college sweethearts!"

Shandy's face reddened. Maybe this wasn't a good idea after all.

"We're just business partners. Our romance ended some time ago."

Tawatha turned her lips down in mock sadness. "That's too bad. I know what it's like to lose the one you love." She leaned closer to Shandy. "I don't know about you, but the love of my life loved another woman. No matter what I tried to do, she was our silent partner. He couldn't get her off his mind."

"How did you handle it?"

"I let it go. I figured if we were really meant to be, we'd be together when the time was right." Tawatha remembered her previous lie. "I also found that when I let the old love go, the universe opened up things for me and Travis. You're gorgeous, Shandy. I'm sure the universe has a new man waiting just for you."

"Everyone says that to me. He's special, but I'm not one of these ghetto women willing to fight over a man. If someone doesn't want to be with me, I don't push it."

Skinny heffa. "You shouldn't push it. You are too delicate and dainty to fight over a man."

"Thank you, Dana. Let's go upstairs to the bedrooms. I'll show you around the rest of the place; we can exchange information when we're done."

Shandy continued the tour. She pointed out the bedrooms, laundry area, and bathrooms to Tawatha. Their conversation flowed easily; she didn't want to be too personal, but needed to assess if the rooms were sufficient enough for her and Travis.

"If you don't mind my asking, Dana, do you have children that will be visiting you? I mean, nieces and nephews? We have a nice play area out back equipped with a tree house, swing, and a bouncy house. James provided these items for his son, and if you have small kids you entertain, I'm sure they'll enjoy playing."

"How is Lil Man?"

"Excuse me?"

Tawatha bit her lower lip. "The little man. How is he?"

Shandy released the nervousness the statement generated, breathed easily, and grasped the staircase. "I thought you said Lil Man. That's James's nickname for his son."

"Oh. I call little boys *Lil Man* all the time," said Tawatha. She moved closer to Shandy. "Are you okay? You are ghost pale."

The stoic front Shandy had maintained since James left came undone, and she placed her head on Tawatha's shoulder. "Dana, I'm in a mess right now." She released light sobs, astounded she felt comfortable confiding in a stranger. "It's…we dated for years, and one night, he left. I knew we weren't on the best terms, but I wanted things to work out for us."

"Let me get you some tissue from the bathroom."

Tawatha darted in the closest bathroom and checked the cabinets for Kleenex, pleased a stash remained. She removed the box, re-joined Shandy, and motioned for her to sit on the floor.

"Oh my God. This is so embarrassing." Shandy shook her head and wiped away her tears.

"Go on and get it out. A good cry is what we women need some-times," said Tawatha. With her attention on Shandy, she passed more Kleenex and rubbed her back. "I'm listening with nonjudg-mental ears."

Shandy didn't know where to begin. She'd pretended she was fine, spitting out Zen sayings and laughing her days and nights away as she conducted business. She couldn't deny the truth: She missed James Dixon. She missed the way he commanded a room with his sexy swagger and easygoing ways. She missed his six-foot-five stature. She met him post-dreadlocks, but she even loved the photos of the pre-James, with oiled locks flowing past his strong shoulders. She missed seeing him every day and discussing business. They spoke daily about the businesses, and she asked about Aruba's condition. Somehow, it was a poor substitute for the man she'd grown to love over the last four years.

"James and I started dating after he and his wife broke up. His wife cheated on him with her best friend's husband, and they eventually married."

Tawatha smirked at the one-sided presentation of the story. "Oh."

"Let me back track. He wasn't this innocent lamb. He cheated on her, too. As a matter of fact, he cheated with this crazy chick that killed three of her four children for him. Can you believe a woman could be so stupid, Dana?"

Poker face. Poker face. "I saw the news story."

"Well, I knew we'd have struggles because he had issues of trust at first."

Because he still wants me, Tawatha thought.

"Finally, we settled into a decent groove and started our little empire," Shandy said, using air quotes to emphasize *little empire*.

"So, if you work so well together and have all these businesses, why did he leave?"

"He left because—" Shandy's cell phone interrupted their girl talk. She stood and removed the phone from her pocket. "Speak of the devil. Let me pull myself together and take this call."

Tawatha's stomach churned. She wanted to snatch the phone from Shandy, tell James how much she missed him, and beg him to come back to her. She angled her body to eavesdrop since Shandy didn't take the call downstairs.

"James, how are you? I have a slight cold and I'm showing the house to a lovely young lady named Dana." Shandy winked her eye at Tawatha.

Twelve minutes later, after blow dryer, hair roller, and invoice minutiae, Shandy brought the call to a close. Before hanging up she asked, "How is Aruba doing?"

Tawatha perked up at the mention of James's ex-wife's name.

"That's good news, right?"

Tawatha waited for Shandy to end the call completely. Aruba's name piqued her curiosity so much she wanted to sneak behind her and press her ear to the call.

"Well, I sincerely hope she gets better, James. I'll send the monthly closeout statement to your new address and email it as soon as I can. Hey, tell Aruba I'm praying for her and hopes she gets better."

She ended the call. "Dana, I am so sorry I dumped on you. I was rude and selfish."

"It's quite alright. I wanted you to pick up where you left off. You were about to tell me why he left."

Shandy looked at her watch and waved away the request. "I really have to go. I've sat here with this pity party and forgot about a meeting I have scheduled with a potential vendor. I have a feeling we'll meet again, so perhaps we can chat later."

Disappointed, Tawatha stood. She walked down the stairs behind Shandy, stopping at the island at Shandy's insistence.

"So, Dana, do you think you and Travis will be interested in renting the place? I'd love to rent it to you if you'd like." Shandy pulled cards out of her purse. "I'll even knock two hundred dollars off the rent and charge thirteen hundred dollars. I'm more interested in having someone stay here for upkeep. A house dies when no one lives in it."

"I'll let him know what I saw and get back with you."

Shandy scribbled information on a card and handed it to Tawatha. "Here is my information. Call me and let me know. Also, here is a VIP salon certificate from me to you. It entitles you to hair services of your choice at our natural or adult salon. Compliments of *moi* and a small token of my appreciation for you indulging my belly-aching."

"Do you and James do hair?"

"I'm not a stylist. He used to do hair, but he handles operations these days. Trust me, there are wonderful stylists on staff. Someone will hook you up."

"Thanks so much, Shandy. One way or another, I will be in touch with you."

They shook hands again, and Shandy escorted Tawatha to her car. She watched her drive and thought if things had been different, maybe she and James could have double-dated with Dana and Travis.

Chapter 21

James had excused himself from Aruba's group therapy session twenty minutes ago; he couldn't bring himself go back inside and wondered if she'd miss him if he left. He made a quick call to Shandy, grabbed a soda and chips from the vending machine, and paced the length of the hall. He wasn't prepared for the spilled truths he heard: Aruba had contemplated suicide when they were married. She felt unattractive because of advances from other women. She felt like she pulled the weight of their marriage during his bouts of unemployment. She felt he didn't love her.

She bore more burdens than he ever imagined, and he didn't realize until now how weary she had grown. *No wonder she was desperate enough to be with Winston. If I could turn back the hands of time...*

More disheartening than hearing Aruba's truth was sitting under the wrath of Darnella Stanton. At Dr. Shipman's coaxing, Aruba discussed circumstances leading to her suicide. As Aruba recounted painful incidents, Darnella folded and unfolded her arms, rolled her eyes at James, and gave Lance "I told you so" looks. Maxine gave her a cryptic look to calm her down. James left the room when Aruba mentioned finding a thong under their living room sofa. Now, he sat in the lobby area, his wilted pride getting the best of him. *Maybe I'm kidding myself by being here. She doesn't want me back, and I don't blame her.*

James's phone rang. Isaak Benford's name brought a smile to his soul. He answered on the second ring. "What's up, Ike?"

"You tell me, Boss Man. I'm getting back with you about the matter we discussed."

"Did you find anything?"

"What's my name? I know low people in high places. I got you covered. You can access your email by phone, correct?"

"Yeah."

"Give me about five minutes to do a file transfer. I'll send it right out. Indybeautyking@aol.com, right?"

"Isaak, the favors are racking up. I'll do what I can to repay you."

"No pay necessary. Katrina said to tell Aruba hello."

"Thanks, Isaak."

James ended the call, nervous about the email. He turned his gaze to the television. Maxine's voice behind him made him nervous.

"Are you rejoining us?" she asked. Aruba's grandmother, supportive of his effort to reconcile with his ex-wife, sat across from him.

"Do you all *want* me back in the room?"

"Of course we do. These are the bumpy moments. You have to go through these to get to better."

"Ms. Maxine, I sounded like a monster in there."

"Ah, you left too soon, son. Had you stayed, you would have heard Aruba talk about pursuing Winston and other things. Nobody's perfect, James."

"Tell Ms. Darnella that, *please*."

"Darnella is the most self-righteous hypocrite I know. And that's *my* child. Don't you let that cheating heifer ruffle your feathers. She has the nerve to sit up like she hasn't done anything."

James, a fellow southerner, remembered what his mother said about relatives: You can talk about your kinfolk, but other people can't. He stayed mum on Ms. Darnella, pressed his lips tightly, and chose not to say what was really on his mind.

"Do you think I can have some time alone with Aruba today? I had a special afternoon planned for her, but after the therapy session, I'm not sure she'll come with me."

"You let me handle the situation. Darnella ain't running nothing here. You might not be married to Aruba, but you two have a child to raise, and it's obvious you still love her."

"I do."

"And she loves you, too."

"She said that?"

"I said you left the room too soon. She said she never stopped loving you; it was taking you too long to get yourself together."

James pondered Maxine's words. "Screwup" could've easily been his name in the marriage. He wouldn't keep a job, frittered away their money, and cheated on Aruba with any woman who had hole and a heartbeat. He hated her for creeping with Winston, but for the first time, he realized how much he'd contributed to her bad choices.

"Ms. Maxine, do you think I'm wasting my time?"

"No." She leaned forward and placed his hands in hers. "It will take some time, but if you want Aruba back, don't give up."

Lance, Darnella, and Aruba appeared in the lobby area. The session had ended, and James looked at Aruba's dejected face. He stood to greet her.

"Aruba, I left the room to handle a little business. Are you hungry?"

"We're about to go to lunch," Darnella snapped. "Without you!"

Maxine stood. "You, Lance, and I are going to the drive-thru at Popeyes so we can be in Harlem when Jeremiah gets home. James and Aruba are going to pick up her meds from the pharmacy and eat something here in Augusta."

"Mama, she doesn't need to be alone with him."

"Nella, let it go. Aruba doesn't need this stress from you." Lance turned to his daughter. "Baby, do you want to go with James?"

She paused, looked at her relatives, and answered, "Yes, I do. I have some things I want to talk over with him."

Darnella pursed her lips. She slung her purse to her opposite shoulder and headed to the parking lot. Maxine and Lance watched her leave, shaking their heads at her defiance.

"Where are you all going?" Lance asked.

"I'm taking her to the pharmacy for her medication and by the house for a meal. I'll bring her back home before nine tonight. I want to spend some time with Lil—Jerry."

"Lord, you sound like y'all are in high school. Take care of her, James," said Maxine.

Maxine hugged them both and left the psychiatrist's office with Lance.

Aruba and James eyed each other, familiar strangers navigating new territory.

"Did I hear you say house? I thought you were staying at a hotel."

"I put business on hold back in 'Nap for a while, and Isaak helped me out with one of his rental properties here."

"Oh."

"By the way, Katrina said hello. I told everyone you're not accepting calls at this time, but everyone is lifting you in their thoughts and prayers."

Not Bria, and definitely not Victoria. "I don't know why. I've let so many people down."

"Who hasn't? Let's look to the future. Can you try?"

She didn't know what to do anymore. She missed having steady employment and an active life. The low-dosage Lexapro lifted her mood somewhat, but it felt artificial. Dr. Shipman recommended diet and exercise to get her endorphins moving and assured her the medicine was not intended to be a long-term fix.

"Where are we headed? For your medication, I mean."

"Deans Bridge Road Walmart."

"I can map it with my GPS."

"Oh, you rented a car?"

"No, I flew back to Indianapolis last weekend and drove back down in my SUV."

Your SUV? Flew without using someone else's credit? When did that happen?

"We need to get going. I'm marinating steaks and I have a surprise for you at the house."

"James, I don't know what to say."

"Say you're hungry."

"I'm starving."

Aruba walked hand-in-hand with her ex-husband to the parking lot. The new James, cocksure and strong, opened the door of his Infiniti QX56, waited for her to be seated, and locked her in. She looked in the backseat of his ride and saw appointment books, invoices, and business manuals. *Who is this man?*

James backed out of the parking lot and headed to Deans Bridge Road. He held Aruba's hand, making sure he didn't say anything inappropriate. Before their first group session, each family member, including Jeremiah, was given a pamphlet about suicide. The statistics were astounding. James had no idea only 10 percent of people who attempted suicide actually died by suicide. Moreover, he found out 80 percent who died had made a previous attempt. He looked at Aruba's attire for the day. Her hair wasn't as matted as it was when he came to the hospital; however, her hair was on his to-do list for the day. His mind drifted back to the pamphlet; the material listed the first six months after hospitalization are critical to the survivor.

It pained him to know Aruba remained at an elevated risk the first year.

"What are you thinking?" Aruba asked.

"About you. I have to make sure you get meds and food in that belly of yours."

"Is that all you're thinking?"

"No. I pictured life without you and how I would have explained it to Jeremiah."

Aruba directed her gaze to the scenic view outside the window. She still tasted the bitterness of the sleeping pills and remembered how they lodged in her throat the night she tried to take her life. She figured no one cared about her; she'd become a burden to everyone and felt the family would be better off without her. It wasn't until her parents and members of her church family held an around-the-clock prayer vigil in her hospital room that she got it. The concern on their faces, the way they each told her how much they loved her and how empty life would be without her, all made her realize how selfish the act had been. In real time, scenes from her life flashed before her in the hospital bed: playing across the street from her parent's house with her childhood friend, Bria Hines; running to meet the ice cream truck and snagging the Good Humor Cherry Bombe popsicle the driver set aside for her; shopping at Belk's for Easter with Darnella and Maxie. Memories of the suicide attempt overwhelmed her. The image that made her swallow the pills was Winston dying in her arms.

James felt her hands tremble and turned in time to see her crying again.

"Let's pull over for a minute."

She didn't respond. She pulled her knees to her chest while James rubbed her back.

Chapter 22

James pulled into a parking space close to the Walmart entrance. Aruba had calmed down and insisted on coming inside with him.

"I can get the meds. It'll take a minute," said James.

"James, I can't stay locked up forever. I made a horrible mistake, but the last thing I want you and everyone else to do is baby me," she said. Her tone was void of her usual spunk.

"Come on in, then," he said. Words from his new holy grail, the suicide pamphlet, popped in his head. *Don't hover and monitor every action of your loved one. Give them a minute to themselves.*

They found the pharmacy area. She handed James the prescription and said, " I'm going to the health and beauty area. I'll be back in a minute."

James dropped the prescription off and decided to shop for a few items for the house. Twenty minutes was enough time to get Aruba some flowers, sparkling grape juice, and her favorite oranges. The aisles bustled with people asking the attendants for greens, peanut oil, sugar, and pecans. It dawned on James that Thanksgiving was near, and a Southern Thanksgiving wasn't complete without fried turkey, pecan pies, and stuffing. He overheard Darnella say she was cancelling Thanksgiving dinner at their house this year due to the "situation"; however, Lance nixed the notion. He told her they had nothing to be ashamed of, and if anything, this year they'd give thanks in a bigger way.

A soft rub on his arm interrupted James's thoughts.

"Well, well, look who's here," said a lovely young woman.

"Hi, it's nice to see you again," James culled his memory for her name.

"Barbara! I sat next to you on the plane," she said.

James checked the immediate area in hopes Aruba wasn't near. The last thing he needed was the appearance of flirting. *This is the worst coincidence.* He couldn't deny Barbara was stunning. His preoccupation with Aruba on the flight distracted him, but this time he saw Barbara for the first time. She wore a lovely ensemble of a two-piece gray skirt suit, black heels, and decorative jewelry. She'd applied just enough makeup to give her medium-brown skin an earthy glow. The one thing he couldn't ignore was how her low haircut accentuated her deep-set eyes and dimples. Her megawatt smile completed her sensuous look. She twirled around as if on the runway, stopping with her back to him as she caressed the nape of her neck. She faced him again, her gaze fixed directly on his eyes.

"Am I rocking this TWA or what?" she asked.

"I told you it would suit you," he said, backing away from the bin of clementines. He looked over his shoulder for Aruba.

"I went to your website and got a lot of information, like you said. Of your products I've ordered so far, I love the Sheanuff Shampoo and Leave-in Conditioner, and the Honey Almond Magic Butter. I'm strictly wash-and-go right now, but you best believe I will be doing twist-outs as soon as my hair grows a little more," she said. She moved closer to him.

"Thanks. I'll let the team know you're pleased with the products. It's always good to know we're meeting our customers' needs."

"It was good seeing you again, James. I wish I could see you more often."

"Take care, Barbara."

He navigated his cart back to the pharmacy area. Aruba sat on the bench in front of the pick-up sign. She had items for purchase in a basket she gave James.

"Do you mind getting these for me?"

"Sure."

He paid for her prescription and the items she'd given him. Aruba blushed at James's ability to pay for the items. When he pulled out his wallet, she saw cash, a debit card, and credit cards. She remembered years of their marriage when she fronted cash and managed their finances. He couldn't manage funds well, and she resented him for his fiscal irresponsibility. Today, she felt embarrassed about the negative thoughts she had regarding him and money. *People can change if they want to.*

"Do you need anything else, Aruba?"

"I got everything I needed. I'm tired. I want to get to your place and take a nap if you don't mind."

"We still need to get your food."

"I'll have a hamburger for now. You said you were making steaks, so I'll dive into those later. I really am sleepy."

They headed out to the car and were startled by a high-pitched voice. "James, one more thing."

They turned as Barbara quickened her pace and headed toward them.

"Your website listed the launch date of the scented, sulfate-free shampoos as the week of Christmas. Is that true? I can't wait to try the Pomegranate Blueberry Quench."

Immediately, James turned to Aruba and said, "Baby, this is Barbara. We sat next to each other on the plane when I flew down two months ago. She did the big chop and was raving about our products."

Sizing up the competition, Barbara eyed Aruba from head-to-toe, looking at her hair, pulled back in an unkempt bun, her dull, unpainted nails, and her dry skin. She continued her visual lashing by turning up her nose at Aruba's sweatshirt, jeans, and athletic shoes. *He won't give me his number for her?* Barbara caressed the nape of her neck again and dismissively said, "It's nice to meet you," offering a limp shake and smoothing out her suit.

Aruba withered under Barbara's scrutiny. She returned the shake. "It's nice to meet you, as well. Your hair is lovely." Aruba glanced at her suit and smelled her intoxicating perfume.

"I know you're going to let him do something to your hair. That's a lot of hair wrapped up in that bun," Barbara sneered.

"As a matter of fact, I'm doing her hair, manicure, and pedicure tonight. When I'm done with her private spa treat, I'm grilling steaks for her. Anything for my baby, Barbara."

Aruba watched as Barbara's face cracked. James stepped up to the plate in such a way she hadn't experienced in years. She felt covered and loved.

"Ummm, I'm gonna be going then. I just wanted to find out about the shampoos." Barbara turned on her heels and headed in the opposite direction.

James held the shopping bags in one hand and placed his free hand around Aruba's shoulder. They headed to his vehicle in silence, both ready to get home. Aruba needed to sleep; James needed to check his emails.

Chapter 23

Tawatha slipped the key in the front door of the carriage house just past seven that evening. She had to process all she'd seen during the day. Talking with Shandy reignited the love she had for James. Being in the space he'd occupied made her realize she belonged with him. Since no one in her family wanted to embrace her, she would find a way to get back in James's good graces. She flipped the light switch and jumped at the sight of Royce sitting in the living room.

"Royce, what are you doing in here?"

"Last time I checked, my name was on both deeds."

His chilly reception stopped her in her tracks. She noticed the active laptop screen and the notepad with names and addresses she'd scribbled earlier. *Damn!*

"Come have a seat, Tawatha. I'd like to speak with you about a few things."

Tawatha took slow steps to the sofa and placed her purse on the floor.

"Lovely outfit."

"Thanks. You said I could wear some of Millie's old things."

Royce nodded. "So, how did it go today?"

"I dropped off a few applications and grabbed a bite to eat. It looks like I'll have to take you up on the offer about helping you with administrative duties. This job hunt isn't going so well. It's hard out here for a felon."

"I see. So, where else did you go?"

"Job hunting and a meal at Jason's Deli." Tawatha snapped her finger. "I also stopped at Sweetie's Gourmet Treats for a cupcake."

Royce placed his head in his hands, lacing his fingers. He sat back in the chair and massaged his temples with his thumbs. He faced her now. Tawatha felt his icy stare.

"Tawatha, do you know what I hate more than lazy people?"

She didn't respond.

"Liars. It bothers me when someone sits in my face and blatantly lies."

"What have I lied about?"

"Jamilah came by earlier today to talk to you. You weren't here, so she came to the main house searching for you. I told her you were out looking for a job. She told me that she had a meeting with your mother and she said you've been stalking them. Naturally, I defended you because surely, the woman I helped wouldn't jeopardize her freedom by doing something as stupid as stalking the people who've done everything except file a protective order against her!

"Since Jamilah has known you longer than I have, and since she insists you have a stalking proclivity, I brought her out here to prove her wrong. Imagine how I felt accessing a laptop *I* gave you to *help* you find a job. Imagine how dumb I felt seeing you use it to stalk your family. *And* James Dixon."

"Royce, let me explain."

He slammed his fist on the coffee table. "There's nothing to explain! Do you realize the danger you're placing yourself in with this behavior?"

She stood and tried to join him in the chair. He held his hands in protest.

"I was so lonely in jail all those years. You were the only one who tried to keep in touch with me. I still have a child, a mother, and two people who were once my best friends. Do you know how it feels to be shunned?"

"No, I don't. But I also know you can't bully or stalk your way into someone's life. If they don't want to deal with you, you can't make them communicate with you!"

"It's been five years."

"It might take five more!"

Royce shifted his strategy. "Please sit down. This argument isn't getting us anywhere. What did you learn about recidivism rates before you were released?"

"Indiana's rate is about 52% within three years."

"Don't you see you'll beat the three year mark sooner if you don't stop stalking your relatives and friends?" Royce walked over to the table, picked up a printout, and handed it to her. "These are Indiana's law from the Stalking Resource Center. I suggest you take the time to read this. The only difference on this sheet and what Jamilah said about your contact is you haven't threatened anyone. If you go back to jail, Tawatha, I can't help you again."

She took the paper from Royce, unable to make eye contact with him. She scanned the sheet, her eyes falling on the words *terrorized*, *frightened*, and *intimidated*.

"I haven't threatened or terrorized anyone, Royce."

"Tawatha, you wouldn't feel terrorized or intimidated if someone sat outside the carriage house watching you, never coming in and never knocking on the door?"

She imagined being the object of such attention. "I would."

Royce sighed. He didn't know if his words carried any weight, but he had to speak his mind.

"Do I make myself clear about this matter?"

"Yes."

"I opened up my home to you because I respected your desire to start a new life. You said you'd learned from your mistakes and you wanted to turn over a new leaf. Don't let yourself down, Tawatha. One more incident, and I'll be forced to ask you to leave my premises."

"Royce, you know I have nowhere else to go."

"The choice should be easy then, right?"

Royce, satisfied with his ultimatum, left Tawatha to consider his words. On his way back to the main house, he saw Tawatha's parole officer park in front of the carriage house.

Chapter 24

Victoria gave her list the once-over again. This Saturday was the first time she had ventured out with Nicolette beyond soccer, dance, and piano lessons. Lillith tagged along, wearing age-appropriate clothing and being calmer than usual. Victoria assumed it was because Bobby traveled to Dallas for some undisclosed business, and Lillith missed her young "Boo Thang," as she called him. This was Victoria's first attempt at making Thanksgiving dinner. With the holiday being one week away, she needed to stock up on staples to make her dinner special.

"Mom, did you want me to find anything else?" Nicolette asked.

"Honey, please get the maraschino cherries from aisle five."

"Grandma, do you need anything?" Nicolette asked.

Lillith curled her lips at Nicolette. "Lillith, do you want anything?"

"Yes, look in the condiment aisle for cooking sherry."

"Okay, Lillith." They watched Nicolette walk away.

"Lillith, why did you ask her to bring you cooking sherry?"

"For my chicken."

"You can't cook."

"Says whom?"

"I said so. Why did you come with us anyway? We're getting Thanksgiving items. This isn't your kind of outing, Lillith."

"Can't an old dog learn new tricks?"

"First of all, you're not a dog, and cooking was never your thing—even when I grew up with you."

"Who has time to slave over a hot oven? Am I wrong for not wanting to sweat out my hair, and chip my nails? And for what? The momentary kudo of 'good meal, hun?' Not Lillith, thank you very much!"

"Lillith, cooking is a gift of hospitality. It's a way of showing those you love you're willing to take the time to do something special for them."

"With the pounds you gained, I see your hospitality from a mile away. I'll admit, though, you've dropped a few. And you look good."

Victoria touched Lillith's forehead. "Thanks." *I'll write this on my calendar. A compliment from my mother.*

"What have you been doing? I mean, what have you been doing to lose weight?"

"I've been walking at the park and working out at Planet Fitness with Yvette."

"Good! You look nice. I may have to join you and Yvette to get rid of this belly of mine."

"Are you okay? You're being very generous with your words today."

"When am I not generous with words?"

"Maybe I should say, you're being kind today. You're good at spewing out a *generous* helping of craziness."

"That's not true!"

"Lillith! You can slice somebody up with your words. I saw you rip cashiers and clerks to shreds with your words the little time I spent with you growing up. Sad to say, I was just like you for a time."

Lillith gave her a sheepish grin. "Bobby said I have a salty mouth."

"So, this kindness is Bobby driven? I should have known a man had something to do with the change."

"It's not just Bobby. It's…it's some other things, too."

"Such as?"

"Nothing I want to talk about in the grocery store. I'll tell you when we get outside."

Nicolette placed the cooking sherry, cherries, and coconut in the shopping cart. Victoria gave Lillith the keys and watched Nicolette grab her grandmother's hand. They left the store, Lillith's smile beaming, sincere. Something was amiss with Lillith, and she couldn't wait to get to the car to solve the mystery.

What a difference five years make, Victoria thought as she swiped her grocery savings card in the self-checkout lane. She eschewed coupon clipping and bargain hunting during her marriage to Winston. The sky was the limit, and she spent as much of his money as she could. Post-divorce, she wouldn't be caught dead without a shopping list, coupons, and her earth-friendly grocery bags. No plastic for her. She rang up her items, swiped her coupons, bagged her groceries, and waited for the receipt to slide out of the receptacle. She grinned wide at the bottom of the receipt's bold black letters: *You saved $388.94 today.* She'd paid sixty-five dollars for almost four hundred dollars of groceries. She folded the receipt and placed it in her wallet.

Bags in her trunk and Harold Melvin and the Blue Notes crooning "I Miss You" from her SIRIUS XM Soul Town channel, she drove home with Emory on her mind. Sans the few text messages they'd shared over the last two months, neither had mustered the courage to get together face-to-face.

"You mind if I turn your music down a minute?" Lillith asked.

"Go ahead."

"Nicolette is mature for her age, so I hope you don't mind if I discuss this matter in her presence."

"What does the discussion involve?"

"Life," Lillith answered.

"Let's stop at the rest area just ahead. I don't want to run off the road." Lillith scared Victoria with her solemn expression.

Victoria found an empty space, parked, and turned to her mother.

Lillith cut to the chase. "I had a mammogram two weeks ago," she said.

"Lillith." She reached for her mother's hand. "What were the results?"

"I'm fine, honey. I did a self-check and thought I felt a lump, had the test, and it came back negative. I sweated bullets after the exam. I had a lot of time to be alone and think."

"Grandma...Lillith, are you going to be okay? I did a report on breast cancer for my science class and I read a lot about chemotherapy."

"I'll be fine. I wanted to get some things off my chest with the two of you. I'm not big on emotions, but I have some making-up to do."

"Lillith, don't get mushy on me," said Victoria. She was used to the foul-mouth, insensitive Lillith. Sensitive Lillith rattled her.

"I'm not getting mushy. I want you to know a few things." Lillith took a deep breath. "I'm sorry for leaving you when you were young. I was hotheaded, irresponsible, and a lousy mother. Something happened to me after your father and I divorced. When I sat in that mammogram and they mashed my toddlers—"

"Toddlers?"

"I don't have girls; I have toddlers. Anyway, I thought about my mother. She died of breast cancer long before they had all this advanced technology and alternative medicine. She suffered a long time before she died. Before she passed, I could literally smell the medication and cancer seeping from her pores. At the end, she talked about so many things she wished she'd done differently. I smelled her smell again during my mammogram, and all I could think about was how I treated you."

Victoria remained silent. She remembered her parents' marriage ending in divorce after her father, Leland, slept with Lillith's friend, Julie Adams. Lillith went into pit bull mode and charged them both in the bedroom after catching them together. Leland shattered her ego by blocking her fists from Julie's face when a fight ensued. Victoria spied the scene in the hallway as Julie scurried past her, naked, bra and panties in hand. Lillith pulled Leland's suitcases from the closet, tossed his clothes from hangers, and gave him ten minutes to leave before she became "homicidal." Leland gathered his things, spotted Victoria in the hallway, and said to her, "Don't let this grown folks' business stop you from loving somebody. Me and your momma… " Leland ended the advice there and trudged down the stairs. Her allegiance tested, she wanted to chase her father and beg him to stay. Instead, she joined Lillith on the bedroom floor. She hugged her mother, willing her heaving shoulders to stop. Lillith's guttural sobs made her hug her mother tighter. They sat on the floor that night until Lillith cried herself to sleep.

"I let the situation get the best of me," said Lillith, snapping Victoria back to the present. "Truth be told, I always tried to make Julie jealous because I knew her husband, Hank, wasn't like Leland. Hank was a hard-working man, but they struggled a lot."

"Lillith, did they struggle like we struggle now? Things are different now that my dad is dead," said Nicolette.

"Lillith, I understand the point you're making, but I don't think we need to have this discussion in front of a nine-year-old," said Victoria.

"When will she ever learn how to be a friend and treat people right? I should have explained to you what was going on during that time. We might have a better relationship now."

"I was ten."

"And you're an adult now, with no husband, and tendencies like mine. Marguerite told me you bragged about your good fortune to Aruba all the time."

Victoria bit down on the inside of her mouth. She didn't realize the conversation would get back to *her* again.

"What does Aruba have to do with this?"

" She's getting the best of you. No one can mention her name without you getting an attitude or flying off the handle," said Lillith.

"She's right, Mom," Nicolette said, nodding.

Nicolette eased back in her seat after Victoria mean-mugged her.

"Take what I'm saying into consideration. I can't undo anything I've done to you, but I can tell you bitterness isn't cute. I ran off and left you with Marguerite after Clifford Rutland promised me the wind, the moon, the stars, and the mountains. I got out to Texas with him and I've lived hand-to-mouth ever since. If it hadn't been for Marguerite giving me a place to stay, I'd still be out there searching. I've wasted so much time."

"Don't you think Aruba should be apologizing to me?"

"I thought you said she called and you wouldn't answer!"

I don't want to hear what she has to say."

"Have it your way, Victoria. Let's get on back to your house so we can put the groceries away and plan the menu."

"Lillith, will you show me how to make the Peach Schnapps cake like you promised?" Nicolette asked.

"I sure will! It's Bobby's recipe and it's real tasty," Lillith said.

Bobby again. She started her engine and headed home, processing all her mother had said. She enjoyed her bohemian years in L.A.

with her aunt, but no one knew how much she longed for Lillith's attention and her presence. Now, Lillith wanted her to let bygones be bygones. She wish she knew how. Even more, she wanted Lillith, Marguerite, or someone else to tell her how to mend her broken heart.

Chapter 25

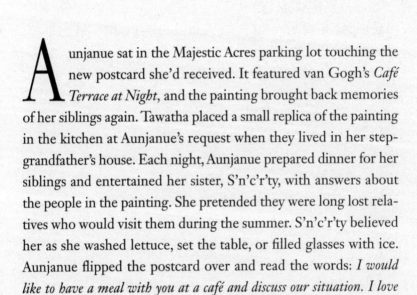

Aunjanue sat in the Majestic Acres parking lot touching the new postcard she'd received. It featured van Gogh's *Café Terrace at Night*, and the painting brought back memories of her siblings again. Tawatha placed a small replica of the painting in the kitchen at Aunjanue's request when they lived in her step-grandfather's house. Each night, Aunjanue prepared dinner for her siblings and entertained her sister, S'n'c'r'ty, with answers about the people in the painting. She pretended they were long lost relatives who would visit them during the summer. S'n'c'r'ty believed her as she washed lettuce, set the table, or filled glasses with ice. Aunjanue flipped the postcard over and read the words: *I would like to have a meal with you at a café and discuss our situation. I love you. I long for us to have a good relationship. Love, T.*

The postcard, nestled between circulars and credit card solicitations, arrived in the mail yesterday. Trembling, Aunjanue climbed the stairs to show Lasheera the postcard, but as usual, she slept like an infant. Aunjanue slipped the postcard in her pocket and went to Mrs. Rosewood's house. Mrs. Rosewood hadn't seen any unusual activity, but promised Aunjanue she'd beef up her watch duties to protect her. Aunjanue stared at the postcard again.

Who does this two days before Thanksgiving?

She tucked the card in her purse, gathered the fruit basket and quilt she'd purchased for Ms. Mag, and headed inside Majestic. The sliding glass doors offered their familiar sights and sounds: lemon commercial cleaner on gleaming floors, the smell of beef pot roast and rice wafting from the cafeteria, and Mr. David Holmes gumming Juicy Fruit, sans his dentures. He waved to her and said, "How are you doing, Felicia?"

"I'm fine, Mr. Holmes."

He wiped drool from his mouth and said, "Happy Thanksgiving."

"Same to you, Mr. Holmes."

She looked in Ms. Mag's spot in the corner, surprised she wasn't there. *She must be in her room.*

She plopped the fruit basket and quilt down at the nurses station and waited for the nurse to finish her call.

"May I help you?" asked the nurse. She gave Aunjanue a warm smile as she waited for her response.

"I'm here to see Ms. Mag. Ms. Maggie Ransom."

"Oh, honey, I'm so sorry. Ms. Mag is under hospice care. You're the young lady from the school, correct?"

"Yes, ma'am."

"I thought somebody called the school and told you. She's been gone two weeks now. She wandered off from the facility after dinner one night. Thankfully, she was out back playing kickball, but we made a mutual decision with the family to help find a more secure setting for her. We had to restrain her a few times, and she went downhill from there. The only thing consistent about her is requesting Felicia."

"May I have the address?"

"Let me check her records. If I'm not mistaken, the family requested to let you know where she'd been moved. They want to meet you."

The nurse double-checked Maggie's chart and read the notes left by the Director of Nursing. She scribbled the name and address of Serenity Hospice on a sheet of paper and handed it to her.

"She's not too far from here. Take I-465 to the Michigan Road Exit. Once you get off the exit, go down about four lights. Serenity is on the left. Can't miss it."

"Thank you."

She took her items and headed to Serenity. First, she was dealing with her mother's stalking, now Ms. Mag's illness. Aunjanue had grown fond of Ms. Mag. She didn't mind being called Felicia, and she didn't mind the periods of sleep Ms. Mag indulged when she visited her. *Dear God, don't let this be the last time I see her.*

She dialed Roger's number, but it went straight to voicemail. Relieved, she ended the call. His life had been fielding scholarship offers from colleges and universities around the country with his parents. Guaranteed a full ride because of his SATs and magic on the football field, he'd grown distant with all the attention he'd received his senior year. He didn't pressure her for sex, but the thought of him being with someone else occupied her mind; her intuition hinted at another girl.

She dialed Lake; he answered on the first ring. "Onnie, are you home yet?"

"Not yet. I went to see Ms. Mag, and she's been placed in hospice. I have a quilt and fruit for her, so when I drop it off, I'll head home."

"Have you talked to Lasheera? I've been calling her, but she won't answer."

"She was asleep when I left home. She woke up long enough to tell me I could borrow the car, then turned over again." She paused. "Is she okay? She hasn't been herself since Mom got out of jail."

"Onnie, I'm not sure," he said. He changed the subject as not to alert her. He planned to get to the bottom of the situation. Soon. "Was Zion home when you left?"

"He said he was bored and went down the street to play video games with Hakeem."

"Good. Do you mind watching him while we go out on our double-date with Caleb and Stephanie tonight?"

"Sure. Roger is out of town anyway."

"Please call Stephanie and have her wake Lasheera up. I don't want to be late tonight."

"I'll call her now."

She ended their call. For the first time in years, she felt alone. Tarsha had been promoted to shift leader at Panera, so their hangout time had diminished. Roger traveled the country with his family every weekend visiting colleges and universities, and Lasheera floated around in a state of disorientation. There was no one with whom she could share the postcards or the ominous feeling she felt. She dialed the Wilson's number. Stephanie always cheered her up with her zany sense of humor. The Wilsons' marriage was only the third one she admired. *If* she ever got married, she'd love to have the type of interaction she witnessed between Caleb and Stephanie. He doted on her, complimented her in public and private, set goals, and acknowledged Stephanie as his strength. The Mosleys' and Lake and Lasheera's marriages were also worth emulating.

She waited for Stephanie to answer their home phone. She was surprised to hear Caleb's voice. "Mr. Wilson, is Ms. Stephanie home?"

"Aunjanue, she's not home right now. Is there a message I can give her?"

"Yes, Uncle Lake asked her to call Auntie 'Sheer and wake her up. She's been groggy and out of it. Ms. Stephanie can get her going."

"I'll tell her to call. She's out getting a mani and pedi."

"Thanks, Mr. Wilson." She waited for him to hang up, but heard him lingering on the call. "Mr. Wilson, is there something else you have to say?"

"Aunjanue, I didn't want to ask this, but I've been worried about you since you got sick in class. Is everything okay?"

No way would she share her feelings with anyone. People would accuse her of being crazy for trying to protect Tawatha, but she couldn't explain her feelings regarding her mother. She trusted Mr. Wilson, but she didn't want to tell him everything.

"Mr. Wilson, it's the situation with my mother."

"I understand. My heart goes out to you and the circumstances. If you need someone to talk to, I'm willing to listen."

"I appreciate it." She waited a few seconds. "I'm headed to see Ms. Mag. She's been moved to hospice, and I have a few Thanksgiving gifts for her."

"I knew she was sick, but I didn't realize she had been placed in another facility."

"I just found out today. I hope I'm not too late. I've grown so fond of her."

"Really, Felicia?" he asked, trying to lighten the mood.

They laughed at her alias.

"Henry, I bet she'd love to see you again."

"No, she wouldn't. I'm the devil, remember?"

They both laughed as Aunjanue found a parking spot at Serenity.

"I'll tell her you said hello, Henry." She said goodbye to him and entered hospice. The nursing attendant gave her Ms. Mag's room number, and her heart sank as she entered the room. A middle-aged woman seated next to Ms. Mag knitted an afghan as she hummed along with Lou Rawls on the radio, singing "You'll Never Find." Aunjanue cleared her throat, and the woman looked up from her project.

"May I help you, Ms.?"

"I'm here to visit Ms. Mag. I'm Aunjanue Gipson, and I brought her a quilt and some fruit."

The woman lifted her glasses to peer at Aunjanue. "You're the one she calls Felicia, aren't you?" The woman stood to shake her hand as Aunjanue confirmed her question with a yes. "I'm Mag's daughter, Hattie. It's so nice to meet you. Have a seat, young lady."

Aunjanue pulled up a seat and placed it at the foot of Ms. Mag's bed. She'd lost a significant amount of weight, and her face had sunken in. Her skin, usually glowing, dulled underneath the light in the room. Rapid breaths made the blanket covering her body rise and fall.

"What's wrong with Ms. Mag?"

"She's on the countdown now. The doctors gave her three weeks. We'll be lucky if Momma makes it to the end of the month." Hattie leaned forward and readjusted her mother's blanket. "She's tired and doesn't want to be here anymore."

"I'm sorry to hear the news. I loved visiting her."

"I believe you kept her alive all this time."

"Ma'am?"

"Momma went downhill after Felicia, our baby sister, died."

"Felicia is dead?"

"Yes. Passed on in 1978."

"All this time I thought she was alive."

"If you listen to Momma long enough, you'll think she is. Truth is, I don't think momma ever accepted Felicia's death." Hattie completed her row of handiwork. "Pass me my purse, dear."

She gave Hattie the purse and watched her dig a wallet from the bag. She leafed through photos, pulling several from the clear wallet sleeves. "Come closer so you can see my little sister."

Aunjanue moved closer to Hattie. She was careful with the photos, as some were fading, and others were crumpled around the edges. As she looked at the alluring young woman standing outside a dance studio in a body suit, ballerina flats, and her hair pulled together in a decorative bun, she understood how Ms. Mag might have mistaken her for Felicia. Felicia's shapely figure appealed to the men standing in the photo's background; they eyed her with hunger and lust. She seemed oblivious to their desires as she waved to the camera.

"Where is she standing?"

"She was outside a dance studio in Detroit. She danced most of her life and wanted to attend Juilliard. Things were fine until her body began to develop. She was a little too thick to do traditional ballet, but I wanted to see her with the Alvin Ailey Troupe. She was a fox, Aunjanue. You couldn't tell her she wasn't Thelma from *Good Times*."

"Who is Thelma, and what is *Good Times*?"

"How old are you, Aunjanue?"

"Seventeen. I'll be eighteen soon, though."

"*Good Times* was a sitcom from the seventies. I bet you can find it on TV Land or TBS." As Aunjanue passed the photos back, Hattie eyed her baby sister. "Now that I'm looking at you, you and Felicia could have been sisters. She was the family flower child— always seeking fun and new adventures."

"If you don't mind me asking, what happened to her?"

Hattie sighed. Recounting Felicia stories made her nauseous because everyone in the family felt they should have done more to save her. "One day, Felicia just up and told Momma she was moving to New York. Momma fought her every step of the way, but she gave in after Felicia told her she was moving in with Daddy's sister, Aunt Rachel. Next thing we knew, Felicia said she was marrying a fellow dancer named Henry Brooks. Momma didn't like Henry from the moment she met him. He stepped in our house for Sunday dinner like he owned the place, criticizing Momma's cooking, our house, and everything about us. Felicia sat there like a little wounded bird—not a chirp in our defense.

"They snuck off and got married, and Henry moved her to L.A. Early one Sunday morning, we got a call from Henry saying Felicia couldn't breathe. *He* said she fell asleep and didn't wake up; the police said Henry killed her after they went out dancing the night before. Henry finally said it was an accident, but Felicia didn't strangle herself. Momma gave up living after that night. She said she aged twenty years after Felicia's funeral."

"She always lit up when I came by to do drawings of her. I understand why now."

"I came down from Detroit to take Momma home. I didn't know she was this sick until I got here."

Felicia's death made her think of S'n'c'r'ty. Another sister gone at the hands of someone else. "I won't disturb you any longer. I wanted to give her these gifts and go home. I'm watching my little brother tonight." She set the items atop a dresser in the room. "May I hug her before I leave?" she asked Hattie.

"You may."

She hugged Ms. Mag and whispered in her ear, "I love you, Ms. Mag. Safe travels on your journey."

Ms. Mag cracked an eye and in a faint, whispery voice asked, "Felicia, what you doing here? Shut Lou Rawls off. I been through with him since he married that white woman. Play that boy with the Bible names."

Curious, Hattie mouthed, "Who's she talking about?"

Aunjanue remembered Mag's love for WTLC 106.7. They listened to the station during visits and drawing sessions. She laughed and answered, "Luke James. She loves his song 'I Want You.'" She switched the station for Hattie as Ms. Mag went back to sleep. Aunjanue squeezed Mag once more and headed for the door.

"Honey, before I forget, I have something for you." Hattie opened a closet door and retrieved a locked box. "Momma wanted you to have this. She said, 'If Felicia comes back, give this to her.'"

"We can't take anything from the residents."

"She's not a resident; she's a friend. I loved the drawings you did of her, and so did she. I don't know what's inside, but let me get the key from my purse."

Aunjanue waited for Hattie to give her the key. She held the box and hesitantly walked away. She stopped again. "Ms. Hattie, what happened to Henry?"

"He didn't go to jail, and we have no idea. Somebody said he moved to Canada. Ever since Felicia's death, Momma swore she had this sixth sense about men who didn't mean women any good."

"Ms. Mag is something else. I'll come back and check up on her before Christmas."

"You can try, but I can't guarantee she'll be here." She gave Aunjanue a warm hug and the key.

"It was nice meeting you, Ms. Hattie."

Aunjanue left the room, box in hand, and headed to her car. Her phone vibrated and she answered when Lake's name appeared. "Are you on your way home?"

"Yes, Uncle Lake. I'll be there soon."

"Don't speed, but get here fast. Your Auntie 'Sheer is missing!"

Chapter 26

Tawatha, still upset after the showdown with Royce, took advantage of Shandy's gift certificate. She sat in the car outside Dixon's Hair Affair talking to herself and looking in the mirror. "The nerve of Royce, accusing me of being a stalker. If he had family and friends who didn't speak to him, he'd want to be in touch with them," Tawatha said to herself. She touched up her makeup.

She kept a stack of "treasures" in her glove compartment, which were mostly Googled items to keep her in touch, or at least at a lawful distance, between herself and family members. Royce stepped up his game to "protect" her; he had placed the Indiana stalking statutes in with her treasures. At the bottom of the print-out, he wrote the words in all caps: *RECIDIVISM. LOSS OF FREEDOM. NOT A GOOD LOOK.* Tawatha perused the paper again, reading the lines he'd highlighted in neon orange. She read the words aloud: "Indiana Code 35-45-10-1. As used in this chapter, 'stalk' means a knowing or an intentional course of conduct involving repeated or continuing harassment of another person that would cause a reasonable person to feel terrorized, frightened, intimidated, or threatened."

"There you go! When have I terrorized, frightened, intimidated or threatened Sheer, Onnie, Momma, or anyone else? Since when did sitting in someone's yard constitute stalking?" she asked herself in the mirror.

A young man tapped lightly on her window, terrifying her. He held a tray of items in one hand as he leaned in with concern. She let her window down.

"You okay, Miss? I saw you talking to yourself and I wanted to see if everything was all right."

"I'm not talking to myself. I had my phone on speaker talking to my dad."

She held up her phone and sucked her teeth.

"Oh. I didn't see your phone." He rubbed his goatee, shifted his tray of items to the left, and presented them to her. "I got incense, DVDs, and CDs. I do purses on Fridays and Saturdays, but this is Thanksgiving week, so I'll get back on my purse grind next weekend. Whatchu need?"

He's cute in a roughneck kinda way. "I'm good. Thank you."

She stepped out of the car and headed toward the salon.

"You are good and fine!" said the young man, and slapped his free thigh as he watched Tawatha switch her massive hips. He ran behind her. "Let me give you my card so you can call me if you need something, Ma."

She looked at his card, blushing at his advances. She read his name and responded, "Waylon, I'll call you if I need anything."

"I gotchu! Whatever you need, I gotchu!" he said and licked his lips.

She entered the salon, taken aback by the elegant surroundings. The last time she was in this location was the night she revealed herself to her lover's wife. She crashed the window with a brick, walked into the opening, and interrupted their candlelit dinner. She assumed the building had just been christened that night, because it was still under construction and contained unopened boxes of products, equipment with tags, and wine bottles plastered with James and his wife's photos. *Time brings about change.*

A receptionist approached her. "Do you have an appointment?"

"Yes, I'm a guest of Shandy Fulton. I made an appointment a few days ago." She fished in her purse for the certificate. "My name is—"

"Dana, right? She's said you'd be in today and to take extra special care of you. Follow me."

Tawatha read the young lady's nametag and said, "Sure thing, Gala."

She followed Gala to an area beyond the impeccably decorated reception area.

"May I take your coat?"

She gave Gala her coat and waited for her to hang it up. A few women looked up from their services at her outfit and gave her a sour look. "Humph," said one, and glued her eyes to *In Style* magazine.

In an attempt to please her onlookers, she slowed her gait, putting extra emphasis in her stride. *Take that, tricks.* Millie had unwittingly upgraded her look from trashy to elegant, and she liked it. The red cashmere body dress went just past her knees. This dress would have been Amish garb in her old days, but she loved how it made her feel like a woman. A silver buckle gathered the dress on the side, leaving enough room to highlight her curves.

A fan in the pre-relaxer process called out, "Girl, you are wearing that dress! The whole outfit suits you."

The other ladies gave the fan fiery eyes, daring her to say anything else.

"What? She does look good!"

She addressed her admirer. "Thank you for the compliment. I wish more women were kinder to each other," said Tawatha, speaking to the young woman but eyeing the other women.

They dropped their heads and went back to their activities, some gossiping, others reading.

Unaware of the commotion, her stylist of the day, Penny, approached her with an outstretched hand. "You must be Dana. How are you? I'm Penny. My chair is over there. The blue one. Have a seat."

She sat in Penny's chair. She'd pulled her hair back in a ponytail. Her hair grew longer in prison and extended to the middle of her back thanks to Faithia's braiding skills. Today, she wanted a new look. Millie's clothes were a great start. The hair had to follow. Penny came toward her, smock in hand, and wrapped it around her.

"It's always great meeting new clients. I'd like to tell you a little about myself."

She nodded, giving Penny the green light to continue.

"I'm Penny Murphy, and I've been with Dixon's two years. I do it all: natural, relaxed, the Devachan, braids, blowouts, and even warm presses if that's your thing. You name it, I do it. I am punctual, so if you continue with me, know that I give clients a fifteen-minute grace period. If you know you'll be late, call me within an hour of your appointment. If you can't make it at all, please cancel within a twenty-four-hour period. Time is precious, so I don't believe in wasting mine or yours. Is that a deal between you and me?"

"Yes." Pleased with Penny's matter-of-fact nature, she asked, "How long have you been doing hair?"

"I've been making magic professionally about ten years now. I started at my dad's feet in his barbershop, and I did unofficial hairdos in high school. I moved to Durham, North Carolina, after high school to attend Dudley, then came back home. The South is beautiful, but the Midwest is my home. I went from shop to shop and made my way to Dixon's about two years after I kept seeing the TV commercials and hearing the radio ads."

"What's so special about Dixon's?"

"Dixon's is a five-star enterprise. Professional service, continuing education, plus, the owner, James, believes in giving us all a stake at personal growth and development. My booth rental isn't too crazy, and he encourages us to branch out on our own and have our own shops. I'm putting together a business plan right now. I hope to go out on my own in about five years."

She blushed at the mention of James's name. "He sounds like a great owner. Does he do hair here?"

"He's out of town handling business right now. As a matter of fact, I've been meaning to ask Shandy when he'll return."

"Oh, that's too bad. I'd like to meet him some time."

"Well, if you remain in my chair, I'm sure your paths will cross. So, tell me about yourself, Dana."

She had rehearsed her new spiel in the mirror along with other personal conversations. "I'm Dana Marin, and I just moved back to Indy after living in Texas five years. I have a seventeen-year-old-daughter, and I'm living with my uncle until I get back on my feet."

Penny eyed Tawatha. "You do not look old enough to have a seventeen-year-old daughter!"

"Thanks, Penny."

"Shandy mentioned you might be renting her old place. How are negotiations going?"

"My boyfriend thinks it might be too much room for both of us, but we're still trying to decide."

"If the two of you entertain, it's a fabulous house for parties. I attended a few parties James and Shandy threw, and I had a ball!"

"Oh, I didn't know Shandy and James were married."

"They're not. They dated for a few years and broke up recently."

"Sound like an ideal couple. I hope they get back together."

Steering the conversation back to business, Penny asked, "What look do you want to achieve, Dana?"

"I'd like a nice shoulder-length cut. Something eye-catching and sexy. Maybe something asymmetrical with highlights or tonal color. Nothing crazy, though."

Penny swiveled her around in the chair. "I think a mild blonde or auburn would bring out your beautiful skin tone." She rotated the chair a quarter turn and ran her fingers through Tawatha's hair. "Are you a fan of Keri Hilson?"

"Ms. Keri, baby? I sure am."

"We can go in that direction if you'd like. I think you'd be gorgeous, and the look would accentuate your eyes, nose, and full lips."

"You think so?"

"Absolutely. The question is, do you really want to cut all this hair?"

"Yes. I'm changing my life in all aspects."

"I like the sound of that, Dana! I think we'll get along fine. It's hard servicing clients who are afraid of change. I'll start with your relaxer. We use all Dixon products here, so I hope you're okay with the product line."

"I'm open to new things. Please, don't burn all my hair out."

They laughed as Tawatha held her head back, allowing Penny to section her hair in four parts. If James had four locations, his own product line, and was away "on business," that meant he was doing *very* well. It also meant he could take care of her, Aunjanue, and Jamesia in their own place. It would take some time to learn hair care lingo and get acquainted with what he did, but she was up for the challenge. She'd make sure this time they stayed together and flourished as a couple.

"Penny, can you answer the phone?" asked another stylist.

Penny grabbed the nearest phone, continuing Tawatha's service. "James, how are you?"

Tawatha craned her neck to listen to the conversation.

"The shears arrived yesterday. We haven't had a chance to complete inventory, but we'll be unpacking everything before next Tuesday. How's everything in Georgia?"

So, he's in Georgia.

"How's your family?"

He'll be back home to me soon. He's just hanging out with my future in-laws.

"I know you've got a lot on your plate, but you have been doing a wonderful job with the Facebook updates. I love the photos of the Georgia clients. The hairstyles are nice. I'm glad you whipped out your clippers and shears again."

I didn't know he had a Facebook page. I'll definitely get the goods on that before I leave.

"I'm doing a new client now, so I'll talk to you a little later."

"Did we talk him up or what!" said Tawatha.

"Yes. I'm sorry for taking the call over your head that way, but we all try and talk to James when he calls. He's down South right now with a family emergency, but he flies back from time to time to handle business here. Dixon's Hair Affair has a Facebook page, and he's been updating photos of the clients he's been servicing there. Shandy updates photos here, so he thought it would be nice to showcase work being done in Georgia, too."

"I have relatives in Georgia. Exactly where is he?"

"He's in Augusta. He's at a salon called Shear Heaven."

"Hmmm, I'll look him up the next time I'm down there. Unless he gets back here, first."

"You should. He's a really nice guy."

"Turn it up!" yelled a client, pointing to the television.

The breaking news flooded the screen on WTHR News 13. Everyone's eyes were glued to the unfolding scene. Bruce Kopp, poised at the news desk, followed the developing story.

"Look at 'em go!" said one client.

"Like they can outrun the police. And on the highway to boot!" said another patron.

"Hold your head still," said Penny to Tawatha. Everyone's attention was drawn to the screen.

"The driver has eluded officers for several miles now," reported Kopp.

The women watched in horror and amazement as a blue Nissan Altima weaved in and out traffic, passing cars at rapid speed. The aerial view of the scene from Chopper 13 mesmerized everyone. Cars drifted to the side of the road to allow the offender and the cops space to continue their journey.

"I bet it's some raunchy juveniles in a stolen car," said an older woman. "Kids don't value freedom worth nothing these days."

"Oh!" The collective gasp came from everyone in the shop as the car hit a guardrail and spun around twice, landing in the opposite direction of the chase. The cops stopped as well. One police officer exited his vehicle, gun drawn, and raced toward the vehicle. He opened the door, and a leg propped out from the driver's side. A young woman staggered from the car. She held her hands in surrender, tottering as if drunk.

Ignoring Penny's admonishment, Tawatha leaned forward. A grounds crew arrived on the scene, and the cops seemed to give instructions to the woman, obviously in a drug-induced haze. Her disheveled appearance couldn't conceal her identity. Tawatha knew Lasheera anywhere. The police officers yanked her hands behind her back, handcuffed her, and grazed her head as they put her in back of the cruiser.

A sick satisfaction overtook Tawatha as she said to no one in particular, "Pot, meet Kettle."

Chapter 27

Aunjanue arrived home just after the CPS van parked in the driveway. She watched a man and woman get out of the van and knock on the front door. Frightened, she ran to them. Lake opened the door, anger etching his face.

"Sir, we are here from Child Protective Services to pick up Zion Anderson." They gave Lake a court order drawn up earlier in the day. "Based on an anonymous hotline tip, reports from Zion's school, and the unfolding news story, Zion is in an unsafe environment."

"Who called the hotline?" Lake asked. His fury rose with each second. He did a visual sweep of the neighborhood and spotted Marvin's car across the street.

"May we come in, sir? We have to do a home inspection and discuss the matter with you."

Lake moved aside to let them in. Zion sat in the den area watching the unfolding news story about his mother. He looked up to see the uniformed man and woman enter the house, followed by Aunjanue. He ran to Aunjanue.

"Mom wrecked the car. It's on the news," said Zion, pointing to the story.

"Come with me a minute, Zion. Let's go to your room while Uncle Lake chats with the man and woman here, okay?" Aunjanue took his hand and headed toward his room. Zion was twelve, but Lasheera accused her of babying him too much. Maybe she did. He'd grown taller and was almost her height, but he was her little brother who needed protection. She'd seen this scene unfold when Tawatha neglected her and her siblings, kept an unkempt apartment, and disappeared for days on end with men she hardly knew. CPS workers took them away for a while to live with Roberta, then returned them when Tawatha promised to straighten up her act. She would explain the routine to Zion to alleviate his fears. Given Lasheera's background, she was sure Zion knew the custom. Lake stood back as the workers inspected the house. He'd gone on a cleaning spree earlier in the day, so incensed Lasheera left Zion by himself again. Had he not stopped by the house to pick up a few items to donate to Goodwill, Zion would have been home alone when CPS arrived. *What's going on with 'Sheer?*

The workers scoured the rooms, noting the cleanliness of the place. They checked the refrigerator for food and inspected the home's overall appearance. They joined Lake in the den area, where he stared into the backyard.

"Mr. Carvin, were you aware of a complaint lodged against your wife from a local pharmacy?"

"No, I wasn't."

"It appears your wife became indignant with a pharmacy tech at Walgreens after she wouldn't refill an Ambien prescription."

"My wife doesn't take Ambien."

"Apparently, she does. She demanded the prescription be refilled, even after it was discovered your wife had the wrong prescription."

Lake recalled articles he'd read about Ambien. He even remembered Roberta taking them for a short time and how she abruptly stopped the meds because they made her jittery and disoriented.

After all 'Sheer has been through with drugs, didn't she have sense enough not to touch prescription drugs?

"So, you're saying in addition to the fact my wife is sitting in jail right now, she's also doing drugs?"

The male worker picked up the conversation. "A few days ago, your wife entered Walgreens with an empty bottle. She'd tried to scratch out the name on the bottle, but of course, prescriptions are identified by Rx numbers. When she couldn't produce proper identification, an argument unfolded in front of Zion and several customers. The incident triggered the first round of allegations."

"First round?"

"Mr. Carvin, are you aware your wife missed a visitation court date with Mr. Marvin Anderson," the woman checked her notes, "three weeks ago on October 29th? This set a bench warrant for her arrest in motion. I'm surprised she wasn't stopped before now. Mr. Anderson stopped by our office on the 30th to discuss the matter with us. He said he came by the house to see if things were okay, and she wouldn't answer the door. He said her car was here, but she never came downstairs. He said Zion came to the window wearing shorts, a T-shirt, and a mismatched pair of sneakers. Zion wouldn't let him; he also refused to say where his mother was at the time."

Lake rubbed his head and clutched the side of the sofa. He wasn't ready for the drama, lies, and deceit being hurled at him at once. There was no need to argue facts. He leaned forward.

"What steps do I need to take to rectify the situation?"

"We will remove Zion from the home temporarily. He will live with Mr. Anderson for a short time until our investigation continues."

"He has to leave right now? Can't you let him stay until after

Thanksgiving? It's only two days away. Please let him stay until then."

"I'm sorry, Mr. Carvin, but he has to come with us now."

Lake walked up the stairs to Zion's room. When he opened the door, he fought to keep his composure as he watched Aunjanue and Zion packing a small suitcase.

"Onnie, why are you packing his things?"

"I've been through this before. It's temporary. Zion will be back with us in no time, Uncle Lake," she said. She met his eyes, hoping he'd mimic the sham.

"You'll get to spend a few days with your father and come back, okay?"

"I thought you said his wife died. He can't cook, and he was hardly ever there when I visited. Do I have to go? And when will Mom get out of jail? This is dumb!" Zion kicked the plastic bucket of basketballs in the floor. He picked up a ball and tossed it in the elevated goal in the bedroom.

Aunjanue patted a space on Zion's bed. He joined her.

"Auntie 'Sheer is a little sick right now, so while you're gone, we're gonna help her get better."

"She's doing drugs again, isn't she?"

"Zion, who said that about Lasheera?" asked Lake.

"I remember what things used to be like when I was younger. Grandma and my stepmom said Mom was a worthless crackhead and a homewrecker. Since Onnie said she's sick, I want to know if she's doing drugs again. She cursed out the lady in the drugstore real bad the other day. She's not herself anymore."

"Your mom isn't doing drugs, Zion," said Lake.

"She's upset with everything going on with my mother. Remember I told you my mom is out of jail? Well, Auntie 'Sheer doesn't want her to harm us. That's why she's been sleepy and distant."

Zion took into account Aunjanue's words. She hadn't lied to him in the past, and he trusted her completely.

"I don't want to go to my dad's."

"I bet you all will have a good Thanksgiving meal at Marvin's mother's house. You'll probably get to see your other relatives, too."

"But I was supposed to play games with Hakeem. His mom said she was getting us Black Friday video games."

"I'll get you two games when you come back. I promise," said Aunjanue. The conversation weighed on her as she fought back tears.

"I'll do this, but you better get my games," said Zion.

He got up and packed two more pairs of shoes.

Lake called Aunjanue outside the bedroom door. "Onnie, will you stay with Zion until I go back downstairs with CPS?"

She nodded. "He just packed shirts and pants. I'll make sure he has everything else packed."

Lake tromped down the stairs in disbelief. He wondered how things had spiraled out of control so quickly. One minute, they were a happy foursome; now they were strangers with a teenager holding them together. The doorbell rang as he reached the bottom step. He answered it, relieved to see Caleb and Stephanie.

"We came as soon as we saw the broadcast. Is there anything we can do?" Caleb asked.

Lake nodded his head toward the den area. Stephanie glanced in the den area, then the van.

"I'm in the middle of an issue right now. Please have a seat in the living room."

Caleb took Stephanie's hand as she wobbled toward the living room. She propped her swollen feet on the ottoman. She counted down the days when the baby would arrive.

"Babes, what do you think is going on here?" she asked.

"Whatever it is, it can't be good with CPS involved," said Caleb.

As they waited for Lake to wrap up his business, Caleb rubbed Stephanie's feet.

Lake rejoined the caseworkers. "We're making sure his suitcase is ready. Are you sure he'll be back soon?"

"This is a mere formality. Depending on the investigation, he may be back in a week, or as long as a month or more."

Aunjanue and Zion appeared in the den area. Zion puffed his chest in false bravado.

"Zion, your father is waiting outside. He will follow us to our office, and after signing paperwork, you'll go home with him," said the male caseworker.

Zion hugged Aunjanue and Lake. Aunjanue kept his suitcase with her as she lifted the Pullman handle. As she rolled his suitcase near the front door, she saw Caleb and Stephanie in the living room.

"Mr. Wilson, what are you and Ms. Stephanie doing here?"

"We came after we saw the news."

She gave an appreciative head bow and continued outside with Zion. Everyone filed outside toward the van. By this time, the neighbors had gathered in their respective yards. Their dismal faces spoke volumes. Even Belinda Rosewood kept her distance, her eyes affixed on Zion. The male caseworker opened the door for Zion.

"I got it!" Zion slammed the door. He lowered the window for Aunjanue.

"You'll be back soon, okay?"

"Coco Soul?" asked Zion.

Aunjanue obliged him with Coco Soul, the handshake they created after she joined the family. The caseworkers and neighbors watched them perform their intricate routine, starting with a scissor move and ending with two fist pounds. She turned away from him and ran inside. Stephanie waddled behind her as she held her stomach.

When they drove away, Marvin trailed the van and gave Lake a sneer as they turned from the subdivision.

"Lake, what's going on?"

"Caleb, I don't know. Man, I..."

"Listen, I'll get Stephanie to take Aunjanue to our house, and we can get together to make arrangements to get Lasheera out of jail."

Lake looked at his friend. "I'm not sure that I want to get her out."

Chapter 28

"It feels like old times," said Aruba to James.

"Is that good or bad?"

"We'll know when everyone arrives in an hour." She pulled a third pan of cornbread dressing from the oven and assembled it next to the other pitch-in items dropped off earlier in the day by relatives who had to work.

The Stanton Thanksgiving tradition, a rotation ritual amongst Lance's siblings, was to take place at Lance's this year. Because of Aruba's suicide attempt, Darnella wanted to do a quiet dinner with their immediate family. Lance favored the tradition instead. This year Darnella and Lance would provide the meats and cornbread dressing, and the guests would bring sides, desserts, drinks, and ice.

"James, are all the tables ready for the children?" Aruba asked.

"Ready and dressed. I bought enough paper plates, cups, and cutlery to feed an army," he said, holding up the turkey-decorated youth plates.

"Those are adorable."

"Oh, I set the trash cans up in the room as well. Jerry has pick-up duty. He'll supervise the younger children and make sure they don't waste anything."

Aruba followed James to the den area. Hours ago, he transformed the sitting area into a kiddie oasis complete with small tables, orange and brown tablecloths, and turkey centerpieces. The plates matched the décor. At least twenty children, ranging in ages from five to twelve, would sit near the dining room and eavesdrop on adult conversation as they did each year.

"I left more cups in my SUV. I'll be right back," said James.

He kissed Aruba's cheek; she rubbed his back and waited for him to leave. Guilt prevented her from returning his affection. She still loved him, but couldn't shake the thought that the last few months were a dream. *Maybe I'm punishing myself too much. Would James be here if he didn't care?* James not only stepped up to the plate, but he owned it. She felt a sense of pride as she watched him conduct business from his home in Augusta. The man she believed in when she first married had come full circle, and it suited him. Still, a niggling voice convinced her at any moment, he might throw up the past in her face and remind her she married another man.

James flipped his trunk, gathered the bag of cups, and sat down in back of his truck. He'd avoided this moment for two months, but he couldn't anymore. He'd gotten so caught up in helping Aruba, working at Shear Heaven, and monitoring multi-state affairs he'd skirted his longing inside. He made sure he was alone before powering up his iPhone. He had a few text messages from Shandy, Isaak, and Mitch. He'd attend to those later. He opened his Indy Beauty King email address and arranged all of Issak's messages. He scrolled down to Issak's message from two months ago marked *urgent*. He counted to ten and read Isaak's message. The file contained two attachments. He took a few deep breaths, then opened the first attachment. He cried at the sight of her. Save a few shades, she and Jeremiah were undeniably siblings. Isaak, thorough with his investigation, said his daughter lived with a good family in

Zionsville, Indiana. She attended private school, an outpouring of her adopted executive father and upper-level management mother's incomes. No longer Jameshia, she was now Hannah Reese. A straight-A student, she enjoyed hiking, arts and crafts, and bike riding. She loved to sing, act, and wanted to have a little brother someday. James wanted to see her, hug her, and if nothing more, hear the cadence of her voice.

"Dad, Mom said to bring the cups in. She's thirsty and doesn't want to wash any dishes before dinner," Jeremiah shouted from the back door.

"I'll be inside in a minute," said James.

He kept the message marked new, and wondered how Aruba would feel about having a daughter.

Chapter 29

Aruba greeted the guests who arrived at two p.m., with Kinsey leading the way. Her other aunts, Mayella and Darshelle, followed closely behind. Her father's sisters were an interesting brood. Kinsey, the sassy one, balanced her famous toasted coconut cake in one hand and a bottle of champagne in the other. Her faux fur color of choice this year was black. She air-kissed Aruba on both sides and continued to the kitchen. Thrice divorced, she loved to shop and watch the world on her massive wraparound porch while drinking scotch or gin. Mayella, the quiet one, quoted scriptures and kept to herself. She shrouded herself in plain dresses, opaque stockings, and polished loafers. Retired six years from the school system as a Home Economics teacher, she spent time in her garden and ministering to the community youth. Lance said she had separation anxiety from teaching because her conversations morphed into cooking and housekeeping tips. Mayella carried a sterilized pickle jar filled with ambrosia she immediately placed in the refrigerator. Darshelle. Well, she was…the different sister. Dressed in her customary overalls, plaid chambray shirt, and spit-shined midnight blue cowboy boots, she came empty-handed, patting her shirt pocket for Virginia Slims and a lighter. She didn't do cooking, kids. men, or working for others. She ran a twenty-five acre farm in Warren County and only fellowshipped with the family during Thanksgiving and Christmas. Standing at six feet three inches, she intimidated men and women alike with her gruff voice and silky black hair, parted down the center and always braided in two large plaits that dusted her shoulders. She brushed past Aruba without acknowledgement and stood with her sisters.

Lance greeted his sisters one by one and offered them drinks.

"Give me my usual, scotch on the rocks," said Kinsey.

"I'll have apple juice," said Mayella.

"You already know," said Darshelle. She took a beer from the refrigerator before heading to the backyard to smoke a cigarette, her boots echoing on the hardwood floors. "Call me when it's time to eat."

Mayella and Kinsey joined Darnella in the kitchen.

"Happy Thanksgiving," said Darnella.

"Same to you," said Kinsey.

"Do you need help with anything?" asked Mayella. "I can get everything together while you all have a seat."

"This isn't home-ec, May," said Darnella. "Go on and have a seat in the living room. We fixed the den area up for the children, so no HGTV for you today."

"I brought some reading materials with me, so I'll be fine," said Mayella.

Kinsey waited for her sister to leave, then sidled next to Darnella. "After all these years, we can't break her from shyness. She's going to die like that, a pathetic bore."

"She likes reading and keeping to herself," said Darnella. She arranged the HoneyBaked ham and deep-fried turkey on separate platters.

"So, I guess I'm the only one who sees a problem with Mayella being by herself. My greatest fear is she'll go to her mailbox, go back inside, and we won't know something happened to her until days later. That's unnatural for a person to keep to herself. Especially with other siblings," said Kinsey. She removed a dessert plate from the cabinet and began slicing her cake.

"What's unnatural," said Darnella, "is out back." She directed Kinsey's attention to Darshelle, now dragging a cigarette and holding court with the neighborhood men. She patted Joe Harris so hard on his back he lost his footing and stumbled forward a few steps. He inched away from Darshelle and rubbed his sore back.

"Between you, me, and the gatepost, Lance always said all Darshelle needed was a penis and a wallet to be complete."

"Stop it," said Darnella. "She is what she is. She doesn't have a lot of trust for people."

"If that's what you call it."

"Help me get this food in the dining room so we can eat." Darnella chided her. "Let's maintain a positivity pact today. No negative talk, okay." She swiped a small piece of ham from the tray.

During a dream two nights ago, Darnella awoke speechless. She struggled catching her breath, and her tongue seemed stuck to the roof of her mouth. It wasn't a cat, but something had her tongue. The first word she uttered after the experience was James. A sign had been sent to keep his name out of her mouth. Or at least be cordial to him. She shuddered at how nasty she'd been to him. She didn't want to see her precious daughter as anything other than innocent; however, neither wore the *blameless* crown. She also remembered Lance calling her a hypocrite. As usual, he made sense.

With dinner splayed on the table and the grace said by Lance, everyone enjoyed their food. Lance sat at the head of the table with other relatives seated on either side. Lance relented and allowed the children to listen to a portable radio as they ate in their designated area. Kinsey dominated the conversation as usual, not one to be drowned out by clanking silverware—or the huge elephant in the room.

"Lance, what did you do to the turkey this year?" asked Kinsey.

"My brine and peanut oil," he answered.

"Now, I'm all for peanut oil, but might I suggest you use a Cajun injector next year? It gives the meat a robust flavor, and it leaves a wonderful aftertaste to the palate," said Mayella, her Home-Ec mode kicking in.

"I'll let you do the turkey next year. I bet it will be delicious," said Lance.

James and Aruba sat next to each other and held hands in between feeding each other. Darshelle gave them an evil eye, but said nothing.

"Have we decided where we're taking the family trip next year?" asked Kinsey. "I'm cruised out, and Lord knows I don't want to be stranded in the middle of the ocean. I can't drink up all that water if something happens at sea."

"I know that's right," chimed in Maxine. "Every other news story is about cruise ships stranded at sea. What sense does it make to pay all that money and be unsafe?" Maxine turned to James. "Will your family be joining us for the trip next year? I miss having your parents, brother, and sister travel with us. We all got along well."

James downed his sweet tea and answered, "If you let me know where you're going, I'll be sure to tell my parents so everyone can coordinate the meet-up location." He squeezed Aruba's hand.

"Thanks, James. I'd love to see them again."

Darshelle belched and refused to excuse herself. Everyone looked in her direction and waited for her to say something. No luck. She finally answered, "What?"

"Now, Darshelle, you know it's rude to belch at the dinner table," said Mayella.

"What's rude is—never mind. Y'all not getting my blood pressure up today," said Darshelle, her voice deeper than usual. She chomped a turkey leg and focused on her dinner plate.

"Lance, tell everyone about possible sites for next year," said Darnella. She hoped her attempt to slice through the tension would be successful.

"I thought of Gatlinburg, Tennessee, upstate New York, or California. No foreign soil, just somewhere we could get a cabin and enjoy fresh air."

"I get plenty fresh air on my farm and in my house—thank you very much," said Darshelle.

Lance smelled the moonshine on her breath now. During her trip to the backyard, someone had slipped her the ultimate no-no. Darshelle could hold beer, but she transformed into a ruder person when she drank moonshine. The family called it "diarrhea of the mouth" when she drank moonshine because whatever came up, came out. Everyone at the table felt eggshells cracking underneath their feet.

"The meal is delicious," said Kinsey. To Aruba she said, "You outdid yourself with the dressing, Hon. It's absolutely splendid."

"I have Aunt Mayella to thank. It's her recipe," said Aruba. James placed his arm around her and ignored Darshelle, whose arms were folded. She rolled her eyes at them and took a few bites of her greens.

"Dressing is incomplete without cream of soup," said Mayella. She radiated with pride at the mention of her recipe.

Jeremiah entered the adult area and approached Aruba and James.

"Mom and Dad, we're done eating. I made everyone put their plates in the trash. May we go outside and play?"

"You may. Keep an eye on everyone and stay in the backyard," said Aruba.

The children ran outside.

"They'll run that food off in no time playing," said Kinsey. "Remember when we all played together as children? Even Darshelle joined in the fun when we were small."

"She did," said Lance. "She outran us all and beat everyone in kickball." He appreciated Kinsey's segue into their other dinner table tradition. "Let's do *Tell Me Something Good*," he said.

"I'll go first!" said Mayella.

"Tell me something good, Mayella," said Lance.

"I'm thankful to have my family here, and I'm thankful the school system called me to work part-time on a permanent basis. They're putting me on the payroll again! I'd gotten bored sitting at home. That's my something good."

"Congratulations, Mayella. I knew they couldn't get along without you at the school," said Darnella.

"Tell me something good, Darnella," said Mayella.

"Aruba is here, and James is helping her get back on her feet every step of the way."

James eyed Darnella with suspicion. He waited for the bomb to drop.

"I've been rude to James, and I wanted to apologize in front of everyone and him." She looked James in his eyes. "I've seen a side of you I didn't know existed. You've matured into a fine young man, and I'm glad you love my child. That's my something good." Darnella turned to Kinsey. "Tell me something good, Kinsey."

"I'm moving to Atlanta in April. I want to be closer to my grandchildren, and the best way to do that is go to them. I love my country living, but I want to try the city a while. Everyone is welcome to come visit me. That's my something good," said Kinsey. "Tell me something good, Lance."

Lance stood, cleared his throat, and faced Aruba. "I'm thankful my daughter is here with us. As our only child, we've tried to nurse every cut, bruise, fall, and heartache she's experienced over the years. Sometimes you take a person's presence for granted and think they'll always be around. Thinking of being without her right now pains me," he said. "I'm glad the Lord saw fit to spare her life so she could be with us. That's my something good. I love you, baby girl."

Aruba's tears mixed with her food. She made her way to her father and hugged him tight. He wiped her tears away, blinking back his own.

Darshelle applauded loudly, her thunderous claps disrupting the moment. "And the Oscar goes to, *my family!* A bunch of people who gonna sit here and pretend it's okay for my *dear* niece to attempt to take a life she didn't give herself." She got in Lance's face.

"This isn't the time or place, Darshelle!" said Lance.

"When will it be Lance? Huh? We're sitting here celebrating like two months ago she wasn't in a seventy-two-hour hold, barely clinging to life. Suicide is selfish! What if she had succeeded? You know what we'd be doing right now? Sitting here blaming ourselves for not loving her enough. For missing key signs, and clues. For not doing enough to help her. Or wait, there would be no dinner. Just a graveside visit where we'd all put flowers on a concrete slab and talk to her corpse. That's torture! How can you celebrate her?"

Darshelle turned her anger on Aruba who stood next to her father. "What were we supposed to tell your son if you died? That his mother got tired of living? She couldn't cope with the ins and outs of life like the rest of us? I guess he was supposed to remember you through pictures, his memories, and ours, right?"

James neared Darshelle with clenched fists. He didn't want to make a scene, and knew he wasn't on his own turf, but he had to defend his woman.

"One more word, Darshelle. One more," said James.

"And what? I'm not afraid of you," said Darshelle.

A flash of rage sparked in James's eyes that made Darshelle back down. Everyone's contemptuous eyes bore into her; she knew she'd crossed the line this time. She headed to the closet for her coat without saying anything else. No one cared about her departure. Everyone's attention was on Aruba, who sat in an empty chair and wept silently. Her family enveloped her.

"She's right. It was selfish, and I'm so sorry," she said.

"What matters is you're here. We can take the rest of the journey day by day," said Mayella, rubbing Aruba's back.

"No one can say they haven't been down in the dumps," said Kinsey.

Aruba's family surrounded her, each touching some part of her body, and all saddened by the sight of her tears. They maintained their unbroken circle as the sound of Darshelle's loud pickup truck barreled down the road and out of the neighborhood.

Chapter 30

"Trick Don't Kill My Vibe" by Kendrick Lamar wafted from Victoria's basement. The dinner dishes were put away. Tupperware bowls of leftovers filled the refrigerator, and Bobby was making good on his promise to teach Lillith how to do the Dougie. Ever since she saw Michelle Obama doing the Dougie with youth, Lillith wanted to learn to do the dance. Victoria's remaining dinner guests retreated to the basement for a Thanksgiving *Blue Lights in the Basement* party. She was proud of the dinner she prepared by herself. Victoria handled a majority of the food alone and had help from an unlikely source: Aruba Dixon. During their friendship, Aruba shared family recipes with Victoria. Victoria bought a recipe box and filed the index cards away, never planning to use them. Relocating to the South, as well as being a single mother, brought out the domestic goddess inside her. Although they ended on bad terms, Victoria always loved Aruba's cooking. Her family members and friends oohed and aahed over the dressing, ham, potato salad, red velvet cake, and other treats. A twinge of loneliness rose when she thought of Emory. He would have been proud of her meal and her continuing effort to lose weight. She was down fifteen additional pounds, had more energy, and was enjoying life as best she could.

"Put your arms out front more, Lillith," said Bobby.

Lillith leaned side to side as she followed Bobby's lead. Yvette, Carl, Foster, and Marguerite grooved to their own rhythms. Bobby gyrated behind Lillith before remembering his audience. He gave Foster a sheepish grin and stopped his raunchy movements.

"Sorry, Pastor," said Bobby.

"Be yourself, young man," said Foster.

Foster cued the music for old- and new-school pleasure. Before he found Christ and became a megachurch pastor, he was a deejay for parties throughout Atlanta and North Georgia. When Victoria asked him to spin records for the night, he gladly accepted.

"How am I doing, Bobby?" Lillith asked. She leaned harder this time, singing along with Kendrick.

"You got it now, Lill," said Bobby. He pumped his fists in the air and feigned a heart attack like his father did at their basement parties.

"Not Elizabeth!" said Lillith. Every blue moon, she and Bobby made a familiar connection, closing the generational gap they shared.

Victoria poured nonalcoholic beverages for the giddy couples. It had been a long time since she felt this happy. Things weren't perfect, but they were stable. Nicolette dined with the neighbor's children today, giving the adults time to unwind. When the doorbell rang, everyone looked at Victoria. Foster turned the music down.

"I told Nicolette to stay next door until six o'clock. She's forever leaving her key, and she never remembers the garage passcode. I'll be right back."

Yvette, Marguerite, and Lillith giggled while Foster, Carl, and Bobby shook their heads. Victoria ran up the stairs, something impossible just three months ago. She flung open the door, ready to give Nicolette a lesson on responsibility.

"Young lady—"

"Nothing feminine about me at all," said Emory. He held a beautiful bouquet of pink, white, and purple roses.

"Emory, what are you doing here?"

"You invited me. I told you I wouldn't be able to make it until after my flight arrived," said Emory.

"I didn't invite—" She directed her gaze toward the basement, shaking her head. There was too much giggling before she came upstairs. "I think we're victims of overzealous matchmakers. Come inside."

Emory handed her the bouquet. "Before I enter, may I kiss you?"

"Are you sure you want to kiss me?"

"Positive."

They fell into their old rhythm, swept up in familiar tongue-locking like old times. He stepped inside the foyer and gave her his coat. She wasn't the only one who'd been working out. He'd slimmed down significantly and looked as handsome as ever. He still had a linebacker physique, and his undeniable swagger remained intact. She took in his tailored, pinstripe suit, decorative tie, and wingtip shoes. *This man can hang a suit.*

Emory and Victoria went to the kitchen. She found a vase from the cabinet and filled it with water for her bouquet. She was beyond playing games and waited for the day they could have a heart-to-heart talk about their relationship. He took a seat at the island.

"Is Nicolette here?" he asked.

"She's across the street. All the neighborhood children were invited over for a big feast. I can't imagine hosting fifty children, but I learned the Danbys have the children over every year. It's their give-back move since they're childless."

"I see." He removed a small box from his jacket. "I brought her a Thanksgiving present. It's nothing fancy. Just something to get her started."

Victoria eyed the blue box. "May I?"

"Go ahead."

Victoria removed the beautiful charm bracelet from the box. Emory blew her away with his memory. During the summer, they vacationed in Hilton Head Island, South Carolina. Nicolette made fast friends with the girls in the adjacent timeshare. One of the girls flashed her Elsa Peretti charm bracelet. She pointed out the heart, Red Jasper Bean, lapis Starfish, rock crystal Tear Drop, and jade Eternal Circle. It was the must-have item amongst the girls during summer. She asked her Uncle Em if he'd buy it for her. He assured her he'd see what he could do.

"When did you get this?"

"A week after our vacation. I planned to give it to her for her birthday, but I didn't get a chance after our breakup."

Victoria didn't know what to say. Emory always included her daughter in their outings and activities.

"Thanks, Emory. She's missed you a lot."

"Have you?"

She hesitated a moment, then responded. "Yes. More than I ever thought I would." She joined him at the island. "Have you eaten yet?"

"Stuffed. We had a big spread at the studio, so I can't eat another morsel."

"I cooked dinner all by myself this year."

"Without my prompting?"

"Yes," she said. They laughed, knowing he ruled the kitchen in his home and hers. "So tell me when I invited you over."

Emory whipped out his cell phone. He opened his text messages and scrolled up to the first message he received from her and read it aloud. "Emory, I'd like to clear the air. Are you available to come by for Thanksgiving?"

Victoria noted the date: November 8, 2013. It was the same date her phone went missing while lunching with Yvette. She searched everywhere for her phone. Due to her newfound thriftiness, she chose not to buy a new phone. She'd just wait until she found the old one. She wasn't attached to her phone and often lost it. She knew it would reappear. *So, Yvette is the culprit.*

"May I?" she asked.

She looked at the trail of messages. Yvette knew her so well that she wrote and responded in her voice.

"Emory, I didn't send these messages."

"They're from your number," he said.

"I had lunch with Yvette two weeks ago, and it appears she snatched my phone for Match.com purposes."

"Duped again, heh?" Emory stood to leave. "At least I'm not being embarrassed in a room full of people this time."

"Stay, please." She took his hand and led him to the living room. After they were seated on the sofa, she faced him. "I'm glad Yvette reached out to you on my behalf. I've missed you so much since the night of the party. I've felt off-balance without you. I didn't realize how much I loved you until you were gone."

"I'm sorry for not responding initially. I felt like a fool proposing to you in front of everyone and you turning me down. Your family and friends pulled together to make the night special, and it blew up in my face."

"Emory, I've been stuck since my husband died. I don't trust anyone, and the minute someone gets close to me, I clam up."

"What does that have to do with me? I told you while we were dating, I'm not your deceased husband, and every woman isn't Aruba. You have to get past your hurt at some point."

"I'm working on it. Believe me, I am. Lillith had a cancer scare which has brought us closer. I understand a bit better why she abandoned me when I was younger. And Emory, the bitterness I feel has physical manifestations. My chest hurts when I think about Aruba or Winston. I can't breathe sometimes, and Nicolette says my face wrinkles when I'm angry. I'm too young to be this mad all the time."

"I agree. You're moving in the right direction. I'm proud of you." He let her words sink in. He hadn't noticed her svelte figure until now. "I'm guessing your weight loss is part of your transformation?"

"Yvette has been dog-walking me, Emory! If we're not at the park walking, we're at Planet Fitness or one of the local CrossFit locations. I didn't know burpees went beyond babies."

"Same here. I love to cook and eat, but it feels like I'm digging my grave with my teeth," he said.

"If you're willing to put up with my mistrustful ways, I think we could balance each other out well," she said.

"Are you willing to try again? I'm talking tortoise pace."

"Yes, Emory, I'm willing to give us another try."

They hugged as the team of matchmakers, who had snuck up from the basement, eavesdropped and high-fived at the sound of the reunion.

Chapter 31

I'm spending Thanksgiving at the Marion County Jail. Lake signed himself into the facility, incredulous his time had been wasted on his wife's poor decisions. Sign-in time was forty-five minutes prior to the visit. During that time, he presented his ID, stood still for the security wand, and had his belongings placed in a locker. He didn't realize how fortunate he was until a ruckus three persons ahead of him broke out. A woman had been arrested within the last three months, so she was unable to visit her daughter. She was escorted from the line by a security officer. His limited experience with the law was aided by Jamilah's expertise. Just as she had helped Tawatha with her legal troubles, Jamilah assisted Lasheera with her case. She was unable to get a bondsman due to the holiday, but she was scheduled to be out of jail first thing Monday morning. She had four more days to ponder her mistakes. Lake, ambivalent about her innocence, wavered about visiting her. He relented after Aunjanue convinced him Lasheera needed him now more than ever. He weighed her words as Lasheera sat behind a glass partition. She pointed to the phone to his left; he picked it up to speak with her.

"Happy Thanksgiving, Lake."

He nodded.

"I'm sorry you have to be here. I know you planned this holiday months ago for us. Dinner was supposed to be at our house with everyone."

"It would be better if you were home."

"I know."

"Why, baby?"

Lasheera shrugged and touched the glass.

"You have to give me more than a shrug. We've been through a lot together, and for the past few months, I've learned more about you from other people than you."

Lasheera bit her bottom lip and watched as Lake planted his elbows on the small space in front of the window. During her time on the streets, she'd convinced herself a man like Lake didn't exist. Not for women like her. She also knew she'd never get married. Too many mistakes had been made; too many slipups had come between her and happiness. The evening she took Aunjanue to an art fair at Lincoln Middle School, she had no idea a teacher would capture and keep her attention. Love, then marriage. The baby carriage bit was altered somewhat since she had a child, but Lake accepted Zion as his own and loved them all equally. The only other incident that topped his undying love was allowing Aunjanue to join their family. He had been good to them, and staring into his loving eyes, she couldn't muster an excuse for her behavior— not a single one. So, she plowed forward with what she could—the truth.

"The police said I did a rolling stop on Allisonville Road."

"Said, or did you do it?"

"Lake, that's the thing. I can't remember. I left the house for something, and the next thing I know, I was being chased by the police."

"Do you expect me to believe you've had all these memory lapses?" he asked.

"I have. It started…" She paused.

"It started when?"

"A few months ago, I picked up the wrong prescription at Walgreens. I meant to take it back, I did, but I'd been having trouble sleeping, and I heard Ambien was good for insomnia."

"So, the Advil story was a lie?"

"Yes."

"So, you haven't been having chronic headaches?"

"No."

"What do you want me to do? How do we move on from this thing?"

Her heart palpitated. She *knew* he would come to the lockup demanding a divorce. She'd seen countless stories of spouses leaving their loved ones in jail. No letters, no phone calls, no money on the books. Her husband, used the words *move on from this thing*.

"You don't want a divorce?"

"I come straight, no chaser, Lasheera. I was minutes away from walking out of this jail and going home. Zion is with Marvin, and Aunjanue is having dinner with Robert and J.B. today."

"What is Zion doing with Marvin?" She moved closer to the partition and placed her hands on the glass.

"Jamilah didn't tell you? CPS took Zion Tuesday. Someone reported the incident you had at the pharmacy, and Marvin reported the fact you didn't appear in court." His hand met hers. "When were you going to tell me about the incident?"

The lies stacked up quickly. She didn't know how much longer she could hold in all the hurts and disappointments she'd experienced. First, she felt inadequate after regaining custody of Zion. Whenever she attended school functions or parent-teacher conferences with him, she couldn't express how her drug use affected her ability to help Zion with his homework. Lake helped him most times, but she wanted to be an active participant with his math and Spanish assignments. There was also the fear of not being able to parent Aunjanue well. When she moved in, most nights were sleepless ones; she and Lake took turns listening out for her as she thrashed back and forth in bed, calling on Tawatha, or her siblings. After the night Aunjanue stayed awake all night because she wanted her sister and brothers to come home, Lake made the stay-at-home executive decision. "Someone has to hold down the fort," he said. *Some fort-holder I am.*

"I don't know when, but I wanted to tell you. I couldn't find the words, Lake."

"How bout, 'Lake I'm stressed and I need your help?'"

"I—"

"Or how about, 'Lake, I'm overwhelmed and I can't do this without you?'"

"Baby—"

"When I said I do, I meant it. The better, the worse, the sickness. But I can't be in a marriage with someone that doesn't talk to me. You know what I've felt like the last few months?"

"What?"

"Like I have a wife who's watching me walk near the edge of a cliff and doesn't have the common courtesy to yell out, 'Hey, wait!'"

Lasheera dropped her head.

"I accepted you while knowing you used drugs in the past. I accepted your son, *our* son, Zion. I didn't mind taking in Aunjanue. But I don't do blindsiding well. Not at all."

"What can I do to make this up to you?"

"Stop lying to me. Be honest. I'm not dumb enough to think you'll tell me everything, but can you at least give a brother a heads-up?" He made a gesture for her to press her face against the glass. When she did, he stroked the side of the partition with his finger, his attempt at caressing her face.

"Is Aunjanue angry with me? Is that why she didn't come?"

"She's not your biological child, so she couldn't come. Since you're getting out Monday, it made no sense to add her to the visitor's list."

"I don't know how I'll face the children Monday," she said.

"With a smile on your face and with humility."

"I've been thinking," she said.

"About?"

"I've been so upset since Tawatha got out. I've ignored her. I've criticized her, and look at where I am right now." She scanned the lockup and narrowed her eyes on the inmates to her left and right.

"You can't compare the two situations. Are you saying you want to see her?"

"I don't know what I'm saying. Maybe I've been wrong. I don't know how I would have felt if you didn't come see me today."

"I'm here. You have to get your priorities together, 'Sheer. We can't stay married if you don't."

"I know."

"By the way, Stephanie took Aunjanue home the other day after CPS took Zion."

"Stephanie and Caleb were there?"

"Unfortunately."

"Now they think I'm a criminal."

"Baby, they stopped by after the news story. Channel 13 viewers saw you being arrested."

"What did they say?"

"Zion and Aunjanue's safety was important to them. Stephanie took Onnie and Caleb stayed with me. No one is judging you."

"What if Stephanie had gone into labor over the stress?"

"She didn't, and it's all good."

A jailer tapped Lake on the shoulder. "Your thirty minutes are up, sir."

"Jamilah will be here Monday for your court appearance. Where is the Ambien?"

"Excuse me?"

"The rest of the Ambien. I don't want any in the house when you get there. Is there a stash I need to get rid of before you come home?"

Not wanting to lose her good thing, she answered, "In back of the closet...in the Jimmy Choo box."

Chapter 32

"Tap it lightly, and make sure the powdered sugar covers the pound cake," Roberta said. "This cake is for J.B., and you and Roger can eat the one with the five-flavor glaze."

"Yes, ma'am."

While Roger and J.B. sat in the den watching sports and talking life, she stayed in the kitchen finishing desserts with Roberta. Aunjanue didn't want to see Lasheera in jail; one adult with legal troubles was all she could handle. The image of Zion rolling away in the CPS van still disturbed her. She knew that ride all too well; Roberta was her refuge after she and her siblings took that ride. Grateful that Mr. Wilson and his wife, Stephanie, invited her to dinner for Thanksgiving, she declined their offer, choosing family instead.

"Grandma Bert, why don't you sit down?"

"I'm fine, Onnie. I need to get these two cakes done before I go back to watching Lifetime. J.B. thinks he's slick watching sports, but he's got another thing coming when that marathon starts."

"You need to sit down. Let me help you to the table." She coaxed her grandmother to sit, the loudness of her shuffling feet filling the kitchen. Her grandmother's step lessened each time she saw her. Roberta plopped in a recliner JB pulled into the kitchen and exhaled.

"Whew. Roberta's no spring chicken anymore!"

"You are a spring chicken, Grandma."

"In my mind."

"In mine, too."

"That cake looks pretty good. Onnie, you did a darn good job today helping me with the cooking. J.B. did his grill-master duties, didn't he?"

"Everything was so good. I'm still stuffed from all the food. I'm not sure when we'll get to dessert."

"In due time." Roberta leaned into Aunjanue. "That Roger is sho 'nuff cute. Got good manners, too."

"He is nice. I'm surprised he came today since he's been so busy visiting colleges."

"You mind if I ask you something?"

"No, ma'am."

"A while back, we talked about, you know, life. You changed your mind yet?"

Aunjanue tried to conjure up the life discussion.

"Which talk?"

Roberta leaned closer. "Are you still saving yourself?"

"Oh, *that*. Yes. I don't want to get pregnant, and I don't want to ruin my future." Aunjanue dropped her voice a few octaves. "The only man I want to have sex with is my husband—if I get married."

Roberta wondered which side of the family birthed Aunjanue's mindset since Tawatha was a product of an out-of-wedlock relationship. Furthermore, Tawatha continued the trend by having out-of-wedlock babies. When Roberta looked at her granddaughter, she saw the realization of answered prayers. She was tired of the women in her family settling for less in relationships and marriage. Maybe, just maybe, Aunjanue would reverse the trend.

"Come here, Roger," Roberta called to the den area.

"Grandma, what are you doing?"

"You mind your business and I'll mind mine," said Roberta.

Roger emerged from the den area. He wore slacks, a nice dress shirt, and a matching tie. He was unlike most of the young men Roberta saw around town who thought sagging pants and wife-beaters gave them the stupid street cred title. Roger, a gentleman and a scholar, joined them at the table.

"J.B. getting on your nerves in there?"

"No, ma'am," he said nervously.

He sat next to Aunjanue and placed her hand in his.

"So, what are your plans for the future, son? I know I'm springing this on real quick, but I'm going somewhere."

He eyed Aunjanue. He wasn't prepared for a pop quiz, and he hoped her face held the answers. No luck.

He stammered. "I've been accepted at IU. I have a full scholar-ship. I plan on studying international business, and I'll be playing football."

"NFL, or a career?"

"Both. I want to explore all my options. My mom and dad said I shouldn't limit myself when it comes to my career."

"How do they feel about my granddaughter? I mean, about you dating her?"

He held Aunjanue's hand closer. "They think the world of her."

"What have they told you about getting married?"

"Grandma!" said Aunjanue.

"Quit harassing those children, Bert!" J.B. called from the den area.

"Keep watching your game!" she shouted back. She refocused her attention on Roger and Aunjanue. "Where was I? Oh, marriage."

"Honestly, ma'am, I don't know if that's even on the radar. I want to get finished with school first. At least get a master's degree. Plus, my dad said the NFL and marriage don't mix. He said to keep my options open in that area, too."

"*Ding, ding, ding!*" Roberta clapped her hands as if she'd won a game show.

Aunjanue and Roger looked at one another.

"I've seen you two all huddled up together, but I wanted to have a heart-to-heart with you all. You don't mind, do you?"

"No, ma'am," they said in unison.

"When I lived in California, I met this man who swept me off my feet. I was a student back then, and you couldn't tell me nothing! I was a bona fide brick house."

"Brick house?" Roger asked.

Roberta curled her lips. "What do you young folks call a fine woman these days?" she asked.

"A cold piece," he said.

"Bam! That was me."

"Anyway, I was a smart student. I had dreams and goals, but I got pregnant, and it slowed me down a little. Actually, I *let* it stop me. If you think about it, I didn't have half the opportunities back then you all have now. All I'm saying is that you should take advantage of your education and go as far as you can. It makes no sense with all this technology, scholarships, fellowships, and everything else known to man, that young folks can't read or write, let alone fill out a simple job application by hand or online."

They nodded in agreement.

"Grandma Bert, may we go in the den now?" Aunjanue asked.

"One last thing. Take your time. You both have plenty of time to do what you need to do. Don't rush into anything you can't handle later on."

Aunjanue didn't see the pep talk coming, but she was glad it happened. No one said anything the last time she was at the Keys' house, but there was tension in the air since her mother had been released from prison. Roger's mother, Eva, wasn't as welcoming as she'd been in the past. His father, Dexter, was still a fun-loving and jovial character, but something was amiss. Her suspicions were confirmed after she heard snatches of their conversation as the couple gardened one evening. She heard her name mixed with the words *unsuitable* and *abandoned* as they pruned weeds. She vowed to enjoy her time with Roger, but she knew they weren't guaranteed a future together.

"Thank you, ma'am," said Roger. They left Roberta and returned to J.B. in front of the television. Aunjanue remembered how much her grandfather like eating cake while watching the game.

"Grandpa J.B., would you like a slice of pound cake?"

"Don't mind if I do," he said.

"Roger, would you like some dessert?" she asked.

"I am full. If it wasn't rude, I'd ask to take a plate home," he said.

"That's not rude at all. I bought take-out plates so we could get rid of this food. We can't eat it all, and we don't need a whole lot of leftovers clogging up the fridge," said J.B. "You *better* take something with you," he said, winking at Roger.

Roger laughed at J.B.'s antics.

Aunjanue returned to the kitchen. In the short time she'd traveled to the den and back, Roberta dozed in the recliner. Aunjanue tapped her shoulder.

"Grandma Bert, go take a nap," she said.

"And miss the marathon?"

"I'll wake you up when it comes on," said Aunjanue.

She helped her grandmother to the nearest bedroom and tucked her in. She went back to the kitchen, cut her grandfather's cake, and served it with a nice, tall glass of milk.

"Roger, I'm going to the car for a minute. I'll be right back." She grabbed her purse.

He waved her away with a smile and mouthed, "Hurry back."

Aunjanue walked outside. She paced a few steps before unlocking Roger's car door. She sat in the front seat, unzipping her bag. The new postcard, a replica of Van Gogh's *The Yellow House*, was tucked inside her oversized wallet. She'd snatched it from the mailbox before anyone could see it. She removed it from her wallet and read it again: *The ones who are supposed to protect you aren't doing it very well. We can be together in our own yellow house. I love you. T.*

The secret of Tawatha's stalking crushed her. She had to find someone to talk to before she lost her mind.

Chapter 33

Since the mountain wouldn't come to Tawatha, she decided to go the mountain. She arrived in Augusta, Georgia, the day after Thanksgiving, suitcase in hand, mission clearly defined. The performances she gave Royce and her parole officer were brilliant, and she patted herself on the back when she was done. Out-of-state travel required written permission from the parole division as well as her supervising officer, and she knew nothing would be as convincing as the death of a family member. Tawatha searched the *Augusta Chronicle* obituaries for the perfect relative and found him in the person of Mr. James Hart. She renamed him Keith "Mack" Gipson, her mother's *brother*. "Uncle Mack" died after falling from his rooftop repairing missing shingles. The rooftop disaster was a good start as Tawatha revised portions of Hart's life story. A little copying and pasting, and she'd crafted the perfect obituary that she printed out for Royce and her PO. She predicted she'd be in Augusta no more than a week, the length of time she'd reserved a room at the Jameson Suites on Claussen Road.

Now, as she sat in the hotel parking lot after touching up her makeup, she took out the folder with the address and directions to Shear Heaven Salon. Shear Heaven, less than seven miles from the hotel, was where she planned to camp out until she saw James. She decided she wouldn't approach him until he was alone, which meant she had to adjust her schedule to track his comings and goings, but she was up for the challenge. She left the parking lot and headed toward the 1700 block of Wrightsboro Road.

She'd grown tired of begging her family to bridge the gap that separated them. Everyone deserved love, and she believed it was time she seized love with the man she truly desired. *"Carpe diem."*

She glanced at her reflection in the mirror, admiring the Keri Hilson hairdo perfectly framing her face. The auburn color and honey-blonde streaks suited her. She wore one of Millie's skirt suits well. Surprisingly, the weather in Augusta was mild, so she ditched her heavy cashmere coat for a lighter one. "I could get used to this city. James and I could buy a house, have another baby, and I could help out with the businesses," she said.

She'd arrived at Shear Heaven faster than expected, so she slowed down in front of the building until she came to a complete stop. She noticed a parking lot on the side of the building, so she moved her car there. The shop window had a light tint, but she saw movement in the building. Activity was light, then again, people were probably Black Friday shopping. She reached in the back seat for her floppy hat and sunglasses. She doubted anyone would recognize her in Augusta, but her disguise was a must, so she never left home without it.

Two hours passed, and there was no sign of James. Hunger pangs rumbled, filling the car with noise she hated hearing. Starvation wasn't an option since long periods of not eating made her nauseous, so she pulled out her phone to search for nearby restaurants. She wanted seafood. She searched online and found Bonefish Grill, her home away from home with Royce, and saw one close to the shop. After mapping out directions, she headed toward the restaurant. "I'll eat and reclaim my post in no time. James has to come by at some point. I'll give him until seven tonight, then I'll go back to my hotel room."

She entered the restaurant, was seated, and perused the menu. Since traveling to a new city was out of her comfort zone, she decided to try a new meal as well. She always ate the same thing every time she dined with Royce. She called her waitress over.

"I've eaten here before, but I want to try something new. What do you suggest?"

"What do you normally eat?"

"The pecan parmesan crusted rainbow trout."

"I'd suggest the sea scallops and shrimp with a kiwi smash."

"That sounds really good."

"I'll put your order in. Be back with you shortly."

Tawatha eyed the patrons and saw what she hated most about dining alone: couples. The majority of the people in the restaurant were paired up, cuddling, holding hands, and staring into each other's eyes. *When will I be able to enjoy that kind of love?* She took out her phone to text Royce. After letting him know she was safe, he texted back: "Having dinner with Millie. We have lots to discuss when you get back." *Royce, too? I guess this means I'll have to find somewhere else to stay when I get back to Indiana.*

Sensing someone staring at her, Tawatha turned toward a table behind her. A man dining alone waved to her and said *hello.*

She said hello as well and quickly turned back to her phone. Her mission was James Dixon, not the man behind her. She tapped on the *Words with Friends* icon, hoping a random opponent or Royce had either invited her to play or continued an existing game. Someone's throat cleared behind her. The man who waved stood near her.

"Do you mind if I join you?" he asked.

"Actually, I have a lot on my mind and wanted to be alone. You understand, don't you?"

"Absolutely. I had to tell you that I think you're beautiful. I saw you when you walked in, and the first thing I noticed was your haircut. It fits your features well. Have a nice evening, Miss."

He returned to his seat. As he walked away, Tawatha took in his neat appearance, dark brown eyes, and calming nature. All he wanted was to join her, but in that moment, she felt there was something different about him. He was the first man in years who didn't say anything about her body or approach her with crass lines. He didn't insist they eat together; he took no for an answer. *You need a paradigm shift.* Royce's words rang in her ears again.

Her food arrived, and she devoured the scallops, shrimp, and kiwi smash. She stretched her eating time out, anticipating James's arrival at the shop.

She flagged her waitress after being beaten down by FrostRubicon in *Words with Friends.*

"I'll have my check, please."

"I'll be right back, Ms."

Tawatha waited for the waitress to return. An older couple two tables over stared into each other's eyes. The man whispered something to her, and she playfully tapped his hand. Since her waitress hadn't returned, she approached them.

"I don't mean to intrude, but I wanted to say you all look wonderful together."

"Thank you, Miss," said the man.

"Fifty-five years of marriage and counting," said the woman. She gazed at Tawatha's left hand and asked, "Are you married, Miss?"

"No, but I hope to be in the near future."

"Don't rush it," said the man. "It's a big commitment that requires trust, honesty, and seeing someone at their best and their worst."

"You said a mouthful," said the woman.

"Thanks for the advice. I'll keep that in mind."

"You're a lovely young woman," said the wife. "I'm sure the man who marries you will be one lucky guy."

Tawatha imagined walking down the aisle with James. "I hope so," she said, and returned to her table.

She pulled her wallet out to pay for dinner. The waitress returned again.

"Miss, the young man at the table paid for your meal and left me a generous tip."

Tawatha turned to thank him, but he was gone.

"Have a good evening, ma'am," said the waitress.

Tawatha left the restaurant, a strange mix of emotions filling her insides. She started her car, unsure of what just happened in the restaurant.

"Paradigms," she said, and headed back to the hotel.

Chapter 34

Darshelle's embarrassing outburst prompted the decision between Aruba and her parents to go to James's house in Augusta. He promised he'd monitor her medication and be with her at all times. They knew Darshelle wouldn't show her face again, but they all agreed a change of scenery would be good for Aruba.

Aruba and James sat at the kitchen table; She packed promo gift bags with Jeremiah as James balanced his checkbook. Shear Heaven loved his promotion ideas. Since he arrived in Augusta and joined the Shear Heaven team, business had increased 62 percent. He tracked numbers so he could stay abreast of the salon's bottom line. The latest promo, Black Saturday, included gift bags to the first forty ladies with Saturday appointments. Each bag contained samples of his hair products, a gift card to a local restaurant, and a raffle ticket for a Christmas drawing for an all-expenses-paid vacation to Jamaica. James advertised the giveaway on WAKB, WIIZ, and WSKP-FM stations, as well as WRDW news.

"Dad, may I use this on my hair, too?" asked Jeremiah, holding up a packet of Perfect Papaya Twisting Crème.

"You could. I don't think you need it though," said James.

"I used it and loved it," said Aruba. "It smells great, and it's helping get my ends together. Thanks for cutting them, James."

"Like I'd let you keep walking around looking like Fanta from *Roots*."

"I did not look like Fanta," said Aruba. She tossed a sample of the cream at him.

"Fanta was fine, but the braids…" said James.

They burst into laughter. Aruba hadn't laughed so much in years. Aruba and James didn't label what they were; they took things day by day. She knew he still loved her; she loved him as well. She wasn't ready to jump another broom, though.

"Are you going to the shop tonight?" she asked.

"No. I have Indianapolis business to handle online, so I won't go back to Shear until tomorrow. If you don't mind dropping the bags off for me after the shop closes, I'd appreciate it. You and Jeremiah can put them in the back storage room for me." He turned to Jeremiah. "We have Pie Day again tomorrow, Jerry."

"Aw, man, again?" asked Jeremiah. He pretended to sulk, tying a tight knot in the bag he held.

"Why do we have Pie Day?" James asked.

Jeremiah huffed. "So I can learn to make my own pie instead of having a slice of someone else's."

"You'll thank me for this when you're a man."

Pie Day, James's entrepreneurship initiative with Jeremiah, happened the last Saturday of every month. He took him to Shear Heaven and gave him a list of assigned tasks to be completed within a certain time. Jeremiah greeted vendors, swept floors, performed inventory, and assisted stylists by stocking their stations with shampoo, conditioners, and gloves. The day culminated with James sending Jeremiah around the corner to a local restaurant for a miniature sweet potato pie. When he returned, James gave him a knife and made him cut a small sliver. The first time it happened, Jeremiah furrowed his brow and said, "May I have the whole pie?"

James responded, "Son, think of this pie as a business. This is what working for someone else is. When someone else employs you, you'll always get a piece of the pie, but you'll never get the whole pie. The sooner you learn to work for yourself, the better off you'll be, and the sooner you can have your own pie."

Jeremiah traipsed away. He was hungry and wanted the rest of the pie, but he'd begun to trust his father enough to believe working for himself was important.

The three of them jumped at the sound of the doorbell.

"James, are you expecting someone?" Aruba asked.

"The only people who know I'm here are your parents, Isaak, Katrina, and Mitch," said James.

"I'll get it."

"No, let me," she said. Dr. Shipman's words came back to her.

"You sure?" he asked.

"Positive. I have to get back to life, right?"

Aruba twisted the gift bag and added it to the others. She smoothed her turtleneck and rubbed her hands over her jeans. James had braided her hair, and she loved not having to wrestle with it every day.

"Who is it?" she asked.

No one responded. She missed having a key hole. She went to the side window and peeked through the curtain. They eyed each other at the same time. She opened the door, her feet firmly planted in the carpet.

"Aruba, how are you?" asked Bria. Bria stood next to her husband, Sidney, holding a beautiful gift basket.

Aruba hadn't talked to her childhood friend since leaving Indianapolis. They'd lost contact after she moved to California. They were neighbors in Harlem, attended college together, and reconnected years later after she hired Bria at State Farm. Their friendship nosedived after Bria learned of Aruba's infidelity. She didn't pretend to understand how Aruba could deceive everyone, and she boycotted her choice of a mate by excommunicating her. Aruba thought of Bria over the years, but she didn't know how to pick up where they left off. She'd try her hand at it today.

"Aruba, we didn't mean to come by unannounced," said Sidney, his ice-breaking attempt.

"Your mother gave us the address, and since we're visiting from Indianapolis, I said I wouldn't let the weekend pass without seeing you. I hope you don't mind," said Bria.

The old friends hugged and Aruba invited them in. James entered the living room and gave Sidney the universal brother's fist pound and handshake.

"Sidney, come join us in the basement. After I handle salon business, I want you to see me put this whipping on Jeremiah in *NBA 2K13*."

Alone in the living room, Aruba offered Bria a seat.

"I brought you a gift basket. I assembled it based on the things you like."

"Thank you. You shouldn't have gone out of your way to do anything for me." Aruba placed the basket on the coffee table.

"It was my pleasure." Bria twiddled her fingers on her legs.

"Why are you nervous? You still do that thing with your fingers and legs, I see."

Bria released nervous laughter and focused on the gift basket.

"I guess you heard about the suicide attempt," said Aruba.

Bria looked at her. "My grandmother told me. She said Maxie called her from the hospital to let her know."

"I figured Maxie told your grandmother. They're still very close."

"I've been a horrible friend. All these years have passed, and I could have at least reached out to you to see if you were okay and needed anything," said Bria.

"I don't think I would have reached out to me either. I let a lot of people down," said Aruba.

"Who hasn't? I shouldn't have let all those years of friendship go because of what happened in your marriage. I didn't mean to judge you."

"It's done. I'm moving forward, Bria. I hope we can put the past behind us."

Bria's shoulders relaxed. Aruba handled the conversation with the grace she always exhibited.

"Look at you, gorgeous!" said Aruba. "You haven't changed at all. Sidney's looking as handsome as ever, too."

"You're as beautiful as always, too. By the way, I'm glad to see you and James back together."

"We're not officially back together yet. He's just helping me through this storm right now. I appreciate him being here—that's for sure."

They fell into the rhythm of the good old days. They swapped tips, caught up on old news, and discussed Indianapolis.

"What's going on in 'Nap?" asked Aruba.

"The Beauty King himself is everywhere. Billboards, television commercials. He and—" Bria stopped short of saying Shandy's name.

"It's okay, Bree. He and Shandy are business partners now. He broke up with her before coming to Georgia to see about me. She calls and checks in with me, also. We're all adults in this situation."

"That's commendable. You know the average woman might be crazy about letting someone like him go," said Bria.

"Yes, the average *woman*. Shandy is a *lady*. I knew she was the real deal when she confessed I kept them from getting closer and that James loved me."

"She admitted it?"

"Yes. She said she always felt like a third wheel. Things are premature, but the old James I knew before I divorced is no more. He leaves his phone near me. I sit near him during conversations, and we actually talk to one another on a regular basis. These are all things we didn't do when we were married. I don't go through his phone, but he keeps it near."

"I hope it works out for you. I always wanted your marriage to work."

"One day at a time. I can't do any more," said Aruba.

"Guess what happened in Indianapolis?" Bria asked.

"What?"

"The lunatic who burned her children in the fire is out of jail!"

"No! How did that happen?"

"A jury-tampering technicality. Someone pulled some strings. I'm glad you and James are out of harm's way with her."

Aruba wondered why James hadn't mentioned Tawatha's prison release. *Then again, when did he have time?* She'd ask him about it later. Prison had a way of reforming or worsening criminals. Time would tell what the walls had done to Tawatha.

"How are things with you and Sidney?"

Bria pulled a small photo album from her purse and handed it to Aruba. She flipped through the photos and turned to Bria. "Who is this?"

"Our child, if the adoption goes through."

Aruba squealed with joy! "A baby? She's a living doll."

"I gave up trying to conceive a long time ago. I wanted to give Sidney a baby so badly, but it wasn't worth the changes my body kept going through. We won't even talk about the outrageous fertility costs. I could feed a small African village with the price of one treatment. So, we did adoption screening, and here we are. The baby was born two weeks ago to a teenage mother. She's met us, has been to our home, and we helped her with prenatal care. We understand she might change her mind, but we're praying the little bundle of joy will join us soon," said Bria.

"You and Sidney will make great parents," said Aruba. I'd love to have a little goddaughter. If not a goddaughter, I'll make a fabulous aunt."

"Godmother, not aunt, Aruba," said Bria.

"I didn't even offer you anything to eat or drink. Darnella would roast me over a spit for my lack of manners," said Aruba. "Would you like something to drink?"

"I would like water or juice," said Bria.

Aruba headed to the kitchen, stopping in her tracks when James yelled from the basement, "I'll be damned!"

Chapter 35

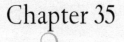

Aruba headed to the basement, Bria close behind. The noise continued once she reached the office area of the basement. James and Sidney stood in front of the computer.

"What's wrong, James?" Aruba asked.

"Jeremiah, go upstairs to your room," said James.

"What about our game?"

"Later. I have to take care of something."

James's authoritative tone sent Jeremiah to his room without further argument. Aruba moved closer to the computer. Puzzled, she said, "Why the noise about your Facebook page?"

James beckoned Sidney, Bria, and Aruba. They leaned in, checking out the hair photo gallery.

"I check the photo gallery every Friday night after Shandy updates it. Low and behold, I find this tonight."

James readjusted the screen. Aruba squinted her eyes at the screen, then gasped. "It can't be. How?"

"If you don't mind going upstairs, I'm about to find out."

Sidney and Bria leaned into the screen as well, staring at Tawatha. Aruba never forgot faces, and Tawatha's face came back to her over the years in nightmares.

"This is the worst kind of trouble, James," said Sidney. "If she's in your establishment, she's probably sniffing around Indianapolis trying to find you."

"Let me get everyone on a conference call, and I'll come upstairs in a few," said James.

The three of them went upstairs, leaving James in the basement.

He paced the length of the basement and tried to figure out how this thorn in his side kept cropping up. He wondered if this could be his payback for trying to find their daughter. Only the private investigator and Isaak knew about his search.

James dialed Shandy. She said she would be in Indianapolis throughout the holiday, so he needed her to coordinate the call. He almost hung up after several rings.

"Hello," she answered. Her groggy voice left him with a twinge of guilt that he'd awakened her.

"Are you able to talk, Shandy?"

"Is something wrong, James?"

"Very." He calmed himself. He couldn't navigate the business at hand if he lost his cool. "Are you near a computer?"

"Sure. Let me get to my desk," she said.

"Log on to the Facebook page." He waited for her to log on, then instructed her to check the Dixon's Hair Affair page.

"Okay, it's the Friday photo gallery. What's new?"

"Anyone look familiar to you?"

Shandy looked at the photos, pausing when a familiar face appeared. "Most of these are regulars except Dana Marin."

"Which one is Dana?" he asked.

"The one with the Keri Hilson cut. She's the young lady I told you who wanted to rent the house," said Shandy.

James ran his fingers through his hair. This nightmare was never ending. "Shandy, her name is not Dana. She's Tawatha, the woman who burned her children in the house fire. The one I had an affair with before my marriage ended."

"James, she's been in the house. I…oh God."

"Shandy, talk to me."

"The gift certificate. She was able to go to the shop because I gave her a certificate for services. You have to believe me when I tell you I didn't know who she was. I would never put you or the workers in harm's way."

"I'm not blaming you, Shandy. She's trouble though. She is certifiable. She will stalk everyone until she gets to me. If she will kill her own children, you know she'll hurt our employees without a second thought or a backward glance."

"We need to act fast."

"Call everyone at each shop and have them dial the conference number in twenty minutes. The code is the same. I'll conduct the call. Who serviced her?"

"Let me look at the photo again." Shandy picked out chairs for each stylist and made sure no two colors were alike. She identified the stylists as such. It made things easier, and when a stylist deserved recognition or a possible reprimand, she knew whom to call upon by color. "It's a blue chair, so Penny serviced her."

"Make sure she's on the call. Tawatha isn't done with her yet, so she needs to be warned."

"I'll join everyone on the call in twenty minutes. James, I'm so sorry."

"Don't be. You had no way of knowing," he said.

James ended the call. He immediately went to work at his computer. He copied Tawatha's image from the hair gallery. He created a Word document with her photo attached to distribute to the four salons in Indianapolis. His banged the keyboard at a rapid pace, upset he couldn't get rid of Tawatha. He typed her real name, alias, and added that under no circumstances should she be serviced. He gave strict instructions to have her escorted off the premises of all the salons should she show up again.

Fifteen minutes later, James, Shandy, and stylists from all his salons were connected by the conference call. He paced as he addressed everyone.

"Thanks for joining us, everyone. I will make this brief since I'm interrupting holiday time with your family, but an emergency has arisen that I have to address. A woman entered our facility and was serviced by one of our stylists. I'll cut to the chase. She is the woman who killed her children in the fire."

Several stylists gasped.

"Penny, are you on the call?"

"Yes, James."

"Do you remember the woman whose hair you cut named Dana?"

"I do. She had a bubbly personality."

"Her name is Tawatha, not Dana."

"I did it?"

"You didn't know Penny. She is dangerous. She is a stalker who will continue coming around until she gets what she wants. Since she's out of jail, I'm not sure what her aim is, but I don't want to take any chances. I've sent everyone an email to your salon addresses. Print out the flyer and place it prominently in each facility. Penny, is she scheduled to come back to see you?"

"I don't have my appointment schedule, but I'm almost positive she's scheduled to come back in three weeks."

"Call her and tell her not to return. Tell her you're overbooked, you've moved on, something, anything. I don't want her in the shop again."

"Okay."

"Does anyone have questions? Concerns?"

A stylist named Janice asked, "How will we know we're safe? She sounds like she'll do anything to us."

"I'm calling Isaak Benford when I get off the call to ask about security. I won't leave any of you in harm's way."

Penny, silent, recalled the conversation she had with "Dana" as she cut her hair. She had to speak up. "James, I did something I shouldn't have."

"What is it, Penny?"

"You called while I was cutting her hair. I didn't know she knew you, so she asked all these questions about you and Shandy, pretending to want to know about the business. She asked if you did hair, and I told her you were out of town on business."

"And?"

"I told her exactly where you were. She knows you're in Augusta doing hair at Shear Heaven."

Moans from the other stylist filled the conference call. James put the phone on mute and slammed his fist on the desk. *Be professional.* He placed the speaker on again.

"Thanks for the heads-up, Penny. I'll have to watch my back."

Penny's voice cracked. "I'm sorry."

Shandy took over. "Who has appointments tomorrow?"

All but two of the stylist confirmed they'd be working.

"I'll stop by all the shops tomorrow to check on everyone. Everyone has my cell number. Call me if you see any suspicious activity. Please be safe, everyone."

"Good night, everyone," said James.

He ended the call and called Aruba, Bria, and Sidney down to the basement again. They sat down and listened to his phone call recap.

"You're telling me there's a possibility that she could come to Augusta?" asked Aruba.

"Yes," said James.

"Aruba, you're welcome to stay with us at the hotel tonight if you'd like," Bria offered.

"I'm going upstairs to get some rest. It's been a rough week, and I'm too tired to run," she said.

"Aruba, it might be best if you go," said James.

"Tawatha would love that more than anything," Aruba said. She hugged Bria and Sidney. "It was good seeing the two of you again. I'm going to bed."

She headed upstairs, and James escorted them to the front door.

"I'd love to see you two under better circumstances. I'm flying back to Indy in a few weeks. You guys still in the same place?"

"We're here throughout the holidays, so we can do something local," replied Sidney.

"I'd like that," said James.

Sidney and Bria left. James stepped outside the front door. He took in the expansive neighborhood, checking for unusual cars and any out-of-order sightings. He'd grown to love the area and the people he'd met on his street. He went back inside, and for the first time since he occupied the home, he set the alarm system and locked all the windows.

Chapter 36

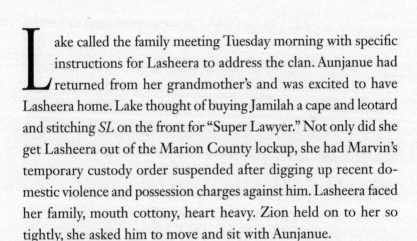

Lake called the family meeting Tuesday morning with specific instructions for Lasheera to address the clan. Aunjanue had returned from her grandmother's and was excited to have Lasheera home. Lake thought of buying Jamilah a cape and leotard and stitching *SL* on the front for "Super Lawyer." Not only did she get Lasheera out of the Marion County lockup, she had Marvin's temporary custody order suspended after digging up recent domestic violence and possession charges against him. Lasheera faced her family, mouth cottony, heart heavy. Zion held on to her so tightly, she asked him to move and sit with Aunjanue.

"I called this family meeting so we can clear the air about some things that have happened recently. Lasheera—" he said.

Lasheera wanted to disappear without addressing the circumstances. What adequate words were there? Stupid? Neglectful? Irresponsible? The children depended on her, and she'd let them down again. Lake told her to speak from her heart; she wasn't sure she still had one.

"Last week was probably more embarrassing for you than it was for me. Being arrested was hard, but having Zion taken away was…"

"Was what, momma?"

"Zion, your father wanted visitation with you, and I didn't say anything about it because I was afraid he'd take you away from me."

"I don't want to be with him."

"I know you don't, Zion, but what have I always told you about rules?"

"You said society has rules we have to follow, or else we're law-breakers."

"I broke the law. I was supposed to go to court and I didn't."

"How long did you know about the court date?" Aunjanue asked.

"At least a month in advance. I thought if I hid the letter, the whole thing would go away. Look at me now," said Lasheera.

Lake sat next to Lasheera and chimed in. "What she's trying to tell us is we need to communicate. Communication would have prevented a lot of the trouble and embarrassment we've experienced."

"Is that why you were sleeping all the time? Because you wanted the whole thing to go away?" Zion asked.

Lasheera sought Lake for her response. His nonverbal cue, a wink, persuaded her to be honest.

"Remember when I got real nasty with the lady in the pharmacy?"

"Yes. You cussed her out! I didn't know you had it in you."

"I was upset because I'd been taking medication I shouldn't have, and I struggled without it. I had someone else's prescription, and after a while, I couldn't stop taking it."

Aunjanue headed toward the stairs.

"Come back, Onnie," said Lasheera.

"Let her go, baby," said Lake. "This is a lot for both of them to absorb."

"Should we wait for her to come back? I don't want to say anything else without her being here."

Aunjanue returned, purse in hand, and sat down on the sofa.

"Where did you go?"

"I went upstairs to get my bag. Since we're having a family meeting, I would like to share something, too."

"Before you share, I wanted to ask if you all would forgive me and help me. I don't want to keep letting you down."

"Yes, ma'am," Zion and Aunjanue answered.

Lasheera sighed. *Do they mean it, or is this to comfort me?* "Onnie, what do you want to share?"

Aunjanue pulled out a colored envelope from her purse. She removed the postcards and held them closely.

"My mom has been sending me these." She passed the postcards to Lake and Lasheera. They read the messages and gave them back.

"May I see them," asked Zion.

Aunjanue shared the cards with him as well.

"How long has this been going on?" asked Lasheera.

"Since she was released." "I received the first one at school, but I got the others from the mailbox. She'll probably stop if I talk to her."

"Do you want to talk to her? Honestly?" Lake asked.

"Yes, I do."

Lasheera imagined being away from Zion, unable to communicate with or see him. She was torn about allowing Aunjanue to see her mother. "Which would you rather do? See her or talk to her?" asked Lasheera.

Without hesitation, Aunjanue responded, "Both."

Chapter 37

"What now?" Jamilah said to her phone. Lasheera's name and face weren't what she counted on seeing so soon after her release from jail. She tossed a shirt she'd gathered in her cart and answered the call.

"Hi, 'Sheer, how are you?"

"I'm fine, 'Milah."

Lasheera's tone bothered Jamilah. When they were children, Lasheera's voice morphed into a guilty sound when she was sorry, or found it difficult to apologize.

"If you're calling to say you're sorry again, save it. Friends help each other out."

"I'm calling for someone else, 'Milah. Hold on a sec." She gave the phone to Aunjanue.

"Hello, Aunt Jamilah."

The sound of Aunjanue's voice made Jamilah abandon her cart in Macy's. She hadn't spoken to her since she fought for Tawatha's freedom. She'd missed her niece, all the children really, but knew it was best to give her space to sort out her feelings. She prayed this moment would come sooner than later, and she welcomed it.

"How are you, Onnie? I've missed hearing your voice and seeing you."

"I've missed you, too."

"Is there something I can do for you?"

"I know I said I didn't want to see my mother or talk to her, but I've changed my mind. Are you working right now?"

"I'm just leaving Keystone at Crossing."

"Would you please take me to see my mother? I don't want to go alone. Auntie 'Sheer said she'd come with me if you'd take us."

"It would be my pleasure. Let me call her first and tell her we're coming."

"Don't call her. I want it to be a surprise."

Jamilah picked up Aunjanue and Lasheera and headed to Royce's house. The stilted conversation picked up steam as Aunjanue shared her college acceptances, scholarships, and prom plans. Her greatest excitement was upcoming participation in the Youth Arts Fair in Nashville, Tennessee. Mr. Wilson had entered several of her drawings in the contest, and her skin glowed as she discussed the possibility of displaying her artwork one last time before attending college.

"I've missed too much, young lady."

"I can show you my latest paintings and drawings if you'd like to see them."

"Still dating that handsome Roger Keys?" Jamilah asked.

"Yes. We're going to the prom in May. You have to help me find a dress."

"We'll make a special Chi-Town trip for your dress. How does that sound?"

Lasheera listened to the interaction between Aunjanue and Jamilah and wondered how it all went downhill. The Three Musketeers felt more like lone survivors these days. Jamilah was busy building her clientele while Lasheera and Tawatha kept her in business. Lasheera never imagined when they were children one musketeer would be put in the uncomfortable position of keeping the others afloat. *I have to make better decisions. This is so unfair to 'Milah.*

"Is he alright?" Jamilah asked Lasheera.

"What did you say, 'Milah?"

"Zion. I asked if he's okay. Marvin wasn't thrilled about giving him up."

"We all need time to adjust to everything."

The weight of her words touched everyone, so they continued the ride in silence. As Jamilah approached Royce's circular drive, she crossed her fingers for a fruitful visit.

"This is where Momma's been living?"

"Yes. I couldn't let her live with me during the court proceedings. Conflict of interest. No one else wanted to open their homes to her."

"I didn't know she lived in a mansion," said Aunjanue.

"She lives in the carriage house out back. I'm letting Mr. Hinton know we're here," said Jamilah. "I don't want to scare him if he sees my car on his property."

They rang the doorbell. Aunjanue only planted flowers and gardened during the summer months. She marveled at the luscious flowers on Mr. Hinton's grounds. *He must have a landscaper. This yard is incredible.*

"May I help you?" An elegant, middle-aged woman wiped her floured hands on an apron and kept the strangers at bay.

"We're here to see—"

"Millie, is it the courier?" Royce said behind the lady's back, interrupting Jamilah's question. He placed his hands on her shoulders as he eyed them. "Jamilah, what a pleasure! Come inside."

Millicent, unsure of their business with her ex, stood her ground in silence. She'd learned more about his generosity in the past month than she cared to stomach, but they were divorced, so she had little say-so in his affairs.

"Jamilah, this is my ex-wife, Millicent Hinton."

Jamilah extended her hand to Millicent, admiring the lovely dress beneath the apron, dainty pearls, and every-hair-in-its-place coiffure. It was obvious Millicent wasn't going down without a fight, evidenced by the coal-black shade of her hair.

"We're baking cookies, so I don't want to ruin your hands. It's nice to meet you."

"Let's all have a seat in the living room," he said.

Aunjanue asked Royce, "Where should I put my shoes?"

"You don't have to remove them."

"I don't want to mess up the carpet, sir."

"It's just carpet. If you'd be more comfortable without your shoes, set them in the corner behind the door."

Lasheera and Jamilah followed Aunjanue's lead and removed their shoes as well. The house felt more like a museum, and they couldn't pay for any broken items. Royce welcomed them into the sunken living room area. They rested on the elegant Queen Anne furniture.

"I'm putting my apron in the kitchen. I'll join you in a moment," said Millicent.

"Royce, this is my friend, Lasheera, and this is Tawatha's daughter, Aunjanue."

Royce shook Lasheera's hand first, then Aunjanue's. He kept her hands in his and said, "Please let me offer my condolences on the death of your great-uncle, Mack. Tawatha told me how close you all were, and I feel horrible about the roof accident."

"Uncle Mack?"

"Your mother left Thanksgiving heading to Georgia for his funeral. The service is today, correct?"

"Georgia?" Jamilah asked.

Millicent joined them in the living room and placed a plate of chocolate chip cookies and napkins on the coffee table. She ankle-crossed her legs and smoothed back her stiff bangs.

"Last week, Tawatha came to me and said she was Georgia bound. She got permission from her parole officer to leave the state, and I helped her with funds for the trip."

Millicent raised her eyebrows but said nothing. She shifted her gaze to the front lawn.

"Mr. Hinton, we don't have an Uncle Mack. Aunt Jamilah brought me here to talk to my mom. I haven't spoken to her since she went to prison, and I wanted to start over with her."

Jamilah felt a migraine coming on. *Was I this dumb thinking helping her would make a difference?*

"Royce, so that I am clear on what you've said, Tawatha left the state without telling me, and said she was going to a funeral?" Jamilah asked.

"Correct."

"When is she expected to return?"

"Friday."

"Have you talked to her since she's been gone?"

"She texted me once, but I haven't heard anything else from her."

"Do you know where she's staying?"

"The Jameson Suites. I have the address and room number. She gave me the info in case I needed to reach her."

Millicent, tired of holding her tongue, addressed the visitors. "Listen, Royce is my ex-husband, but he's a good man. Your friend has taken advantage of his kindness, and I don't think it's fair. He's been shunned by many of his friends for harboring a felon, and all she seems to do is lie to him every chance she gets. I may be over-stepping my boundaries, but I want her off this property. Are either of you willing to take her in?"

"Millie!"

"Don't *Millie* me. You're the only one who can't see she's making a fool of you! Our daughter is dead, and Quinton will probably walk the streets doing drugs the rest of his life. You can't undo what's happened!"

Millie's anger humbled Royce. She kept a stoic face throughout their marriage and never raised her voice. In the span of four sentences, he felt more concern from her than he did throughout their marriage.

"I was only trying to help her," said Royce.

"You've done more than enough," said Jamilah. "We all have."

Millicent faced them once more. "I'll ask again. Are either of you in a position to take her in? This may be Royce's house, but I made it a home. I'm not going to let some ungrateful maniac destroy it."

"She can live with me," said Jamilah. "Lasheera has a husband and two children at her home. I live alone since my parents died. I have more than enough space for her."

"Good. Follow me to the garage. I'll get some trash bags, and we can gather her things. After today, she's banned from the premises."

Jamilah excused herself and dialed Tawatha's number. After four rings and voicemail, Jamilah said, "Be ready in the morning. I'm taking a flight to Augusta late tonight and bringing you home. Your foolishness ends today."

Chapter 38

Tawatha drove past Shear Heaven a third time. No sign of James. A police car parked on the side of the building deterred her parking. She only wanted to lay eyes on him and see if he was doing well. *Maybe he's back in Indianapolis. Maybe there's another Shear Heaven in Augusta.*

She headed back to the Jameson Suites. She'd drive back to Indianapolis tomorrow. If she was lucky, she would be able to catch James at one of his locations. She was tired of being alone and wanted someone to love her. Royce had told her he was having dinner with Millie, but she didn't prod him for details.

She looked down at her phone and saw four missed calls from Jamilah and a voicemail message. *I'll respond to her when I wake up from my nap.* Tawatha took the elevator to her room. Royce's paradigm advice made more sense. She kept doing the same thing and getting the same results. *How do you do things differently?* Different is what she'd discuss with Royce when she got back to Indianapolis. She opened her room door, shocked to find Jamilah sitting at the desk.

"Jamilah, what are you doing here? How did you get in my room?"

"I am your attorney, and you did leave the state of Indiana without notifying me."

"I didn't have to notify you."

"The front desk manager is clueless about legal proceedings. Get your things so we can go."

"Go where?"

"Home."

"I'm not leaving until tomorrow. I'm taking care of business here."

Jamilah folded her arms. "What business is that? James Dixon?"

Tawatha averted her eyes.

"Took a little digging, but I found out he's been here a few months with his wife."

"He's divorced."

"With plans to remarry." Jamilah calmed herself. She knew Tawatha was unstable; she had to complete the task at hand. "Did you listen to my voicemail?"

"I was going to listen to it after my nap."

"I'm here to pick you up, Tawatha. We're going back to Indianapolis, and you're moving in with me until I can help you find a job and get a place of your own."

"I have a place to stay."

"Not after yesterday."

Jamilah took photos from her purse and gave them to Tawatha. She'd photographed the packed items now stored in her garage in the boxes and bags Millie supplied. The packing was done in less than two hours, and Millicent went back to the main house, brought cleaning items out, and insisted on cleaning the carriage house from top to bottom. She wanted no traces of Tawatha in the home.

"How did my things get in your garage?"

"Millicent, Aunjanue, and Lasheera helped me pack your things. Funny thing is, Aunjanue decided she wanted to see you and talk with you. Imagine how surprised we were to find out you were attending your Uncle Mack's funeral."

Tawatha bit her bottom lip.

"Wait, it gets better. You made Royce look like a complete idiot in front of us and his ex-wife. All this time he's tried to assuage his guilt over his daughter and his cousin by helping you, and this is how you thank him and us.

"Your family and friends have bent over backward to help you, and this is the thanks we get?"

"You don't understand. James loves me! He just hasn't accepted it yet."

"Shut up, Tawatha! Do you hear yourself? Do you know how crazy you sound?"

"I'm not crazy!"

Jamilah lowered her voice. In grade school, the best way to reach Tawatha or help her comprehend an idea was writing it down. Her spoken, faulty rationalizations were cleared once she saw a written concept. Well, most of the time. Jamilah found a tablet next to the Bible in the hotel desk drawer.

"Sit down, Tawatha."

"I'm fine standing."

"What did I say?"

Tawatha sat at the desk as instructed. She flipped the tablet back a few pages. "I need a pen."

Jamilah fished in her purse for a pen, flinging it next to the tablet.

"Make two columns on a sheet of paper. Mark one side for James, the other for family and friends."

Tawatha obeyed. She wanted to get the exercise over and to drive by Shear Heaven once more.

"What's the point?"

"Write down all the pros James has added to your life. On the other column, write down all the pros your family and friends have added to your life. When you're done, flip it over on the back, and write down all the cons James has added, then all the cons your family and friends have added. Take all the time you need."

Tawatha scribbled away. Jamilah resisted the temptation to look over her shoulder. She walked over to the window, observing oncoming traffic and the maintenance crew in the parking lot hauling trash bags. Prison should have stopped Tawatha's fantasy thinking, but it didn't.

Thirty minutes passed before Tawatha put her pen down. "I'm going to the bathroom. I'll be back."

Jamilah waited for her to lock the door before picking up the list. Jamilah's eyes deceived her. She hadn't given Tawatha enough credit. Under the pros, and beneath James's name, she listed: Jameshia. Under her daughter's name she read, "Nothing else." She read the laundry list of blessings beneath family and friends' names. "Love, support, beautiful children, a place to stay." Jamilah stopped reading. She didn't flip the page. She waited for Tawatha to come out of the bathroom.

"What time are we leaving?" She wiped her swollen eyes and put the list in her pocket.

"Our flight leaves later tonight," said Jamilah.

"But I drove down."

Jamilah faced her friend before dropping another bomb. "Royce has made arrangements to have to car shipped back to Indy. He asked that you clean it out and leave the keys with the driver."

Chapter 39

Aunjanue locked the postcards in the back of closet. Her mother was at Jamilah's. *Why discuss the cards?* She folded sweaters, organized them in her drawer, and went back downstairs with Lasheera and Stephanie. She sat next to Stephanie and rubbed her belly.

"Stephanie, this baby will be here well before Christmas," said Lasheera.

"I'd welcome it, but I think Caleb wants his son to stay in the womb for nine more months. I think he may be the one who faints when I go into labor," Stephanie tried to get in a comfortable position on the sofa. "Where are you going tonight, Onnie?"

"Tarsha's coming by and we're going to the movies. We might get something to eat, too. I told her I wanted something other than Panera."

"Friends with hookups. Sounds like my kind of night," said Stephanie. She shifted again in her seat and grimaced.

"Are you okay, Ms. Stephanie?"

"CJ is on fire tonight!"

"What did you feed Caleb Jr.?"

"I had to have Los Rancheros. I love the spicy chicken nachos, but they don't love me. I'm feeling that meal in the worst way."

"When are you due again?"

"Christmas Eve," said Stephanie. She couldn't mask the throbbing pain in her lower abdomen. "Onnie, please help me to the bathroom."

She led Stephanie to the guest bathroom. Lasheera, worried about Stephanie's sweaty face, went to her medicine cabinet for Tylenol. She waited for Stephanie to sit again before offering the meds.

"Do you want me to call Mr. Wilson?"

"No. He's enjoying himself with Lake and the fellas. Leave him alone. I'll be fine. It's the spicy nachos."

"You sure?" asked Lasheera. "I'm sure Lake would rather we call than watch you suffer."

"I'll lean back for about an hour. The pain subsides after a while."

Aunjanue had another couple's crush moment. She thought it was considerate of Stephanie to let Caleb have time with his friends. The few men her mother dated were smothered by her constant calls, texts, and pop-up visits. Stephanie brought lunch to Caleb, and he in turn sent flowers to her job. She knew this because she heard him on the phone from time to time calling Poppy Florals.

"Ms. Stephanie, how did you and Mr. Wilson meet?"

Stephanie's facial muscles relaxed at the question.

"I met Caleb four years ago in Florida at a birthday party for a mutual friend. He was handsome, studious, and taught seventh-grade art at a school near my old job. I'll admit, sparks didn't fly at first. For him, that is. I actually asked her for his number because I thought he was so handsome. My friend called him the "mystery man" because no one knew a lot about him. He was a handy man in the neighborhood as well as a teacher. We had a few dates… had some fun. But Onnie, he became super excited when I told him my job was transferring me to the Midwest. He said he always wanted to live in the heartland of America. He proposed, and here we are."

"I love Caleb," said Lasheera. "He loves you so much. You can see it in the way he looks at you, the way he talks about CJ being born. You're one of the lucky ones."

"And Lake is chopped liver? You've got a good husband, too," said Stephanie.

"Correction. We're both lucky. Lake has stuck by me through so much."

"Amen," said Stephanie. She gave Lasheera's arm a playful punch.

The doorbell interrupted their revelry. Aunjanue opened the door for Tarsha, who came into the living room carrying a large bag of yellow apples.

"Look at the working girl," said Lasheera. She stood, hugged Tarsha, and tugged on her Panera hat.

"Mom asked me to bring you these apples. Onnie mentioned you loved this brand, so Dad brought two bags back from his last business trip."

"Thanks, Tarsha," said Lasheera. "Don't you want to keep a few?"

Tarsha smiled, revealing her braces. "Two more weeks and I'm done with these. Until then, no apples, popcorn, or candy."

"Ah, the beautiful smile you'll have when you walk across the stage," said Lasheera.

"Mom and Dad say the same thing." Tarsha turned to Aunjanue. "Girl, let's go. I have to be back at work at six in the morning."

Aunjanue and Tarsha left, both giggling like they were in elementary school. Stephanie watched the door and waited for them to leave.

"I'm glad they're gone."

"Why?"

"I need to talk to you in private. Aunjanue thinks the world of Caleb, so I didn't want to be negative." Stephanie paused.

"What's going on?"

"You've had a baby, so you know how hormonal women are. I feel like a big-nosed whale. I have swollen cankles; my face is filled with acne, and I can barely move from point A to point B with taking a leak."

Lasheera exhaled. "Steph, I thought you meant the man was cheating or something."

"I could accept that, Lasheera. I'd divorce him, but I'd understand."

"Well, what is it?"

"I feel I'm not enough for him. I also get the feeling he doesn't want the baby."

"Hormones times ten. That man loves you. Give me an example of him not wanting *his* child."

"Intuition. I can't describe it any other way."

"Yep. Hormones. Talk to me when you have something concrete." Lasheera popped the top off the Tylenol. "Take one for your intuition and take a nap until the boys get home."

Stephanie took the Tylenol with the Sprite Lasheera had poured earlier.

"Since you're so sure of my situation, please tell me about the day of the arrest. We haven't discussed it, and I've been wondering how you've been."

"Short version. I got the wrong prescription at the pharmacy, and I started an affair with Ambien. When I tell you it felt good, I mean it *felt good*. The longer I took it, the less I remembered. People claimed to have had conversations with me I couldn't recall. And the resting. All I needed was a Pamper and a bottle of warm milk. Best sleep I've had all my life!"

"Really."

"I think it was the Tawatha situation. I hate blaming her for everything, but we're all on edge."

"Caleb told me she was stalking you all."

"The only reason I'm open to talking to her now is because Aunjanue wants to rekindle the relationship with her. Get this, she's been sending Aunjanue Vincent van Gogh postcards. Van Gogh is Onnie's favorite artist. Tawatha left them at school and in our mailbox."

"Why not knock on the door?"

"She knew better. I wouldn't have let her in."

"What makes you so sure you want to have a relationship with her now?"

"Something has to give. I'd do anything to compromise for the children."

CJ kicked Stephanie hard. She rubbed him and realized she had at least eighteen years of compromise ahead.

Chapter 40

James promised himself this would be the last lie he told Aruba. He did have salon business to handle in Indianapolis. It was also true he had supplies to order, sites to secure, and prospective stylists to interview. What he refused to share was the real reason for his flight back to Indianapolis.

Isaak called him with details of the plan a week ago. He'd left Jeremiah and Aruba in Harlem with her parents. He packed his suitcase, nervous, and afraid the plan might backfire. He couldn't postpone things. It was now or never.

He opened the salon at noon. He cancelled all the appointments and waited. Isaak and Katrina entered Dixon's Kiddies and Tweens around one. Katrina's face lit up when she saw James. She embraced him and Isaak gave him their usual soul brother's shake. Katrina, mug of tea in hand, sat in one of the chairs.

"Are you nervous?" she asked.

"As nervous as I've been in all my life," said James. "How did you pull this off?"

"I told you I know low people in high places," Isaak joked. "Seriously, I've known Brandon Reese for years. It wasn't until things happened with this situation that I realized he'd adopted her. I remember him saying in passing his wife wanted a child, but his soldiers were out of commission. Next thing I knew, I saw them out at dinner with a beautiful daughter in tow."

James remembered her pictures. He wanted to see his daughter. When he learned she was performing in the Indianapolis Children's Choir Christmas Concert, he thought of ways to see her performance. He and Isaak put their heads together, and soon, devised a plan to give her a small gift and see the concert as well.

"We have to leave, but I wanted to stop in and check on you," said Isaak. "If you want us to stay, we will."

"No, I'm fine."

"Call us if you need us," said Katrina.

As they left the salon, Camille Reese entered Kiddies and Tweens holding Hannah's hand. She was a tall, regal woman who carried herself like a queen. She wore an elegant red-and-black wool winter coat with black fur surrounding the collar. When she removed her coat, James noticed her lovely figure in a gray, tweed winter business suit. Her hair, swept in an updo with loose curls framing her face, accentuated her medium-brown complexion. Hannah took in the surroundings as her mother approached James.

"You must be James Dixon. I've seen your commercials and always wanted to bring Hannah here." They shook hands as Hannah moved closer to him.

"I'm Hannah Reese. It's nice to meet you," she said, shaking James's hand. "I'm singing in the concert tonight!" Hannah flashed a toothy grin and giggled as she placed her hands over her mouth.

"You are?" He gave Camille a knowing smile. "What will you sing tonight?"

"I'm singing 'The First Noel' with the choir," she said. "I had to audition, and I beat out a lot of other girls. My daddy said I'm an awesome singer."

The punch hit James hard. *My daddy.* He maintained his composure and addressed Camille.

"How would you like her hair styled, Mrs. Reese?"

Camille looked around the shop for other children. "Is Hannah the only child getting her hair done today?"

"In this salon, yes. A friend of mine, Isaak Benford, owed your husband a favor, so we closed the shop down for Hannah to get her hair done. She'll also get a clear manicure and pedicure if you'd like."

"Mom, may I?"

Camille didn't like the idea of children getting manicures and pedicures, but Hannah was excited about the concert, and Camille didn't see why she shouldn't allow Hannah this small luxury.

"Okay, Precious. Just this once."

"Hannah, if you'd have a seat in the chair over there, I'll be with you soon. I need to discuss your hairdo with your mom."

Hannah skipped over to a seat and rifled through a stack of children's hair magazines. Satisfied with one, she sat in the chair and flipped through the pages.

"Is there a specific look you'd like to achieve?" he asked.

"I hope this doesn't sound pompous, but she'll be singing in the front row, so I want her to have an eye-catching look."

"Updo or something down?"

"She has such lovely hair. I want her to have bouncy curls. *Toddlers & Tiaras* turned me off from updos."

They laughed at her joke. "I can do that. I'll wash, blow dry her hair, and use Marcel irons. Are you okay with that?"

"Perfect."

"I have food in the break area if you're hungry, and you may watch television if you'd like."

"I'll sit here and watch Hannah get her hair done."

James joined Hannah at her chair and placed a smock around

her. He pumped up the chair so he could examine Hannah's hair. He released her flowing mane from a single ponytail down her back.

"Tell me something about yourself, Hannah."

"I'm a first-grader at St. Roch."

"I bet you're a smart girl."

She nodded as James parted her hair. He decided he'd do large curls for the concert.

"I like going to school, and I like learning. Mommy said I didn't need to attend Head Start or kindergarten because I'm gifted."

James liked her confidence. "I need you to come with me to the bowl so I can wash your hair, Hannah."

Hannah followed James to the bowl, holding the flowing cape close to her body. She scooted up in the seat as he lathered her hair.

"Do you do a lot of little girls' hair?" she asked.

"Not as much as I used to, but I do hair for boys and girls."

"I told Mommy and Daddy I want a little brother. They said I'm all they need."

"I'm sure you're a joy to have around," he said. He blotted her hair, escorted her back to her seat, and blow dried her hair. She sat patiently as he completed the task. The front door opened as he warmed the curling irons. Camille stood, kissed a tall man in a heavy winter coat, and took his coat. They exchanged words as he gave Camille his briefcase.

"I see you're busy with my princess, but I'm Brandon Reese."

"James Dixon. I do have my hands full, but it's nice to make your acquaintance."

"Daddy!"

Brandon planted a quick peck on Hannah's cheek and sat with Camille. They chatted, and James noticed the loving air between them.

"Are you coming to the concert tonight?" Hannah asked.

"No. I have business to take care of, but I know you'll do a wonderful job singing."

"I wish you could listen to me sing," she said.

"If the concert still airs on television, I'll watch you tonight. Deal?"

"Deal."

James finished her hair, gave her a pedicure and a manicure, and gave her a kiddie bag from the stockroom. He kept bags prepared for boys and girls who frequented the shop. Her bag contained products and a ticket to the Children's Museum of Indianapolis. James watched her run to Brandon, who stood with open arms.

"Daddy, do you like it?" She twirled around to show him her concert hairdo. Her big curls bounced as she whirled.

"Princess, you are the most beautiful girl in the world!"

She blushed and covered her mouth. "Thank you, Daddy."

"What do I owe you?" Camille asked, reaching for her purse. She touched Hannah's hair. "You did an amazing job. I'll be bringing her back here again."

"It's on me and Isaak. No charge."

"I thought Isaak was kidding with me about this," said Brandon. "I'll give him a call after the concert tonight."

Brandon slipped Hannah's coat on. They left the salon, a picture-perfect family. Hannah, holding her father's hand, hung on his every word. Spent from seeing his daughter and unable to reveal his identity, he pondered the meeting. He knew that it could be the last time he saw her, unless he squirmed a way into their lives. *Too complicated.*

A strange emotion overtook him. He locked the front door and reclined in a styling chair. He sat for hours, rehashing how he'd arrived at being a man who'd have no contact with one of his children. He spied his watch and turned on the television. The Children's Choir aired the Christmas concert each year. He waited for the live broadcast to start. He didn't have to wait too long as Hannah stepped to the microphone with the younger children.

She sang "The First Noel" with the choir, and James imagined she sounded like an angel. Their voices blended well, and he watched his daughter as the camera panned over the children. She stood down front. The camera zoomed in on her. Too painful to continue watching, he turned off the television as she sang, "born is the King of Israel."

Chapter 41

"Emory, this is the craziest thing we've ever done!" Victoria yelled over the Christmas Eve crowd.

"Well, you waited until the last minute to get your mother a gift!" he shouted, his pitch as loud as hers.

They made their way through Phipps Plaza, practically walking sideways in the sea of last-minute bargain hunters. Victoria gripped Emory's hand tighter and held her purse close. Christmas time was thieves' paradise, and she didn't want to give anyone reason to think she had money to spare.

"What does Lillith like?" he asked.

"Besides Bobby?"

Emory gave Victoria a stern look, not pleased with her criticism of Lillith's mate.

Victoria huffed. "She likes purses, perfume, and chocolates."

Emory pressed his fingers to his temples. They were close to most of Lillith's loves. *Decisions, decisions.* Emory pointed to the Coach store. "Let's go in and get her something here. We need to get back home before it's too late."

They ducked into Coach, greeted by a friendly salesgirl.

"May I help the two of you find something?" she asked, her face screaming, *let's do this so we can all go home.*

"I'm looking for a nice purse for my mother," Victoria answered.

"What's her style?" asked the salesgirl.

"Nothing too flashy, but not exactly conservative. A nice, middle-of-the-road bag will do fine," said Emory.

"Sounds like she might like a hobo bag. Follow me," said the salesgirl.

They followed her to the back wall, admiring the displays of shades, purses, and wallets.

Victoria rarely left home to shop on Christmas Eve. In her past life, all her Christmas shopping was done by December 1st each year. Emory put off shopping this year; they agreed they'd give homemade gifts to family and friends. Lillith practically begged for a new purse. Victoria thought it would be a nice gesture after her cancer scare.

The salesgirl pointed out the hobos and left them. "Take your time and let me know which one you like," she said.

Victoria picked up several purses. Money wasn't an object. She'd make sure Lillith loved her gift. Victoria's hands collided with another woman's hands as they both reached for a sand-colored hobo.

"Oops...we've got greedy fingers," the woman said to Victoria. "You go ahead. I have two already in different colors."

"I'm sure the storeroom is stocked," said Victoria. They laughed. Victoria's laughter subsided when she looked at the woman. They recognized each other.

"What's your name?" Victoria asked.

"Bria Hines," she answered.

Victoria was sure it was Bria. Bria's lips clamped shut, making the silent moment more awkward. She looked for Sidney to rescue her, but he'd disappeared.

"How are you, Bria?" Victoria asked.

"I'm well, Victoria. And you?"

"I'm fantastic. I'm shopping for my mother with my fiancé, Emory," she said.

Emory had wandered off near the men's items.

"What brings you to the Atlanta area?" Victoria asked.

"Sidney and I are visiting his relatives throughout the holiday season. We'll be here until the New Year. We'll go back to Indianapolis on January 5th. We plan to hang out and watch the peach drop," said Bria. She continued to search for Sidney in the crowded mall.

Victoria didn't want to postpone the inevitable. With grit and determination, she asked, "How is Aruba doing?"

A pall fell over Bria's face. "She's doing better."

"As opposed to?"

"Victoria. Did you know—" Bria paused. "Let's step outside the store a moment."

Victoria gained Emory's attention and pointed to the door. She followed Bria to a bench where they sat.

"Have you had any contact with Aruba?" Bria asked.

"Not since Winston's funeral. She's tried to call me, but I didn't want to talk to her."

"She tried to commit suicide a few months ago. Sidney and I went to visit her last month in Augusta."

"She's in Georgia now? When did she move back?"

"A few months after the funeral. She's with her parents and James right now."

"James is here, too?"

"He's back and forth between here and Indianapolis. He came back to check on her and Jeremiah."

"I'm genuinely sad to hear about the suicide attempt. I wouldn't wish suicide on anyone."

"I always wanted you to know I felt badly about how your marriage ended."

Victoria suspected Bria was trying to dump her abetting guilt.

"Well, what's done is done. Cloakers are as guilty as the cheaters."

"Excuse me?"

"Cloakers. Covers for guilty parties."

It took a minute for the accusation to sink in. "Are you accusing me of helping Aruba cheat?"

"Didn't you?"

"Victoria, I had no idea Aruba was cheating until the night of her birthday party. I learned the truth at the same time as everyone else."

"That's news to me. I assumed…"

"You know what they say about assumptions," Bria snapped. *Not on Christmas Eve.*

"Listen, I'm sorry. I've had a hard time with all of this. Seeing you again brings up unpleasant memories. I didn't mean to offend you."

"No need to apologize. I don't agree with what Aruba did or how she did it, but it can't be undone. I've thought of you often and wondered how you and Nicolette were doing."

"You have?"

"Yes. I liked getting to know you when you lived in Indianapolis. We didn't hang out much, but I really liked you."

Bria's words came as a shock. Victoria always assumed Aruba's friends resented her status and lifestyle. "Why didn't you ever say anything?"

"I liked you; *you* didn't seem to be too fond of women," said Bria, pointing a playful finger at Victoria's chest.

"Was it that obvious?"

"Oh yes!"

Bria and Victoria chuckled at Bria's response.

"I've been told that before. I'm working on it."

Sidney tapped Bria's shoulder. She stood. "Honey, do you remember Victoria Faulk?"

"I do. How are you, Victoria?" He shook her hand. "It's good seeing you again."

"Having a party without me?" Emory asked as he joined them at the bench.

Victoria held Emory's hand. "Bria and Sidney, this is Emory Wilkerson."

"It's nice to meet you both." He waited for Victoria to reveal her friends.

"We knew each other in a past life," she joked. Turning serious, she said, "These are good friends of Aruba's, honey. They're celebrating in Atlanta for Christmas and New Year's."

"Maybe we'll run into each other again," he said. "Baby, I went ahead and bought your mom the hobo. You ready to go home?"

"I was ready hours ago. Let's fight this traffic, Em."

Victoria looked at Bria again. "Bria, tell Aruba I said hello."

"I have a better idea. Why don't you tell her yourself?" Bria tore a sheet of paper from a small tablet in her purse and jotted Aruba's phone number down. "I'm sure she'd love to hear from you."

Bria and Sidney disappeared in the middle of the last-minute shoppers, leaving Victoria staring at Aruba's number.

Chapter 42

Tawatha tramped to Jamilah's house from Cracker Barrel, feet aching, back sore, and ready for a good, hot bath—or a good foot soaking—whichever one she mustered the strength to perform first. Tawatha resisted Jamilah's strict house at first, but the rules sounded better than going to a homeless shelter, Jamilah's second alternative for her. Since bringing her back from Augusta, Jamilah had helped her find a job as a server at Cracker Barrel, purchased her a used Toyota Corolla, and helped her establish a savings account. Jamilah gave her a one-year deadline, marked in red on a calendar that sat in her bedroom, to save money and get an apartment of her own. Tawatha wanted to crawl on all fours, but she took slow steps her bedroom.

She passed by Jamilah's bedroom and waved. "I'm home, 'Milah."

Jamilah looked up from court briefs and returned the salutation. "How'd it go today?"

"Same old thing. It's Christmas Eve, so we were packed beyond belief. I'm glad we closed early."

"You ready to go to dinner at Lake and Lasheera's?"

"I thought that was tomorrow night. Christmas dinner."

"No. They have a Christmas Eve tradition."

"I am dog-tired. Do I have to come?"

"Yes. This is the first night we'll all dine together, remember? Ms. Roberta and Mr. J.B. are coming, too."

Tawatha groaned. "May I get an hour nap? Please?"

"We've got plenty of time. I'll wake you up in an hour and thirty minutes. I know it takes you forever to doze off."

Tawatha headed to her bedroom. She took off her work Naturalizer shoes and rubbed her feet. She splayed her tips on the bed and counted out the day's bounty. When she'd tallied the dollars and change, her tips came to $95.18. She fell back on the bed, wondering when things would change. She missed being at Royce's, but he no longer accepted her calls. The final text message he sent her said, "I only want to see you once you're back on your feet. Stay strong. I know you can do it." *Back on my feet. How long will that take?*

Tawatha turned over on her stomach and imagined how the night would unfold. Her contact with her family had been so-so since returning from Augusta. A quick visit here, a phone call there. Nothing substantial. She thought the camaraderie would flow, that some of the good memories from years past would replace the distance they now experienced. *Who am I kidding?*

She'd been banned from James's salons. Shandy had taken out a restraining order against her, and she no longer felt comfortable doing drive-by surveillance. James was becoming a far-off memory as well. She worked, came home, watched TV, and started the next day all over again. Jamilah knocked on her door.

"May I come in?"

"Sure."

Jamilah came in, still dressed in her lounging clothes. "It's written all over your face. What's wrong?"

"Nothing."

"Tell that lie to someone who doesn't know you. Come on and talk to me."

Tawatha blinked back tears. She intended to nap and get ready for dinner, but her world felt off-kilter."

"I wish you hadn't gotten me out of jail."

"Why?"

"What good am I?" Tawatha covered her face, embarrassed she'd let Jamilah see her cry.

"You're getting your life back together. It takes time, Tawatha."

"Nobody wants me here," she said.

"We want you here. We want you stable and able to cope with reality. You can get help."

"A shrink. Is that your answer?"

"No, that's your answer. How do you think I got through my parents' deaths?"

"You've always been so strong. You graduated college, got your own place, and you're building a name for yourself."

"And I'm neurotic, moody, frustrated, tired, and some days, I want to chuck it all and live in the wilderness."

Tawatha sat up. "You do?"

"Of course, but I imagine how disappointed I'd be in myself, and how disappointed my parents would be if they knew I gave up."

"It was easier for me in prison. I had a routine, a system."

"You have a routine and system here, too. You need to give it more time." Jamilah paused. "May I ask you something?"

"Yes."

"I rarely hear you mention the children. Why?"

"I see them everywhere. I hear their voices. I smell them. I was never fit to be anyone's mother, and I try not to bring them up because they're better off without me. Not the way they died. If I could do things over, I would have stopped at Aunjanue and gave her up for adoption. I loved them, I didn't know how to raise them. Even with a good village, I was a lousy matriarch."

"I wished you'd voiced that opinion years ago. There were other options instead of what happened." Jamilah rubbed Tawatha's back.

"What should I do at this dinner tonight?"

"Be yourself."

"What if they don't want me there?"

"Lake and Lasheera wouldn't have invited you over if you weren't welcome."

Butterflies fluttered in her stomach again.

"Let's get dressed and go. I've got your back."

"Let me get my nap, and I'll be good as new."

Chapter 43

Aunjanue went to the mailbox. The postcards had stopped coming, so she didn't mind taking the walk to bring in the mail. Tawatha's presence at dinner would be the first time she'd been with the family at length since her release. She was excited and afraid. Her biggest concern was her grandmother. Roberta promised to be cordial, not mention the children, and embrace Tawatha at least once. She had a good feeling about the night. They'd experienced so many ups and downs since September that Christmas had to be a gift. It had to be.

Aunjanue brought the mail inside and went to her room. She had less than an hour before dinner started. The family, along with the Wilsons, would be having Christmas Eve dinner. She sorted through the mail and would take the household mail downstairs after she dressed. She sifted through the letters, coming to an oversized envelope addressed to her. It had no return address, and she couldn't make out the postmark. She gently opened the envelope with the decorative letter opener she'd received after her siblings' funeral. Her room was filled with an assortment of things people gave her to soothe her conscience. If Tawatha sent another item, knowing she was coming to dinner, she would scream.

She whiffed the floral scent of the envelope before opening it. She unfolded the neat letter as another document fell on the bed. She read the letter aloud:

Dear Aunjanue:

This is Hattie, Maggie Ransom's daughter. I'm writing you to let you know Mom passed away the second week of December. I called the school to ask for your address. They were hesitant to give it to me, but I told them about all the wonderful drawings you sketched of Mom, and they gave in. Her last days weren't so good. She was in and out of consciousness, but she still spoke of you. In a moment of clarity, she asked if I had given you, "Felicia," the box. I told her I did, and that you appreciated it very much. She said she knew you needed it more than she did. I've enclosed an obituary from her home-going service. It was lovely. My siblings all came, and we sat around sharing memories of Mom. I hope you are having a wonderful holiday. Thanks so much for caring for my mother and being there when she needed family most.

With deepest gratitude,

Ms. Hattie Ransom

Aunjanue unfolded the obituary. A younger version of Maggie stared back at her, her mouth fashioned in a confident pout. The black-and-white photo of Maggie must have been taken during her single days. Her ring finger was empty. If Aunjanue guessed her age, she'd say twenty. Her soft, clear eyes were innocent, calm. She read details of Ms. Mag's life and wished they'd met at a different time. She placed the obituary back in the envelope and put it in her drawer. Silent, she reminisced about her elderly friend. She'd never opened the box, and decided to wait until her graduation day to do so.

Aunjanue took the family mail downstairs. Zion was in charge of bringing the cooler from the garage. She was responsible for setting the table. She went outside to the shed to get a set of goblets Lasheera had placed on the top shelf last Christmas. She entered the shed, climbed the ladder, and found the goblets. She lifted the box and touched the gold rim of the crystal glasses. She held on to the top shelf as she looked out the window.

Across the street she saw the Wilsons' car. They were parked just below Belinda Rosewood's house. She squinted to get a better look. Stephanie's arms flailed wildly as she got in Caleb's face. Caleb struck the dashboard with his fists. She pointed a finger in his face, opened the door, and slammed it with such force Aunjanue felt the power in the shed. Stephanie waddled up the walkway carrying an MCL bag. Her contribution to tonight's dinner was three dozen yeast rolls. Stephanie, a severe asthmatic, bent down, patted her chest several times, leaned her head back, and shot several bursts in her mouth from an inhaler. Aunjanue climbed down the ladder and ran outside to meet Stephanie. *She was so angry. I know she must have left her coat in the car.* Aunjanue noted she only wore a raspberry maternity dress with matching tights. She was shoeless, and she'd lost an earring at home, in the car, or the driveway. Only one sparkling, burgundy autumn leaf dangled in her ear. She stepped in front of Stephanie, whose head was lowered.

"Ms. Stephanie, let me get the bread." Stephanie caught her breath, plastered a smile on her face. "Aunjanue, how are you? I didn't see you there."

She grabbed the bag. "Do I need to get your coat and shoes?"

"No!" Stephanie said. Her brusque response sent Aunjanue two steps back. Stephanie softened her tone. "I didn't mean to be snippy." She looked back at the car where Caleb sat, staring straight ahead.

Lasheera joined them in the driveway. "Stephanie, where is your coat? Hurry up and come inside." To Aunjanue, she said, "Go to the car and get Stephanie's things."

Lasheera led Stephanie inside. Caleb opened the door, handed

Aunjanue the coat and shoes, and closed the door, never acknowl-
edging her presence with a greeting.

She took the coat inside. Lasheera had fashioned a pallet on the
floor where Stephanie lay in a fetal position. Aunjanue noted the
wet floor.

"Onnie, call everyone and cancel dinner. Stephanie's in labor."

Chapter 44

Stephanie's labor lasted fourteen hours. Lake, Lasheera, Aunjanue, and Caleb sat in the waiting room. The doctor came into the waiting area with great news about CJ.

"Are you with Stephanie Wilson?"

"Yes," they said in unison.

"Mother and baby are doing fine. You may go to the nursery and see him."

Everyone joined Caleb. With his anger lessened, he went to Stephanie's room where a nurse provided him with a gown and gloves. They stood outside the nursery, eyeing a room full of babies. Swaddled in a blue-and-white striped blanket and a blue knit cap, CJ cried and kicked in his clear bassinet. The nurse wheeled CJ to the window. Caleb looked at his son.

A nurse passed by them and Caleb, pointing to CJ asked, "May I take Baby Wilson to our room?"

"I'll wheel him down in a minute."

Caleb headed to their room, quiet, withdrawn.

"What happened earlier?" Lake whispered to Lasheera.

"I don't know. I looked outside and Aunjanue was helping Stephanie bring in bread. She came inside, her water broke, and we got her here as fast as we could."

"I've never seen Caleb so silent. I wonder what happened."

"Probably new-father jitters. Did you see anything, Aunjanue?" Lasheera asked.

"No. Only Ms. Stephanie coming toward the house with the bread." *I can't believe they argued. They wouldn't want anyone to know.*

They waited and walked down to the room. Stephanie held CJ in her arms. Aunjanue watched the baby's head rotate as he sucked milk from a bottle. Stephanie stroked his curls. Caleb sat next to her, both admiring their baby.

"May I hold him?" Lasheera asked.

"Of course," said Stephanie. "Get used to him. He'll be at Aunt Lasheera and Uncle Lake's house a lot. Aunjanue, get ready for your babysitting time." Stephanie's weak voice indicated they didn't need to wear out their welcome or her.

"Caleb, may I speak with you outside a minute?" Lake asked.

"Sure."

Caleb removed his gown and hat and followed Lake down the hallway. The found a corner on the opposite end of the hall to chat.

"Anything you want to talk about?"

"I'm a little stressed about the baby. I want us to be good parents, but I'm afraid I'll make mistakes and do something that doesn't please Stephanie."

"Get ready. It's coming. Parenting isn't for punks. I'm not a biological parent, and I know it's a huge job. You'll be fine. You've got a great village to help you. Your problem will be if you decide not to call on us for help."

"What if I do a lousy job?"

"A baby is on-the-job training. You'll fall into the rhythm."

"I hope so. I'm going outside for some fresh air." Caleb went back to the room, put on his coat, and left the hospital.

Lake walked back down to the room. "Lasheera, I'll be in the lobby area if you need me."

"Thanks, baby," she said. She shifted the baby on her right shoulder to burp him.

"May I hold him?" Aunjanue asked.

"Yes," said Stephanie.

Aunjanue held CJ. She took in his fresh, powdery scent. She followed suit and cradled his head as Stephanie and Lasheera had. She sat back in the chair and placed the baby across her lap. She replayed Stephanie and Caleb's lovers' spat. With her image of them forever changed, she rubbed CJ's back and thought, *If they can play the masquerade, so can I.*

Chapter 45

Seven months had passed since Aruba's suicide attempt, and she was finally unthawing. She pulled along the curbside of Delta's arrivals at Hartsfield-Jackson in Atlanta and waited for James to arrive. The curbside Nazis blew whistles and kept traffic moving. She spotted James in business attire as usual. He flagged her down as she circled the area again. When he called, James said he had a surprise for her, for them. She had dropped Jeremiah and Aaron off at her parents' home hours ago.

She'd spruced up today and enjoyed the warm weather. Still in one-day-at-a-time mode, she enjoyed the moments she shared getting to know James again. When she stepped out of his vehicle to switch places with James so he could drive, she enjoyed the catcalls and whistles from men admiring her beauty. He tossed his suitcase in the backseat and playfully mocked her by rolling his eyes.

"Did you have to come out looking so fine today?"

"What did you want me to look like?"

"Just the way you are. I want people to know I have good taste and you're mine."

She held his hand and rubbed his face. He veered into I-75 traffic.

"Where are we going today?"

"I'm doing a little business and wanted you to join me."

"What kind of business?"

"It's a surprise, remember?"

James headed toward Duluth to meet his sister, Teresa. His brother, Marvin, gave up his garage business and was doing civilian work in Afghanistan. Teresa still held on to her wedding planning business. Today, she promised to meet with James and her ex-sister-in-law to make party plans.

"Are we meeting Teresa for pleasure?"

"Don't ask another question."

Aruba popped the glove compartment open and took out a list of properties in the Atlanta area. She still hadn't committed to remarriage, but she liked James's suggestion they start over again in a neutral area. Not Augusta. Not Indianapolis. Atlanta was large enough for James to expand his clientele as well as make inroads with their relationship. He asked Aruba to print out a list of "dream" properties, homes she could see them living in some time in the near future. She stayed within price ranges on the lower end. She wanted to contribute to their way of life if they reunited.

"Check out Mrs. Fisher," James said.

Teresa stood outside her office as they pulled into her commercial property. Teresa refused to take back her daddy's name and kept her married name on the marquee. She was Teresa Fisher, wedding planner extraordinaire. She ran to the vehicle, opened Aruba's door, and swept her up in her arms. Teresa's ex-husband wasn't one for fellowshipping. He kept Teresa isolated, only wanting her to mingle with clients or others when it benefited him. When they divorced, she vowed to make up for lost time with all the relatives and friends she'd shunned over the years. She'd start with her brother, James, and work her way around.

"If I didn't know any better, I'd swear you two were still married," she said. She made Aruba stand back so she could inspect her outfit. "Still on your game, I see."

"I have a little help from someone who loves me," Aruba said.

Teresa pretended to throw up. "Come in here before you two make me gag," she said.

Teresa led them to her office. She'd laid out several party themes on her desk as well as on her computer screen. "Check these out and tell me what you think," Teresa said.

Aruba eyed James. "Why are we here again?"

He faced her and held her hand. "You said you weren't ready to remarry me. Would you at least consider having a party?"

"A party?"

"Yea, babes. Something like a Back Together Again party. A party my family and yours can mix and mingle so they know we're trying to mend our relationship. Teresa has agreed to help us with the planning."

"Whew, I thought you were going to propose again. I can do a party!"

Teresa slid the party ideas toward them. The tropical themes were the only ones that elicited further discussion.

"How about mid-summer?" Teresa asked. "We could do something in the downtown Atlanta area, or maybe at one of the wineries in North Georgia if you'd like."

"We have enough time to think about it, James."

"I have to meet with a possible vendor in about thirty minutes, so Teresa, if you could get us going with this selection, we'd appreciate it."

"I'm so happy you two are together again. I always saw great things in store for the two of you. You'd be amazed at the number of people who wished they could reconcile," said Teresa.

James hoped Teresa wasn't referring to her ex. Teresa seemed so much better off without him, but he'd never tell her.

"We're rolling, Teresa. We'll be in touch."

Aruba and James left the office, headed to the meeting. James, sensing a change in Aruba's attitude, turned the music down.

"What's wrong, Aruba?"

"Secrets."

James waited for her to explain.

"I think secrets kept us from having a good marriage in the past. I know we divorced, and I moved on, but I've kept some things from you. One thing in particular."

James looked at his watch. He would reschedule the meeting. He wanted Aruba to know her feelings mattered.

"Can we pull over a minute?"

He stopped at the next exit and pulled in a gas station. "What do you have to say?"

"I haven't been completely honest with you about everything, James. I neglected to tell you that when I moved to California, I got pregnant shortly thereafter. Winston and I had just moved, and I miscarried before his disease took effect. I didn't want to go on carrying that albatross around my neck. I didn't have the child, but it's something I thought you needed to know. Even if we date and raise our son, I don't want us to have secrets and lies between us like before."

"I agree."

"Especially with Tawatha out and crazy."

"You're right."

"Is there anything you need to tell me? I mean, we've been through the best and the worst. I think I can handle anything you share with me."

James saw Hannah singing, her voice rising and falling with the choir. He remembered running his fingers through her locks and hearing her giggle. He gazed at Aruba and held her hand. "Baby, I lied to you about my salon trip a few months ago."

Aruba sighed but continued to gaze into his eyes.

"Since we're laying our cards on the table, you need to know I had a daughter with Tawatha. The state made her give up the child for adoption, and she's with a good family. Her name is—"

"Hannah Reese," said Aruba. "She looks like you. You left your messages up on your iPhone and I saw the message from Isaak. I've known for quite a while. I followed Tawatha's story and when I read she'd had a child…"

"I didn't know how to tell you, Baby."

"You just did. That's what matters most. I just wanted to know if you'd be honest with me. I still love you, but I don't want to go back to the lies we lived in the past."

"I did her hair and wanted to hug her so badly. I never thought I wouldn't raise a child I fathered."

"Life is funny, James. I have a feeling your paths will cross again. I feel in in my bones."

They sat in silence at the gas station until dusk fell. At Aruba's prodding, they drove off, both wondering how James could find a way to do something meaningful for his daughter.

Chapter 46

Aunjanue packed her bag for the Youth Arts Fair in Nashville. The school van was scheduled to head to the fair later in the day; Mr. Wilson was driving her down early to set up her drawings. Aunjanue was excited to leave early because her paintings would be on display. She hoped to sell a few drawings to boost her savings account. She loved setting up her artwork so that it would look just right.

"Onnie, I made blueberry pancakes! Please come down and eat before you leave," Lasheera yelled upstairs.

"If you don't come down, I'm eating my share and yours," said Zion.

"Don't touch my pancakes! I'll be there!"

Aunjanue sat on her suitcase. She packed as few clothes as possible. Over the years, she left room in her suitcases to store artwork and other crafty items she'd found. She joined Zion at the table.

"Zion, do you want me to bring you a souvenir?"

"Bring me something with Nashville on it," he said.

They ate their pancakes in silence. Aunjanue wolfed her pancakes down and headed back upstairs. She brought her bag downstairs and set it next to the console table in the foyer. The four-day trip would be a welcomed break from her studies. Next weekend, she'd travel to Chicago with Jamilah to buy a prom dress.

The doorbell rang, and Zion raced to the door.

"Mr. Wilson is here," he called out over his shoulder.

Caleb stepped inside the foyer.

"Caleb, come on in," said Lasheera. "Would you like some blueberry pancakes?"

"I ate before I left home. Stephanie made a feast for me. I may have to make Aunjanue drive if I fall asleep," he joked.

"How is CJ doing?" Lasheera asked.

"Growing like a weed and drinking milk like we own a cow," he said. He pulled up CJ's photos on his iPhone and showed them to Lasheera. She scrolled through them, admiring how much he'd grown over the last four months.

"Aunjanue, do you have your phone charger?"

"Yes, Auntie 'Sheer."

"Do you have enough spending money?"

"Uncle Lake gave me some money before he left this morning."

"Nashville's not too far, so call me if you need anything." Lasheera addressed Caleb. "You said Mr. Johannsen was driving the school van with the other students. What time are they supposed to leave?"

"They should be heading to Nashville in two hours. We should have Onnie's art-work set up at the fair in time enough to join everyone later tonight for dinner."

"Drive carefully and take care of our girl."

Zion and Lasheera hugged Aunjanue as Caleb took her bag to his car. She waved and jumped in the front seat.

"We should be in Nashville in no time," said Caleb.

They pulled out of the driveway. Aunjanue searched her purse for Ms. Mag's black box. Instead of waiting until graduation, she decided to open it in her hotel room in Nashville. She'd been apprehensive because so many memories of Ms. Mag came flooding back to her. She missed her old friend and thought time alone would be perfect to reminisce about the Silver Fox, the family's name for Ms. Mag.

"Have you ever been to Nashville?" Caleb asked.

"A few times for football games and once to the Grand Ole Opry. I've always wanted to see the city."

"We could probably tour the city if you like. You should rest up first."

"I will. I didn't sleep well last night."

"Why not?"

"Well, things have gotten better with my mom, but I miss my family as I remember it." She paused. "Did I tell you Ms. Mag passed?"

"You didn't. I'm sorry to hear of her dying. She was so fond of you, Aunjanue."

"I feel like a part of me died. I've never had an older person take to me the way she did. It's like someone I love is always being taken away from me."

"You're still blessed to have a family unit."

"I know." Aunjanue yawned.

"Someone is sleepier than they let on." Caleb joked.

"I'm taking a nap if you don't mind," she said.

"Go right ahead. I'll wake you up when we get to Nashville."

Chapter 47

The Three Musketeers were at it again. Jamilah hosted an old-school party and invited Lasheera over. Tawatha picked the television shows and Lasheera picked the music. Jamilah made sure to have all their favorite foods and card games. They'd buried the hatchet after each agreed to move forward. It made no sense to hold on to the past.

"Lasheera, when is Onnie coming back?" Tawatha asked.

"They should be back Sunday. I am so glad Lake and Zion went away for the weekend. I can hang out with you two tonight, then I get the house to myself for the next three days. Can someone say *heaven?*"

"Lasheera, you know you can't survive three days without your family. I can see you crawling back over here before midnight to hang with us and eat up all my food." Jamilah joked.

"For that, I'm locking the door and staying inside. Try and come by if you like."

Tawatha placed the DVDs on the table. "We have *Soul Train*, the hippest trip in America. *The Jeffersons. Friends. Frazier.*"

"Tawatha, I do have cable," said Jamilah.

"I know. If we're having an old-school party, we should watch episodes we've seen and recite the lines like we did back in the day," said Tawatha.

"Leave it to you to complicate things," said Lasheera. "We did have fun reciting those lines, though. I remember the time we all deepened our voices and kept saying 'The Help Center' like Louise Jefferson."

"Yea, we did! Ms. Roberta got so upset with us for repeating it," said Lasheera.

"Not to mention the crazy shenanigans of Dee on *What's Happening!* If that had been my sister…" said Jamilah.

"Lasheera, that actually was you. You were never good at keeping secrets," said Tawatha.

Jamilah placed hot wings, pizza, breadsticks, and drinks on the table. They feasted, laughed, and challenged one another.

"'Sheer, I never thanked you and Lake for doing such a great job with Onnie. She turned out well."

"She was easy to raise. She has morals and a genuine desire to do what's right."

"Thank you," said Tawatha.

"Since you brought up the subject, I don't mean to step on your toes, but I want to thank you for something," said Lasheera.

"Oh, boy." Tawatha shifted on the floor.

"I'm glad you stopped sending Onnie—"

A loud bang on the door interrupted their conversation. The banging continued.

"Who is it?"

"Do you think it's Momma?" Tawatha asked.

"I don't know who it is, but whoever is banging on my door like they're crazy better have a darn good excuse."

Jamilah walked to the front door, yanked it open, and called to Lasheera and Tawatha at the sight of Stephanie standing at the door with CJ.

Chapter 48

"We're here," said Caleb.

Aunjanue focused her eyes in the hotel parking lot. The Fair-field Inn and Suites. She wasn't familiar with the hotel, but sleep called her, and she was ready.

"I have your key. I'll get your bag while you get inside. My room is next door."

Caleb grabbed her bag from his car. Aunjanue opened the door and waited for Caleb to bring her bag in. He set it next to the side of the single bed in the room.

"Will you wake me up in about an hour?" she asked.

"Sure. Have you decided what you want to eat?"

"I don't want fish, and I don't want chicken. We can come up with something in between. I just want a snack before everyone gets here later."

"Sounds good."

"Wait one second. I have to go to the bathroom, then I have to give you something out of my bag. I'll be right back."

Aunjanue took her purse in the bathroom. She texted Chloe, asking her to bring the set of colored pencils she'd loaned her. She waited for Chloe's response. She went back out to the room to give Caleb the sketch pad she'd accidentally taken from class.

"I have a sketch pad to return to you, Mr. Wilson. I took it by mistake and I wanted to make sure I gave it back." She handed him the pad as her message alert sounded. "It's probably Chloe," she said.

She opened the message. "THE TRIP WAS CANCELLED TWO DAYS AGO. WHERE ARE YOU? DIDN'T U C MY FB POST?"

Caleb snatched the phone from her hand, pushing her on the bed. He restrained her, scaring her as she struggled to break free from his grip.

"Don't fight me. I'm not going to hurt you. Promise me you'll stop moving."

"Mr. Wilson, what are you doing? Please don't hurt me."

"Do as I say and you won't get hurt!"

She tried to breathe, but the weight of his body constricted her. She stopped moving.

"I'm sorry to handle the situation like this, but this was the only way I could be with you."

"Mr. Wilson, what are you talking about? I don't want to be with you."

"Aunjanue, why are you acting this way? After all the sacrifices I've made for you. After all I've done to be with you."

Her grandmother's Oxygen network marathons came rushing back to her memory. Police said not to fight an assailant. To pretend to go along with the ruse. Mr. Wilson had to feel the thumping of her chest. She also thought of Chloe's text. No matter how many times she told her friends she didn't do Facebook, Twitter, or Instagram, they didn't believe her. They assumed she lurked under an alias; however, after her siblings died she shut down all her social media avenues after being harassed by well-meaning but eerie people who wanted to make sure she was okay.

Slightly above a whisper, she asked, "What sacrifices are you talking about?"

"Do you know how long I've wanted you? Do you know how long I've wanted to be with you?"

Caleb held her tighter around her waist. "I fell in love with you the day I saw you on the news at the funeral. You looked so vulnerable. You were left by yourself by a whorish, selfish mother who cared more about running the streets than she did about you."

Tears trickled down Aunjanue's face as he held her closer.

"Who do you think sent you the postcards? Who do you think wrote your mother all those letters in prison?"

"Mr. Wilson!"

"My name is Todd. Todd Sibley. Not Caleb Wilson. Todd Sibley. If we're going to be together, you need to know who I really am and what I'm about."

"Please let me go."

"Get up!"

Todd took her to the bathroom. He made her watch as he flushed her cell phone down the toilet.

"We don't have to worry about anybody calling us back. We're going to leave when it gets dark, so until then, relax."

Aunjanue's hands trembled as he held her closer and took her back to the bed.

"Take your jeans and shirt off."

Aunjanue did as she was told. She placed her jeans and shirt in the chair and shrank beneath his leering. He ogled her body and asked her to turn around. No man had ever seen her without clothes, not even Roger. She was determined to play it safe and follow instructions. The look in his eyes, cold and distant, frightened her. He'd always been gentle and kind toward her. Now, she stared at this stranger who'd preyed on her from the day they met. She watched him disrobe as well. He placed his clothes on top of hers.

"Come here, Aunjanue."

She walked toward him. He'd overpowered her on the bed, and she didn't want to exert herself before coming up with a concrete plan. She stood before him.

"Touch me, right here."

He pointed to his chest, and she noticed the tattoo of Van Gogh's *Café Terrace at Night.* The tattoo, a perfect replica of the painting etched just above his heart area, moved with the thumping of his heart.

"Aunjanue, you're my heart and soul. I love you so much."

She leaned in closer, noticed he'd etched her birthdate in the yellow awning above the diners, and fainted.

Chapter 49

C J extended his chunky arms toward Lasheera, having grown accustomed to her babysitting him. Stephanie's hair jutted wildly across her head. She clutched her inhaler, sprayed it twice in her mouth, and staggered into Jamilah's living room.

"Sit her down on the couch," said Jamilah.

Jamilah and Tawatha steadied Stephanie until she was seated; Lasheera rocked the baby. Stephanie struggled to breathe. She pointed to the front door, but couldn't utter a word.

"Stephanie, breathe," said Tawatha.

CJ whimpered and played with Lasheera's necklace.

"Help me," Stephanie finally managed. "The car."

"What do you need from the car?" Jamilah asked.

"The trunk."

Tawatha ran to Stephanie's car. She didn't have time to play twenty questions, and she didn't want Stephanie to have a severe asthma attack on her watch. Glad Stephanie had left her doors unlocked, she opened the door to flip her trunk and noticed a black-and-grey steamer trunk in the back seat. She dragged the trunk out of the car and trudged it toward the house. She managed to hoist the trunk and drop it in the hallway. It was too heavy to carry. She joined Jamilah on the sofa with Stephanie.

"It's Aunjanue. She's in trouble. Call her. Call the school. Do something!" Stephanie said. She sprayed her inhaler a second time.

"She's gone on the trip. She'll be back," said Lasheera.

"You don't understand! Dial her number now!"

Lasheera laid CJ across her lap while she dialed Aunjanue's number. "It went straight to voicemail."

"He's done something to her! I know he has!"

"Slow down, Stephanie, and start from the beginning. You're not making any sense," said Jamilah, rubbing Stephanie's back.

"The night I went into labor, Caleb and I had a horrible fight outside your house, Lasheera. We'd been moving the last of some items from the house to a storage unit. He always went to the unit alone, but this time, I went with him. I normally sat in the car, but I went inside to see what we had in the unit and what we could purge for a yard sale this summer. I moved a few things around and found an old steamer trunk. I touched it, and Caleb went ballistic!

"He accused me of snooping and told me never to put my hands on his things again. He moved the trunk from the unit. I didn't know what had happened to it until I went in the attic tonight to store some of CJ's things. I had a bad feeling about it, so I cut the locks."

"Let me pull it around here," said Tawatha.

Tawatha pulled the trunk near the center of the floor. She looked to Stephanie for permission to open it. Stephanie wiped her face and dug through the items, taking out a huge stack of documents.

"Lasheera, several months ago, I told you Caleb seemed hesitant to date when we first met, but warmed up to me when he found out we were moving to the Midwest. This probably explains why."

Stephanie pulled out clipping after clipping about Tawatha, Aunjanue, the court case, and the verdict. She passed the items to the others as they looked on in horror. Articles about Aunjanue's academic accomplishments, her likes, and her goals were magnified.

On a separate sheet of paper, Caleb jotted notes about Aunjanue's favorite foods, her favorite artist, and her secret fears. He'd compiled the facts from magazine and online interviews conducted over the years. Lasheera's stomach knotted when she turned over a box of Vincent van Gogh postcards.

"Caleb did this, not Tawatha," she said.

"Did what?" asked Tawatha.

"For months, Onnie received postcards with messages we assumed were from you. Each card was signed *T*. Everything coincided with your release, so we knew you did it, Tawatha," said Lasheera.

Stephanie removed a huge manila envelope from the trunk and unfolded several documents.

"I came straight here with the baby, but Jamilah, I need you to take this and do a search on your computer."

Jamilah took the information to her office as Tawatha held the baby. Lasheera dialed Lake and paced the floor. Jamilah typed in the name on the birth certificate and waited for search results. Todd Sibley's name appeared in multiple hits, all with the title of registered sex offender next to it. Jamilah printed out the information and ran back into the living room.

"His name is Todd Sibley, and he's a registered sex offender."

"That can't be!" said Lasheera.

Stephanie's hands, shaking and barely able to straighten out the documents, passed around information again. The falsified birth certificate, teaching credentials, and degree all bore the name Caleb Wilson. Additionally, he'd placed stars by names and numbers with the word references underlined.

"We have to alert authorities and the school right now! If necessary, we need to drive to Nashville," said Tawatha.

Chapter 50

Aunjanue awakened with a cool facecloth on her forehead, her head nestled in Todd's lap. Still in her bra and panties, she shivered as his clammy hands traveled the length of her body.

"I see you're okay," he said. "It took you a little longer to come to." He kissed her forehead and put the facecloth on the nightstand.

"Please let me go, Mr. Wilson," she said. Fresh tears fell from her face. "I promise I won't say anything. This will be our secret."

"It's already our secret, Aunjanue. And stop calling me 'Mr. Wilson.' I told you my name is Todd. We'll be on our way after dark." He pulled her from the bed and pulled the curtain back. "Do you see the blue car over there?"

"Yes."

"I drove down yesterday and parked it across the street. I made sure I had an alternate way to leave so we could start our new life together. Aunjanue looked at the car and faced Todd. "May I use the bathroom?"

Todd escorted her to the bathroom door. His confidence rose as he knew no window was in the bathroom. He'd spent weeks selecting their location and plotting his scheme so he could be with the woman he truly loved. His plot to be with her was paying off. He went out of his way to befriend Lake as he pretended to search for a teaching mentor. He paid a hefty price to create an alias, a false degree, an alternate birth certificate, and another social security number, but she was worth it. He hated marrying Stephanie, lying next to her each night, pretending to love her, procreating with her, but the façade allowed him to get closer to Aunjanue. He rubbed his hands together at the realization of his dream coming true.

"I'll stand outside until you come out. You have five minutes. I'll come in after you if I have to, Aunjanue. Do you understand?"

She nodded and went to the bathroom. She relieved herself, fear causing her legs to tremble. Her mind drifted back to years past and her judgment toward those who'd been kidnapped or abducted. She recalled thinking how stupid they were for not calling the police, for not fighting their attackers, and for not being strong enough to break free. As she looked around the windowless bathroom, her mind raced one hundred miles a minute thinking of ways to get out of the situation. She knew her family was looking for her, but wondered how could she reach them. She thought of banging on the wall so someone next door could hear her, but the rooms to her left and right had been unoccupied hours earlier.

"Aunjanue, are you okay in there?"

"Yes… Todd. I guess I drank too much earlier."

His silence, coupled with the shuffling of his feet away from the door, made her relax. She wished she could talk with Roger, Tarsha, or Lasheera. So many voices and moments had been taken for granted. She'd give anything to see those she loved in that moment. She flushed the toilet, washed her hands, and went back to the room. She felt Todd's eyes on her as she sat on the edge of the bed. He sat in the chair in the corner, still in his underwear.

"You can lie down and rest."

"I'm too scared."

"Have I ever hurt you?"

"It's not a matter of you hurting me; you're scaring me."

"Aunjanue, I don't want to scare you. I love you."

"You don't know me. You don't love me."

"Don't say I don't love you! Don't tell me I don't love you, and I've given up everything for you!"

Panic stricken, she winced as he punctuated every word with emphasis while shouting at her.

Seeing the fear in her eyes, he sat next to her on the edge of the bed and pulled her into a tight embrace.

"Shhhhh. It's okay. I didn't mean to shout at you. You have to trust me, okay?"

She didn't acknowledge his request. She looked around the room.

"Where are my clothes?"

"I put them away for safe keeping."

"I want to go home."

"We're going home when it gets dark. You'll like the place I have for us. We can be together and start a new life. Won't you like that, Aunjanue?"

Her stomach churned again. She fell back on the bed and willed the fresh batch of tears to stop falling.

He crawled in bed beside her, holding her again. He rubbed her hair and wiped her tears, placing light kisses on her forehead.

"It's going to be okay, baby. I promise I'll take good care of you. I promise."

Chapter 51

Principal Gordon and the authorities met Lake and the women outside the school. Tarsha and Roger joined them as well. He followed proper procedure by sending out an automated message throughout the district about Aunjanue's status. Students came to the school and milled around discussing the matter, surprised Mr. Wilson was a predator. Authorities confirmed the abduction, and after getting a description of the car, Aunjanue, and Todd Sibley's true identity, issued an Amber Alert. The community, as well as the students, were terrified knowing one of their own had vanished under horrible circumstances.

"How was he allowed to go away in the first place?" a concerned mother asked.

"He is a family friend. We thought he was a family friend," said Lake. "We had no reason to suspect he'd harm her."

"Is there a way we can trace the car?" Lasheera asked.

"We are in wait-and-see mode," said Principal Gordon.

Lake held Lasheera's hand, resisting the urge to pace the school grounds. He felt responsible for not being home when Caleb came to pick up Aunjanue. If he'd been able to look Caleb in the eye, man to man, he might have seen something that would have tipped off his motives.

"You all have to let the authorities handle the matter," said

Principal Gordon. "I know you want to find her, but going to Nashville won't help the situation and may, in fact, put all of you in greater danger."

"We can't sit here and do nothing," said Lake. Lake thought of the images of Aunjanue that would be distributed nationwide. Her mental and physical maturity belied her years. "What if someone thinks she's an adult?"

"Didn't you say she doesn't turn eighteen for two more weeks? An Amber Alert is acceptable as long as the person abducted is seventeen or younger. Technology has evolved so much the alert will be issued via emails, smartphones, and television. Someone has seen or knows something. We'll find her," said the police officer.

Hours earlier, the family had pored over recent photos of Aunjanue. Tawatha was allowed to pick out photos that would be distributed to the media. Lake felt guilty after discovering there was no such thing as a Youth Arts Fair in Nashville. Todd created the bogus event, even going as far as creating an event website. He generated interest amongst the art students, then sent personal letters to the students two days before the event stating it was cancelled. Lake wondered why the other students hadn't conveyed the message to Aunjanue. He also wondered how he missed a key planning event, since he was so attuned to the art functions at the school. If something happened to Aunjanue, he'd never forgive himself.

"Should we go home and wait?" asked Lasheera. "Being here at the school is doing nothing for me."

"You may go home if you wish. We'll be in touch as things unfold," said the officer.

Lake drove Lasheera home. Zion had stayed behind with Roberta and J.B. The family agreed he'd seen enough the past few months and shouldn't bear the burden of Aunjanue's disappearance.

Roberta and J.B. turned off the televisions and radios, and against their usual routine, allowed Zion video game time.

En route home, Lake's phone rang. He recognized the officer's number.

"Mr. Carvin, the car was found in Gallatin, Tennessee. No sign of Aunjanue or Todd Sibley, but it was abandoned in the Holder Family Fun Center parking lot."

Lake waited for more information. "Was there anything in the car?"

"Vehicle is empty," said the officer.

"Thanks for the call, officer."

Lake ended the call. He looked in his rearview mirror and noted Jamilah's car. She transported Stephanie, CJ, and Tawatha. *How can I be strong for my family?*

"What's on your mind, Lake?" asked Lasheera.

"I feel so guilty. All this time, I've befriended this man thinking he wanted my advice, my guidance, and my wisdom. Baby, think of all the times we've shared things about Aunjanue with him. Think of all the times he's been in our house, eating our food, and traveling with us. Now that I recall our conversations, he always cared more about her well-being than Zion's. Almost in an macabre way. I shrugged it off since everyone protected her after the fire."

"You can't blame yourself, Lake. We were all blindsided."

"If something happens to her, I'll never forgive myself, 'Sheer."

"She'll be fine, Lake. She's strong and resourceful," said Lasheera, trying to convince herself more than Lake.

They pulled into the driveway and were met with a familiar yet heartwarming scene. Their neighbors stood outside in a show of solidarity. Belinda Rosewood approached Lake's car, the usual spokesperson for the street.

"We heard about what happened," said Belinda. She leaned into the driver side and said, "James Ford, three doors down, said he would be on the lookout tonight when he does his run down to Nashville."

"The trucker?" asked Lasheera.

"Yep. He happens to do his runs to Nashville on Fridays and Saturdays. He said he'd call if he hears of anything," Belinda said.

"Thank you, Belinda," said Lake.

"You all come on over to my place. We all got together and fixed some food for you all. I know you might not have an appetite, but you'll go crazy sitting in there, staring at the walls, and waiting to hear something. We cooked some things and bought a few other items."

Jamilah pulled in behind Lake. She exited the car, followed by Stephanie and Tawatha.

"We're going over to Belinda's," Lake said to them.

Jamilah, familiar with Belinda's hospitality, followed her family across the street, grateful that community still reigned in their lives.

Chapter 52

The Ghoul. That was the nickname Aunjanue gave Tawatha's most hideous boyfriend. The Ghoul, whose real name was Jacob Curry, wore too much cologne, had three missing digits on his right hand, and sat in the living room in their La-Z-Boy playing with a platinum signet ring on his left ring finger. The *J* in the center of the ring caught the light as he twirled it and munched pork rinds. Aunjanue remembered the night Tawatha gave the performance of a lifetime to restore their electricity.

Aunjanue was ten, and the lights had been shut off for almost a month. Tawatha had sworn the children to secrecy about the lights so Roberta wouldn't lecture Tawatha or provide the money with strings attached. She'd come to rely on her steady stream of men to provide groceries, stock the pantry, or help her with tires or gas for her lemon. Aunjanue channeled Tawatha from the night, the way she leaned into Jacob, or Big Jake, as she called him, and rendered him putty in her hands.

"Todd, hold me tighter," said Aunjanue.

His body stiffened at her command. Her body had relaxed, and she caressed his hand. "What did you say?" he asked.

"I asked you to hold me tighter. I like the way your body feels next to mine," she said.

The landscape had changed. He'd braced himself to fight with her for the rest of the night, to use the drugs in his bag to sedate her if necessary. He hadn't anticipated surrender.

"What are you saying, Aunjanue? Are you playing games with me?"

She faced him now. She traced the delicate sketching of his tattoo with her fingers. She circled the numbers of her birthdate on the café's awning, pleased that his body shivered at her touch. "I'm tired of pretending I don't have feelings for you. I've cared for you since the first time I met you."

"Don't play head games," he said.

"Todd, I mean it. Look at how handsome you are. You're sweet, kind, loving, and you always have my back when it comes to my well-being," she said. Tawatha spoke those same words to Big Jake.

Todd kissed her forehead, pulled her hair behind her ears. "I've wanted you so badly."

"How did you know I was the one for you?"

Todd sought the right explanation. He heard the words of his arresting officers during past run-ins. They called him a predator, a molester, but he wasn't. He loved *those* girls in a different way; Aunjanue was special. He wanted to give her his all, to protect her. "When I first heard of the situation with your family, my heart went out to you. I sat in my living room watching CNN and saw photos of your house burning. I hated your mother for doing what she did to your brothers and your sister. I didn't realize she had one child living until I saw you at the funeral.

"You and Tarsha held hands before you went inside the church. In that moment, I knew I had to protect you, to make sure no one else did anything to harm you."

She let his words soak in as she resisted the urge to vomit. "How did you get here? I mean, to be my teacher?"

"I taught school right out of college. I came from a long line of professors and teachers, so it was natural for me to pursue the family tradition. I was fine at first, but I lost my teaching license in Connecticut after a girl accused me of impregnating her."

"Did you?"

"She wanted it. She was sixteen, and her family neglected her. They made her have an abortion, and I spent a year in jail for statutory rape."

"Oh."

"No, Aunjanue, don't take it that way. I didn't love her like I love you," he said.

"What about Stephanie?" she asked.

Stephanie. Todd had moved to Florida after his Connecticut jail release to get away from his criminal history. He didn't register with the State of Florida as a sex offender, and he kept the contact information for a man inmates called Shadow. Shadow's specialty was creating new identities. Birth certificates, social security numbers, addresses, and credit histories—if he could name it, Shadow could do it. After receiving a six-thousand-dollar cash payment, Shadow transformed Todd Sibley to Caleb Wilson. New teaching license in hand, he quietly taught art at a small middle school in Ocala, Florida. At a birthday party for a fellow teacher, Stephanie approached him talking a mile a minute about her career as a banker, her love of baking, and her investing expertise. She asked him on a date. When he declined, she persisted. He passed the time away with her to keep his growing feelings for the teens around him at bay. He loved girls between the ages of twelve and fifteen. They were no longer little girls, but not quite women. They were moldable. When he learned Stephanie had received a job transfer to Indianapolis, he proposed, knowing his chance to be with Aunjanue was imminent. Lake was a prominent figure in the funeral photos as well, so he sought him out as a mentor. Lake and Lasheera's guardianship of Aunjanue sealed the deal for him.

"Stephanie was a bump in the road. I should have never gotten her pregnant, and I regret marrying her. I should have come to Indy, told you what you meant to me, and took my chances."

"Don't you love CJ?"

"I do. I wish I could be the kind of father he needs, but I know that's impossible," he said.

"You know we have to move, right? We can't be around family like this. What would they say?"

"After getting to know you, I also admire how mature you are. The other girls didn't understand the need to keep our love quiet, but you do."

"Telling will ruin our good thing," she said, and moved closer to him. Tawatha had assured Big Jake their secrets were safe from his wife as well.

His heart raced. She felt the rapid movement of his chest and placed her hand over his heart.

"What's wrong?"

"I've wanted you for so long. I don't want to let you down."

"You won't."

Hours passed as Aunjanue massaged Todd's shoulders and held him close. She thought of Tawatha's next move from so many years ago. Big Jake splayed four crisp, hundred-dollar bills on the table that night. He told her to get the lights turned back on and use the remaining money for groceries. Big Jake, ready for pay-back, took Tawatha in his arms to whisk her away to the bedroom, but she made a bathroom pit-stop.

"Todd, I—"

"What is it, honey?"

She hated the words *honey, sweetie,* and *doll.* She pushed past the irritation and said, "It's that time of the month. I need to go the restroom to, you know…" she lied.

"Aunjanue, I didn't know." He released her body as if it were rotted fruit. *I wish I had known about her cycle.*

"I'll get my purse and change. I'll be right back."

Aunjanue took her purse from the chair and went to the bathroom. She turned the faucet on and scrounged around in her purse for a sharp object. She knew a fingernail file would make a small dent in her plan, but she couldn't find it. Lasheera gave her a hard time about keeping a junky purse; today she understood why. Were it not for moving the church programs and her mini sketch pads around, she would have missed it. She removed the black box from her purse and set it on the counter. She'd kept the key in a separate compartment in her bag. She removed it and opened the box for the first time. Photos and paper filled the top of the box. She turned the water off and sat on the toilet to view the pictures. Ms. Mag, her husband, and Felicia stood outside a church on Easter. The red brick façade of the church was the perfect backdrop for their pastel ensembles and the huge Easter basket Felicia cradled. Aunjanue flipped through photo after photo, then shifted to the strips of paper underneath the photos. Ms. Mag had scribbled illegible messages on the slips. *Felicia. Fight. Don't let Henry get by.* Aunjanue set the papers aside and noticed a second compartment in the box. She unlocked it as well, then noticed the items. She slipped one of the items in her bra, flushed the toilet, and rejoined Todd in bed, cradling his back. He removed her arms.

"Did you take care of what you needed?"

"I did. Is everything okay? You seem different all of a sudden. Did I do something wrong?"

"A woman's cycle is an intimate time. I don't want to disturb your flow of life."

"You're not disturbing me."

"Listen, I'm going to get some ice."

"Wait, don't go." She undid the bed covers, wrapped herself in a sheet, and asked Todd to lie down. He listened to her; his discomfort increasing as she mounted him.

"I wanted to thank you for bringing us here. We're going to have such a good time. I've waited a long time to be with you. Close your eyes so I can kiss you."

He smiled and did as he was told. She removed the mace from her bra and vigorously sprayed his face. He screamed and rubbed his eyes, clawing and grasping at the air to find her. He made it to the floor and stumbled. She kicked him, held the sheet tighter to her body, and grabbed her purse. She ran from the room and didn't care who saw her, or what anyone thought. She took the stairs to the front lobby, grateful they'd only gone to the second floor.

"Please help me!" she said to the front desk clerk. "The man I came with is my teacher and he tried to rape me."

The clerk eyed her suspiciously, then remembered the Amber Alert.

"Come back here in the office while I call the police."

Aunjanue followed her, giving her key information about the situation. Her heart raced, and all she wanted to do was hear her family's voices.

"Ma'am, please let me call my family before the authorities get here."

The clerk obliged and gave Aunjanue the phone and privacy.

"I'll be waiting right out here 'til the police come. I won't let anything happen to you."

Chapter 53

Todd Sibley was arrested outside Fairfield Suites in his underwear. Authorities found passports and a large amount of spending money in the trunk of his second vehicle. One officer held up a pair of handcuffs from the car. Aunjanue, still inside the hotel, stared straight ahead, her voice never rising above a whisper. She sipped on hot chocolate the clerk had given her and was grateful her clothes were retrieved from the trunk of Todd's car.

"You're a very brave young lady," said the officer. "It took a lot of quick thinking on your part to bring this guy down. He's wanted in three states."

Aunjanue nodded and looked at her watch. Hours had passed, and she felt a bit of relief that one predator was off the streets. Still, she couldn't wait until Lake and Lasheera arrived.

"Did you want to lie down?" the clerk asked.

"No, I'm fine right here."

She didn't want to see the television, nor could she stomach anything news related. First, her mother, then Lasheera, and now the Amber Alert. It seemed they were magnets for drama and strife. She sat in the hotel wondering how she could put an end to the chaos that was her life. She would be leaving for Spelman in August, and she wanted nothing more than the last five years of her life to disappear.

"Onnie," Lasheera said as she walked into the hotel's office.

Aunjanue's face beamed as Lasheera walked in the room. She was equally excited to see Lake and Tawatha. For the first time, she'd felt kinship with Tawatha.

"Aunjanue, I'm so sorry this happened!" That was all Lasheera could say before the tears fell. The four of them fell into an embrace, and Aunjanue, still shaken, wished they could stay clustered in the circle forever. She never wanted to be left alone, nor was she sure she could trust again.

"Tarsha wanted to come, but her parents wouldn't allow it," said Lasheera.

"Ditto for Roger. They said they would come tomorrow if you are up for company," said Lake. "I told them that would be your call."

"I'm not up for company. I want to go home and stay there. I was only one class away from completion. I hope I'll be allowed to take the class at home."

"Don't isolate yourself, Onnie," said Tawatha.

Aunjanue stared at Tawatha. After all the resentment she harbored for her mother, she looked at the woman who saved her life. Had she not witnessed Tawatha's errant behavior, or opened the black box and embraced Ms. Mag's gift from the grave, she'd still be in Todd's hands.

"I'm not isolating myself, Momma. I need time to sort things out."

Lasheera ended the tension. "We have a long ride to Indianapolis in the morning. Let's get a room here in the city tonight and head back tomorrow."

They agreed and left Fairfield Inn, the family forming a shield around Aunjanue.

Chapter 54

Victoria gave her invitation to the receptionist at the ball-room entry. She checked them in, Faulk, party of four, and directed them toward the Grand Ballroom.

"Are you nervous?" Yvette asked.

"Not really. I'm more… I can't explain it. It's not nervousness, though. I want to get this over."

"We're here for backup," quipped Emory.

"You need armed guards if this thing goes downhill," said Carl.

Victoria sighed and punched Carl's arm. They were seated at table forty-one, and made their way through the ever-growing crowd.

"Check out this setup," Yvette whispered to Victoria.

"It is very elegant," said Victoria.

The tropical theme was breathtaking. Emory, Carl, Victoria, and Yvette sat at an oblong table decked in white linen and pink and yellow plumerias. Lush greenery filled the room. The warm and inviting evening, perfect for a party, was just the right vibe for the night's happenings.

"All we're missing is a beach and sand," said Emory.

"Speaking of which, don't forget the Cancun trip in July. I've taken off work for some fun in the sun," said Carl.

Victoria smiled at Carl. This would be the first time she'd taken a couples trip since her divorce. Victoria scanned the faces and saw a few familiars. "There's Aruba's grandmother, Maxie," she said to Yvette. "I'm going over to speak to her."

Victoria made her way to Aruba's grandmother. Maxie stopped talking midsentence to greet her.

"Victoria! I'm so glad you made it. I saw your name on the guest list and hoped you'd be here."

"I wanted to be here. After I ran into Bria, I missed the fellowship we used to have." She pointed to her table. "I'm over here with my friends, Yvette and Carl, and my fiancé, Emory. Would you like to meet them?"

"I most certainly would."

Maxie made her way through the crowd, greeting friends and family members, and hugging a few of the neighbors who'd driven to Atlanta from Harlem.

"Everyone, this is Maxie, Aruba's grandmother. Maxie, this is my friend, Yvette, and her husband, Carl. This handsome stunner is my fiancé, Emory Wilkerson."

Emory kissed Maxine's hand. "It's nice to meet you, Maxie."

Maxie feigned dizziness. "You still know how to pick 'em."

She sat at the table with them and made small talk. She stopped the waiters and took champagne from the tray. Carl, Yvette, Emory, and Victoria followed her lead.

"This party almost didn't happen," said Maxie.

"Why?" asked Victoria.

"You know my granddaughter is a stubborn old mule. She's still not ready to remarry, but James insisted on some celebration to let family and friends know they'd reunited."

"That's awesome," said Victoria. After five years, she spoke sincerely and wished Aruba well.

"Here they come now," said Maxie. "Old lovebirds."

Aruba and James entered the ballroom arm in arm. The crowd stood and applauded. Victoria took in Aruba's Greek goddess attire. The white, Grecian silk dress stopped just above her knees. Her diamond headpiece accented her thick Goddess braids perfectly. The love flowing between Aruba and James was undeniable as they greeted guests throughout the room. When they neared Victoria's table, Aruba's face lit up. She embraced her old friend with a lingering hug. Victoria welcomed the tight squeeze.

"You look incredible, Aruba. It's good to see you also, James."

James greeted Victoria as well. "I'm glad you came, Victoria." James eyed her guests.

"Excuse my manners. These are my friends, Yvette and Carl. This is my fiancé, Emory."

The word fiancé widened James's eyes. "Nice to meet you all." He turned to Aruba. "Baby, I'm going to check on the drinks. I'll be back." He kissed her lips and headed to the bar.

"Aruba, may I speak with you in private?"

Yvette winced at the request. "Are you sure this is a good time, Victoria? It's a party, after all."

"It's okay," said Aruba.

Victoria followed Aruba to a room in back of the ballroom. She'd rehearsed her speech a million times at home, but decided to speak from her heart. Aruba smoothed her braids and took a seat on a sofa in the room.

"I want to get this off my chest while I have the chance. I have been so angry with you since my marriage ended that I didn't know what to do. When Bria told me about the suicide attempt, I had a change of heart. If you had died, I would have never gotten a chance to see you face-to-face to start the healing process, and I would have never got a chance to say, I forgive you."

Aruba teared up.

"I blamed you for so many things. I hate to admit this, but I did wish you had died. The thought of you taking your life brought me back to reality. Jeremiah would be motherless, and a lot of people would be without your friendship."

"But I did so many horrible things to you."

"Winston and I had been distant for a long time. I think the attention you gave him made him realize he was missing genuine partnership. If it hadn't been you, it would have been another woman."

"Don't let me off the hook."

"I'm not. I wouldn't wish your payback on anyone."

Aruba cried now. Victoria found some Kleenex and gave them to her old friend.

"I didn't mean to make you cry. I wanted you to know everything is all right."

"I'm happy for you and Emory. He seems like a wonderful man."

"He is. I got a winner. Trust me when I tell you I won't take him for granted. By the way, it's good to see you and James back together."

"We still have a long way to go, but I didn't realize how much I still loved him until…"

Victoria held her friend's hand, hoping the mention of suicide wouldn't darken the conversation. This was supposed to be a happy time.

"Wait, you hear it?" asked Aruba, patting her feet.

"Theme song, right?"

Donny Hathaway and Roberta Flack's "Back Together Again" wafted in the room.

"James has it playing at the top of every hour with the sole purpose of everyone doing the Electric Slide."

Aruba saw the concern on Victoria's face.

"Come on, Victoria, it's a group dance. You can do it. You can dance next to me."

They doubled over in laughter, reminiscing about Victoria's lack of rhythm.

"You lead the way, old friend," said Victoria

"Gladly," said Aruba.

They joined everyone on the dance floor. Emory took Victoria's hand, leading her through the steps. James and Aruba danced next to them, the four of them pumping their fists and reciting lyrics. *"Doo doo doo doo doo, Doo doo doo doo yeah, Ooh, ooh, ooh, ooh, ooh, ooh, ooh, ooh, ooh. Back together again."*

Chapter 55

Families descended on the Indiana State Fairgrounds for North Central High School's graduation. Aunjanue mailed out invitations three months ago, and she was pleased at the response she'd received from family members and friends. Her greatest joy came when her grandfather, Shirley Gipson, RSVP'd. Now confined to a wheelchair and in constant need of an oxygen tank, she was elated he'd agreed to make the trip. She was also excited that her aunts and uncle, Candice, Connie, and Carson, would be attendance.

Tawatha helped her dress for the special occasion after Aunjanue requested her presence. Lasheera couldn't mask her disappointment, but she relented, hoping their mother-daughter relationship would be mended over time. Tawatha asked Aunjanue to step back for one last glance.

"You look beautiful, baby. The dress suits you. You're a chip off the old block."

"Thanks, Momma. Help me zip up my gown."

Tawatha helped her zip up the gown and place her cap on. Aunjanue took in the bittersweet moment. She wished her siblings could be there to see her walk across the stage to receive her diploma. The "They're smiling down from heaven" cliché wasn't soothing her today. If they were alive, they'd run up to her, give her a bear hug, and rip her cap off or play with her tassel. Those were the siblings and memories she embraced.

"What are you thinking about, Onnie?"

"S'n'c'r'ty, Grant, and Sims. I wish they were here."

"They are. In spirit."

"Momma, give me my perfume," she said, ignoring Tawatha's words.

Tawatha sprayed Aunjanue with Shower Fresh. She wanted Aunjanue to do as little as possible on her special day.

"I'm going to join everyone else in the stands," she said.

"Remember, Momma, no screaming or yelling in the stands. You'll be removed from the stadium if you do."

"We'll be as quiet as church mice. I promise."

Aunjanue shook her head. She knew how loud her mother was, and she didn't want to be embarrassed.

"Who's in the stands?" she asked.

"The family and Stephanie."

"I didn't think she'd accept my invitation. I feel terrible about what happened with Ca… Todd."

"She wants to make things up to you. She feels guilty about bringing him to the city."

"I can't wait to hold CJ later tonight. I bet he's getting chunkier by the day."

Tawatha closed in on the space between them. "Onnie, I'm so proud of you. Not just on your graduation, but weathering so many storms. You've had to deal with more drama and pain than most people will ever experience. I want you to stay strong."

"I'm not strong, Momma. I want better than I've seen all my life."

"I've said it a million times, but I'm sorry about the fire. I'm trying to do better, baby. Jamilah hooked me up with a counselor, and I'm working now and taking care of business for myself."

"I know, Momma."

"I'm trying to apologize for bringing all those men around when you all were small. I wanted you all to have a father figure, but I didn't know how to do it without sacrificing myself."

"Momma, do you know you saved me from Todd?"

"What do you mean?"

"I remembered how you pulled a fast one on Big Jake one night. How you fooled him into giving you money for the lights and the groceries. I heard everything and saw how you used him."

"I…"

"Don't be ashamed. I used the same game on Todd. He fell for it and thought I loved him. I wouldn't be here with you if I hadn't seen you work your magic."

"I'm embarrassed. I'm not that person anymore, Onnie. I'm trying to get better day by day."

"It's good you've had a paradigm shift."

"You sound like Royce." Tawatha unzipped her purse. "By the way, he sent you this card and gift. I'm sure it's money inside. He delivered it to Jamilah since I've been banned from his premises."

"I'll send him a thank you card with everyone else's." Aunjanue adjusted her cap once more. "I have to join my classmates. Thanks for your help, Momma."

Tawatha left the bathroom and waved to Tarsha and Roger, who were outside waiting for Aunjanue. She watched as the three of them joined the processional.

"How is she doing?" Lasheera asked. Tawatha sat in the family's designated rows in the stands.

"She's nervous but ready for this night to be over. She says she's okay, but I'm worried about her."

"How's my granddaughter doing in there?" Shirley asked.

"Our granddaughter is doing well. It's good to see you, Shirley," said Roberta.

They gave each other a knowing glance that said time had healed the wounds between them. J.B. held Roberta closer.

Lake and Lasheera held CJ. Stephanie was quiet, paranoid the family blamed her for the incidents that unfolded. She wanted to attend the graduation because she'd grown to think of the Carvins as family. She refused to visit Todd in jail, and filed for divorce the night of the arrest. There was nothing he could say to her or her son, and there would be no turning back with him. He'd made a fool of her, knowing he preferred young girls instead of women. Perhaps she could make it up to Aunjanue in time.

The processional started. Lake, Lasheera, Tawatha, Jamilah, Zion, and Roberta beamed with pride as the students walked into the stadium. Roberta pointed out Aunjanue to the family. They'd made a pact to be quiet and not embarrass her.

The program became a blur to Lasheera. Filled with thoughts of the day they'd taken guardianship of Aunjanue, she enjoyed the movie playing in her head about Aunjanue. The dreams she had after her siblings died. The first time Belinda Rosewood coaxed her out of the house for cookies, lemonade, and a movie. The first birthday party she had with the neighborhood children who insisted they spend the night to make sure she was okay. Caleb coming by to check on her. Her first date with Roger. Aunjanue and Zion horse playing. It all unraveled in real time, moments blissful and painful.

"Here she comes," Jamilah whispered in her ear.

"Aunjanue Maria Gipson" said Principal Gordon. Aunjanue walked across the stage, shook Principal Gordon's hand, received her diploma, and flipped her tassel to the left side.

The family stood, holding up a sign that read, "Congratulations, Aunjanue! We're so proud of you!"

She looked in the audience and found her family. She waved to them and smiled. She took her seat and pinched herself. She found Tarsha and Roger on their designated rows and waved to them. The sign her family held caught her eye again. She'd dreamt of this moment for years, when her family would be reunited. Cordial. Loving. One.

About the Author

Stacy Campbell was born and raised in Sparta, Georgia, where she spent summers on her family's front porch listening to the animated tales of her older relatives. She lives with her family in Indianapolis, Indiana. She is the author of *Dream Girl Awakened*. You may visit the author at www.facebook.com/stacy.campbell.376 and on Twitter @stacycampbell20, or visit her website at www.stacy loveswriting.com.

If you want to discover what set events in motion,
be sure to pick up

Dream Girl Awakened

BY Stacy Campbell
AVAILABLE FROM STREBOR BOOKS

[1]
Owed to Myself

May 21, 2008

Aruba propped up the girls in a Miracle C-cup, checked the smooth, waxed bikini line in her thong, and released her shoulder-length hair from a barrette, proud she'd made an appointment at Aveda Fredericks to iron out her leonine mane of curls earlier in the day. Just as she slipped on her dress, Jeremiah called from the door, "Mommy, you smell good."

As she turned, she stopped mid-smile at the sight of Jeremiah perched atop James's shoulders.

"Yeah, Mah-mee, I haven't seen you this beautiful since—well, you're always beautiful. Are you trying to make me jealous?" asked James, hoping to elicit a smile. "Where you going looking so good?" James was careful not to offend her. He needed to get back in her corner, back into her accommodating thighs.

"Just a company function. Won't be out too late. One of us has to work in the morning. May I have five more minutes to get dressed? *Please*."

James walked out the door with Jeremiah blowing kisses at Aruba. She balled her fists at James's back. *Ten years and this is the best I can do. Ten years of hanging my hopes on this man's dreams. Ten years of supporting him and he won't even keep a decent job. Was I that dumb in 1998 thinking James was the best I could do? It all ends tonight. Definitely! I have one year to accomplish my goal, to make things better for myself and my son. Mind-blowing sex can't make up for all I've endured with this man.*

She shook her head in disgust as her mind drifted back two weeks. That Wednesday, James ambled into the great room, parked himself on the sectional, and sprinted into his usual discourse on the job market, the Edomites—his term for the oppressors—and how he never got a chance to shine. He grabbed a 40-ounce from the fridge and proclaimed, "Edomites always tryna keep a brotha down!"

She glared at him as he jumped up, then paced back and forth in the living room, his steel-toed boots leaving small tracks in the carpet.

"I'm glad I walked off that fucking site. Ain't no way in hell I'ma settle for fifteen dollars an hour under those conditions."

"You did what?" she shouted. She counted the cost of his latest job loss, then grew angrier. She knew she'd have some explaining to do since her Uncle Walstine had put in a good word for James at Hinton and Conyers Construction.

"You know how those Edomites do. Segregating *us* to the high, roofing positions while they let the young bloods, the young *white* bloods do the painting and drywalling."

She counted to ten, then remembered Jeremiah was still at Angels in Halos, near Indianapolis. "Maybe I'll discuss this when I get *our child* from day care!"

"Aruba, baby, I forgot about Jerry. Lemme go—"

"Forget it, James! I'll deal with you when I get back."

Aruba grabbed her keys, stormed out the house, and rushed to the center. As she weaved in and out of traffic on I-465, she tallied the twenty-five-dollar-per-minute late fee steadily accruing. Just as she approached the Allisonville Road exit, Mrs. Timmons, the day care director, rang her cell.

"Is everything okay, Aruba? Big meeting today?"

"Yes," she lied, hoping to stay in Mrs. Timmons's good graces. "I've been traveling my region, training for State Farm nonstop. Things have been hectic at the office."

"Not to worry, Aruba. I'm here with Jeremiah and he's playing with Lyric Austin. They're having a blast."

Aruba sighed, unsure of how she'd atone for yet another lie told to cover for James. Before she could exhale with relief, Uncle Walstine's name and number flashed on her caller ID. "Mrs. Timmons, I'm around the corner. See you soon." *Better get this over now.* She swapped from Mrs. Timmons to her uncle.

"Unk, how's it going?"

"You know damn well how it's going! Works-when-he-feels-like-it James just ruined my good name at Hinton and Conyers. I had two more *good* prospects lined up and he goes in there ranting and raving about the Edomites—and Hinton and Conyers are black folks!"

"Unk, I had no idea—"

"Save it. We told you that boy was no good when you brought him around. 'Bout the best thing you got outta that union was Jeremiah!"

"That's not fair, Uncle Walstine. I've been try—"

"Trying. Working like a dog to take care of that…" Walstine paused. "I'm just saying, baby girl, I'm tired of seeing you work so hard. You need to be in a relationship where you complement, not supplement."

"Thank you. I understand how you feel and I'm so sorry about what happened. I'll talk to James about it. I promise."

With that, they said good-byes. Aruba retrieved Jeremiah, went home, and chose to say only hello and good-bye to James for the next two weeks. His romantic overtures; yellow, long-stemmed roses; and candlelight, homemade dinners were met with no enthusiasm. The more she looked at James, the more she thought of Winston. She knew she couldn't give James the silent treatment tonight. She had to weave her web, lay a foundation for the new life she and Jeremiah would soon come to know.

Aruba decided tonight was perfect to take what she deserved—her friend Victoria's husband. After all, Victoria whined about Winston morning, noon, and night. Aruba mimicked Victoria's complaints as she applied makeup to her soft cheeks, compliments of an organic honey-almond facial.

"Aruba, Winston's never home."

"We've moved three times in four years with his practice and I'm tired."

"He only gives me a three-thousand-dollar allowance each month."

"You wouldn't understand unless you've walked a mile in my Manolos, Rube."

Aruba grunted at *that* statement and double-checked the night's game plan sprawled across the bed: MapQuest directions to the conference center where Winston would conduct a presentation on cardiovascular breakthroughs; Winston's favorite CDs—Glenn Jones's *Forever: Timeless R&B Classics*, Boney James's *Shine*, and Charles Hilton Brown's *Owed To Myself*—she had heard wafting from his home office; the last pay stub from James's fifth job in seven months; Winston's favorite perfume, Flowerbomb; photos of her son, Jeremiah, and Winston's daughter, Nicolette, at a Mocha Moms outing. Tonight she had bigger salmon to marinate and pan sear. In one swoop she tossed the plan in her oversized bag and threw on a trench coat. She exhaled deeply when James and Jeremiah reentered the room.

"I wanna come, Mommy," said Jeremiah. Aruba marveled at her three-year-old's obsession with following her.

"Mommy and Daddy will take you to Great Times this weekend. Okay?"

Jeremiah wiggled from James's shoulders as he reached for Aruba's arms. "Mommy and Daddy gonna talk this weekend?"

Embarrassed that her child had noticed the distance between them, Aruba hugged him, and said, "Yes, we're gonna have lots of fun. Pinkie promise."

Jeremiah wrapped his left pinkie finger with Aruba's, and said, "I'm happy. Daddy said you were in an itchy mood." Jeremiah's tendency to drop beginning letters saved yet another fight brewing between his parents.

James, sheepish and remorseful, chimed in, "You know how I get when I'm mad. I'm sorry."

Aruba waved him off without acknowledgment and headed to the garage. James and Jeremiah followed her, giggling and singing "Sesame Street."

Aruba faced James before she entered her SUV. "How 'bout this tune, James. Happy Birthday to me. Happy Birthday to me," Aruba sang and poked her chest.

James thwacked his forehead, embarrassed he'd forgotten her birthday.

"I was gonna get you a gift, but you know I'm a little light right now. I'll get you something soon. I promise."

James tried to lighten the mood as she started her vehicle. "Baby,

I'm gonna get another job. I promise," he said, his eyes pleading, sincere.

She backed out of the garage into the driveway, waving to them both. She blew Jeremiah a quick kiss. *Yeah, you'll need a job when I'm done with you. I owe this to myself.*

[2]
Ready or Not, Here I Come

Aruba circled the Marten Hotel parking lot until she spotted Winston's Range Rover. According to Victoria, Winston wrapped up his speeches like clockwork. The Lilly Conference Center, housed within Marten, was the spot of many lectures and speeches Winston facilitated. He didn't mingle too long with colleagues and headed home when he wrapped up his talks because he wanted to respect his wife and marriage. Since his scheduled speaking time was seven-fifteen, Aruba anticipated he'd walk out the front door at approximately eight-twenty-two. That gave her enough time to swing around to the Half Price Books entrance, turn on her hazard lights, and wait for Winston to cruise by since she "accidentally" ran out of gas. She'd even taken care to leave her gas can home. No need to make his job easier. She had inroads to make. As she waited in the hotel parking lot, she received a nod from the heavens: raindrops. A few sprinkles multiplied, fell heavier, and relaxed her. *I couldn't have planned this any better.*

She leaned back, queued Glenn Jones in the CD player, and pondered her circumstances. She thought of Jeremiah and how much better off he'd be with Winston as his father. Vacations. A bigger house. Private school. Legitimate playdates and outings with Mocha Moms and the women she'd charmed in Victoria's neighborhood. As Glenn Jones gave Toni Braxton a run for her money belting out "Another Sad Love Song," she superimposed herself in Victoria's role. Aruba whipped out a note pad, scribbling out house rules for her new life: Greet Winston with a hug and a kiss each morning. Treat Alva, our nanny, with the utmost respect. Give Winston head and sex whenever he wants it, not just for procreation. Be frugal with our finances, so we can retire and travel. She continued scribbling, this time pronouncing her new name. Mrs. Winston Faulk. Mrs. Aruba Faulk. Aruba Aneece Faulk. She rolled the titles off her tongue respectively, settling on the first name. Mrs. Winston Faulk sounded sexier, glamorous. A hell of a lot better than Aruba Dixon.

"Mrs. James Dixon." She shuddered at the pronunciation of her married name, her pathetic reality. Not that she always felt that way. She still glowed at the memory of meeting James ten years ago. She'd just slit open a box of Cuisinart toasters in JCPenney's housewares department. She gazed at the towering display rack lacking Foreman Grills, quesadilla makers, and pizza stones. She dragged a stepladder from the corner, climbing up to make room for the just-arrived stock. As she descended the ladder, a rich, baritone voice below called out, "Excuse me, are you Kenya Moore?"

Aruba sighed at the tired line she received from men and women. It was true. She could be Kenya's twin. Same banging body. Same hazel-green eyes. Same smile that made men whip out their wallets and spend cash or swipe credit cards after Aruba convinced them their wife, girlfriend, significant other, or boyfriend just *had* to have the latest gadget in their kitchen. The same smile either stopped women in their tracks while spitting out the refrain *bitch*, or made them sidle next to her, and say, "My son in the military will be home on leave next week. Can I bring him in to meet you?"

Aruba steeled herself to face what she knew was an older gentleman. She formed the image in her mind: Dark. Short and stocky. Horn-rimmed glasses. Balding head. Hoodwinked, she turned to find a totally opposite vision: A dreadlocked god who stood at least six feet seven inches tall. He beckoned her to descend the ladder. He was a little too light for her taste, but handsome just the same. As she climbed down, she eyed the blue Nike warm-up suit that hinted of days spent at Gold's Gym. The white muscle shirt he wore accented six-pack abs. She got lost in those perfect white teeth, those blue-green eyes that danced. *Our kids would have gorgeous eyes.*

"What would a former Miss USA be doing in Penney's?" she asked, unable to mask her attraction to him.

"I was serious. You look—"

"Just like Kenya Moore. I get that often."

Not one to allow lapses in conversations, James continued, "I'd love to get my hands in your hair sometimes."

"Excuse me?"

"Everyone wants a stalker, right?" James smiled and handed Aruba a business card. "I'm a barber and stylist and I'm looking for new clients."

She eyed the card. "Wow, do you go around hitting on every woman in South Dekalb Mall?"

"Only the beautiful ones."

"Gee, thanks." Aruba turned to walk away as James grabbed her arm.

"Just kidding. Let's try this again. Hi, I'm James Dixon. And you are?"

She hesitated as he extended his hand. Something about his spirit made her smile. "Aruba Stanton."

"Really, I'm here because my moms sent me to get," he pulled a slip of paper from his pocket, "a Black and Decker Steamer. Ever since Mom's sugar was diagnosed, she's been steaming food, watching her weight and whatnot."

"Good for her. Several of my family members have diabetes and it's no joke."

Aruba moved the ladder aside and directed James toward the steamers. They chatted, exchanged pleasantries, life tidbits. James shared that he was from Atlanta, grew up in the Bankhead area, and had a younger brother, Marvin; an older sister, Teresa; and dreamed of owning a string of beauty salons one day. He knew he'd succeed because black men and women liked to look good. Aruba sweetened the conversation by adding she was from Harlem, Georgia, a junior at Clark-Atlanta University majoring in mathematics, and an only child. The pleasantries continued until a little old lady called out, "Miss, will you help me find a Wilton cake decorating kit?"

"So may I call you sometimes, Miss Aruba?"

"How 'bout you give me your number and I'll call you?"

"You gonna brush me off like that?" he joked. He asked for the business card again and scribbled a number on the back. "This is my home number and my cell. The number on the front of the card is the shop I work out of."

"Leaving no stone unturned, heh? I promise, I'll call," said Aruba, holding up the peace sign.

He watched her guide the older woman leaning on a cane to a different section of the department. Aruba waved one last time.

The thought of that wave lulled her back to the present. *I should have never called him.* Glenn Jones crooned, "Where is the Love?" She eyed her watch. Eight seventeen. She crept out of the hotel parking lot, drove down to the entrance of Half Price Books, stopping as she pressed on the hazard lights. She waited. Hoped. Wondered if the positioning was right. Whether he'd know it was her. Just as she thought she'd lost her mind, that her life with James had in fact created this lunacy attack, she noticed a shiny black Range Rover pass by, slow up, then cruise backward in her direction.

Showtime!